WAY OF THE HATCHET

Book One of The Hatchets Trilogy

by Edge O. Erin

Contents

Disclaimer

Acknowledgements

Chapter One: Missing

Chapter Two: Numbskulls

Chapter Three: Hooked

Chapter Four: Walkabout

Chapter Five: SinglePass

Chapter Six: Kayak Kid

Chapter Seven: Swatfly

Chapter Eight: Stones

Chapter Nine: The Walking Wounded

Chapter Ten: Nearly Clueless

Chapter Eleven: Brickwallaby

Chapter Twelve: First Date

Chapter Thirteen: Wagons Ho!

Chapter Fourteen: In Deep

Chapter Fifteen: Horseplay

Chapter Sixteen: Grave

Chapter Seventeen: Passion and Poison

Chapter Eighteen: Identification

Chapter Nineteen: Hal Stead

Chapter Twenty: h

Chapter Twenty-One: Rammed

Chapter Twenty-Two: Bacon, Beans, and Beaver

Chapter Twenty-Three: Bait

Chapter Twenty-Four: Freepool

Chapter Twenty-Five: Rogue
Chapter Twenty-Six: R.I.P
Chapter Twenty-Seven: Charm
Chapter Twenty-Eight: Anagram
Chapter Twenty-Nine: No Farmer in the Dell
Chapter Thirty: Neighbors
Chapter Thirty-One: Proposal
Chapter Thirty-Two: The Blót
Chapter Thirty-Three: hQ
Chapter Thirty-Four: Sunk
Chapter Thirty-Five: Stretched
Chapter Thirty-Six: Road Rage
Chapter Thirty-Seven: Rewind
Chapter Thirty-Eight: Figurine
Chapter Thirty-Nine: Room to Run

DISCLAIMER

"Way of the Hatchet is a work of fiction. While set in British Columbia and Montana, place names (towns, communities, roads, etc.) are fictitious. Any resemblance to actual events or persons, living or dead, is entirely coincidental."

ACKNOWLEDGEMENTS

To my editor, Michaeli Knight, thank you for your keen eye, expert analysis, constructive criticism, and grammatical greatness. If one should encounter any errors, the author takes full responsibility from his last round of "fixes."

Chapter One: Missing

Debra McGown, 21, from Jasper Springs, Montana, has been missing since June 17th. Authorities are asking anyone with knowledge of her whereabouts to please come forward. The family has offered $100,000 to anyone providing information leading to her whereabouts.

The article had a picture of the dark-haired young woman that Ethan knew to love horses, spaghetti, iced coffee, and her 12-year-old cat, "Mr. Scruffles." Debra was known to read to seniors in her community.

The fact that Jasper Springs, Montana, was two hours south of his town of Glyph's Gulch, British Columbia, didn't take away from Ethan's interest in the case. There were too many unsolved cases, unanswered questions, and unrecovered bodies over too many years in southeastern BC, southwestern Alberta, and northern Montana. There had to be some link. Sadly, he was sure this wouldn't be the last 'Debra.'

"You want me to grab you a coffee from the bakery, Ethan?"

"Huh?"

"Want a double-double?"

"Ah, ya, sounds good, Bert. Thanks."

Ethan watched his right-hand man bounce his big frame down the concrete steps of the bland, one-story RCMP detachment. He remembered having Bert's agility, and perhaps he was still fitter than most guys his age; however, Bert Dawton was 25 and 250 pounds, whereas Ethan was 55 and 190.

Though he had poured over the McGown file at least ten times, RCMP Sergeant Ethan Birchom pulled the paperwork from his desk drawer and read the summary report again:

NAME: Debra Jane McGown
DOB: 2004
HAIR: Black
EYES: Brown
HEIGHT: 5'7"

WEIGHT: 150-lbs
SEX: Female
RACE: Caucasian

IDENTIFYING MARKS: A scar on her right knee from surgery done to repair an MCL after a skiing accident. A small birthmark on her left shoulder, just to the side of the neck, and a black cat tattoo on her right forearm.

Ethan surmised the tattoo was of Mr. Scruffles.

REMARKS: *McGown was last seen wearing blue jeans and a white shirt. She may have worn a red rain jacket and been toting a carrier with her cat.*

DETAILS: *The Jasper Springs Police Department in Montana are seeking help from the public to locate Debra Jane McGown. McGown was last seen on Saturday, May 3, 2023, around 10:00 a.m. She left her home on Applecrush Road in Jasper Springs, Montana, and was seen getting into a dark blue or black pickup truck (model and year, indeterminate, but it may have been a 70s or 80s GMC or Chevrolet.) McGown has not been seen since and has not had any contact with family and friends. Anyone with information regarding the whereabouts of Debra Jane McGown is asked to call the Jasper Springs Sheriff's Office at (717) 555-5717.*

Given Jasper Springs proximity to the Canadian border, you may contact your local RCMP detachment, dial 911, or contact a US or Canadian consulate.

Unfortunately, in Canada, they seldom got leads for victims south of the border; that didn't mean Ethan wasn't determined to help. Plus, it was yet another case that hit close to home.

"Might as well call Caroline." He announced to Twix, another key member of his team.

Twix moaned a sound Ethan interpreted as German Sheppard for "Sure," and Ethan dialed the Jasper Spring's Sheriff's Department.

"Good day, Officer Birchom."

Sheriff Caroline Leadshat was thirteen years younger than him but had received many more accolades — and probably received twice his salary.

"Howdy, Caroline."

"Let me guess: you're wondering if we've received any new leads on Debra McGown."

"Yep, that, but I figured I would check in on ya, given last week's close shave."

For whatever reason, her officialdom often resulted in him using old sayings, something he knew he had been guilty of since he was knee-high to a grasshopper. *Ah, there I go again...*

"All is well, Ethan, thanks. Bulletproof vest absorbed the shot, and yesterday we nabbed the perpetrator."

"You're quick, Caroline. Good work."

"We got lucky."

From his experience, it was unlikely Caroline "got lucky." It was as if catching criminals was in her DNA. Her success rate at solving violent crimes was off the charts.

"I doubt good fortune had anything to do with it, Caroline," he teased. "Any idea why he was after you?"

"I'm sorry, Ethan, I can't comment —"

"— on an ongoing investigation." Ethan finished her sentence, which he regretted, so he quickly added, "My bad for asking. I should know better than to pry."

"No worries, eh?" Her use of "eh" was often contextually wrong, but he enjoyed her saying it just the same.

"So, Caroline, I found a missing person's report from '93. Girl from Winnipeg was thumbing to Vancouver and vanished. It appears she was last seen near Cardston, Alberta, which is somewhat off the beaten track if you're going to Vancouver."

Caroline's "Hmm...interesting" was all he needed to continue.

"The American border is just south of Cardston. Could be she ended up in Montana?"

9

"It's not impossible." It was a minor concession, but it was enough.

"Can I send you what I have on it?"

"Of course."

"You never know where it might lead."

"That's right. I appreciate you staying on top of all these missing people. So many girls..."

Ethan knew why she cut herself off, but the reminder — any reminder — always registered in his heart.

"Anyway, I have to go, Caroline, but I'll email you what I have."

"Very good. We *will* catch him, you know."

"Thanks. Have a good one and be safe."

Setting down the phone, Ethan rubbed the wiry salt-and-pepper stubble on his chin, closed his eyes, and looked two decades into the past.

His daughter, Chelsea, was in her yellow sundress, chasing an orange and black butterfly across the yard. Her giggles were heart-melting magic. She nearly snatched the butterfly before she stumbled and crashed to the ground.

Ethan got up, half expecting Chelsea to cry, but nope, Chelsea brushed off her knees and dress, smiled at him, and resumed pursuit of the butterfly.

Little kept Chelsea down. Ethan and his wife, April, hadn't expected to have kids, so Chelsea was a surprise, an exceedingly pleasant one.

Ethan unbuttoned his shirt pocket, pulled out a small horse figurine, and placed it on the table in front of him. He raised it up on its back feet and whinnied. Chelsea always loved it when he did that, but often teased him too: '*Dad, I love you, but your whinny sounds a lot like a laughing hyena!*'

Chapter Two: Numbskulls

The Hatchet-wielders called their forced labor 'Numbskulls.' As he lacked a formal education, he initially didn't understand the word. However, over time — and exposure to more and more Numbskulls — he knew what to expect from them: not much.

They were, as he understood, '*dead-between-the-ears.*' Yes, they could perform basic tasks, such as feed the stock, shovel manure, pick rocks and vegetables, but they were only partially 'present.'

It was beyond his understanding what, at their core, separated Numbskulls from Hatchets. Physically, they were much the same; mentally, they were not. While Hatchets seemed to grow smarter over time, Numbskulls got dumber. He had noticed some developmental differences, so maybe that explained it.

Here on the ranch, Hatchets were born, reared, mentored, and, while occasionally disciplined, they were treated with respect. Hatchets were small and grew, not only in size, but in knowledge and confidence.

Numbskulls arrived fully-formed, did not get hugs, and were harshly disciplined — sometimes so severely they could not walk afterwards. Occasionally, they were pulled apart by forces he did not understand, only that he had, at times, been part of the *pulling*.

Even though he, like all those of his kind, was bred to be strong, unyielding, and obedient, the act always turned his stomach.

Generally, life for his kind was simple: do as you were told, and you would be left alone. Yes, sometimes there was heavy work, as there had always been on grassy and arable lands that fringed wilderness, but there were also pleasant day trips. All their needs, including those of a more carnal nature, were met. Life was predictable.

At least, it had been until a few weeks ago.

A Numbskull called Mork recently assigned to him was being fawned over by a young male Hatchet named Fetter. Fetter had even pulled Mork away from her menial duties and treated her to the same food the Hatchets ate, not the pasty glop provided to the other Numbskulls. Their intimacy increased and nourishment, care, and affection washed away Mork's stupid — at least mostly.

From his emotionally detached perspective, the 'relationship' was permitted, but their senses told them some of the Hatchets were displeased. Only now, as Mork stood across from an older Numbskull brought in from another ranch, did he sense engagement from the audience. Some in the bleachers above the pen even looked excited. The women in the dusty horse pen each held a hatchet and was tied to the ring's center pole by a 50-foot length of rope.

He'd seen this before, but never involving two Numbskulls. Normally disinterested in these sorts of affairs, he nonetheless poked his head through the fence to observe the spectacle.

A pistol shot rang out to start the proceedings. Although the dim Numbskull surely must've heard the sound before, she panicked and began running around the pen. Mork, wisely, or perhaps instinctively, lifted her rope and let the dunce run by.

"Run to the center, Runny! Run to the center!" yelled a woman from the stands. After receiving disapproving looks from the others, the overzealous, visiting Hatchet, promptly sat down and crossed her arms. In his experience, some Hatchets could be as dense as the Numbskulls they administered to.

It had been a very hot, dry summer, and as Runny ran, fell, scrambled on all fours, and ran again, fine dust wafted up, coating the sweat-dampened skin of all concerned.

After Runny ran by a second time, Mork dashed with her rope in hand to the center pole. Once there, she lifted the rope attached to her waist and draped it over the top of the chest-high, black pole. Mork then chopped at the rope with her hatchet, which must've been dull, for she was making little to no headway.

The crowd remained silent, except for Fetter's enthusiastic clapping. Runny stopped in her tracks and, slack-jawed and confused, looked up at the clapper. Then she smiled and began dancing, clapping her free hand against the side of the hatchet.

Looking up at those seated around Fetter, he could see faces flushed with anger or embarrassment. Clearly, Runny's actions, if not the entire affair, wasn't being viewed favorably. An elderly man got up and laid a hand on Fetter's shoulder. He could see Fetter wince, and then stop clapping. Almost immediately, Mork stopped her chopping and Runny, her running. The same old man yelled out, "Axe! Work! Axe!"

Both Runny and Mork were stunned, Runny looking at her keeper, Mork at Fetter. With an agility he was used to seeing out of even the oldest Hatchet, the elder hopped the wood rail fence into the ring. This time his "Axe! Work! Axe!" was accompanied by two gunshots, with the bullets whizzing just over the heads of the competing Numbskulls.

Runny, hatchet raised, took off like a shot from a canon. Once again it was in a circle, presumably mimicking the horses she'd witnessed training in such an environment. As for Mork, sweat from her brow mixed with tears, and she chopped so wildly that she missed her rope and hit herself in the shin. The self-inflicted blow caused her to cry out in pain and fall to the ground. Fetter rose swiftly from his seat, but just as quickly was ushered down by those around him. Nobody dared interfere with a hatchet contest.

Runny's rope, taught as it was, caught Mork in the behind and drove her head into the post. She slumped to the ground. All the while, Runny continued her mindless course of concentric circles. Mork regained her 'senses,' navigated Runny's ropes, and, eyebrows furrowed, determinedly rose to her feet.

Fetter bellowed a "Yes!" and resisted protesting arms as he stood up and clapped.

Encouraged, Mork resumed chopping at the rope. Blood from her forehead and shin dripped to the ground, mixing with the manure and murder of days gone by.

The collective action of Runny spiralling ever inward and Mork stepping and stomping made the dust so thick that the Numbskulls became mere shadows. A minute later, the suspended silt had totally engulfed them — their being evidenced more by their grunting and coughing as their movements.

Fortunately, a breeze kicked up and a few minutes later the Numbskulls reappeared. Some people moaned; others laughed. Hatchets seldom laughed; Fetter *definitely* wasn't laughing. Mork was now pinned to the post by Runny's rope, and they were face-to-face at the center post.

Mork had almost chopped through the rope and Runny hadn't chopped once, though she had mastered the axe-clap. Then, Runny noticed that Mork was frantically chopping at the rope, and with an innocent smile, began chopping her 'playmate's' rope.

Success! She had helped Mork cut the rope! At the realization, a wide, satisfied grin came across Runny's face; she liked this game!

Freed from her rope, Mork stepped behind Runny. Everyone in the crowd stood up. Looking up at the young man, Mork then clobbered Runny over the head with the back of her hatchet.

As Runny collapsed, Mork raised her hand and hatchet in victory. This satisfied the onlookers, especially Fetter, who raced down the steps, leapt over the top rail, ran to Mork, and embraced her tightly.

As the young couple hugged, two other Numbskulls dragged Runny away. Perhaps she was knocked out; maybe she was dead. It didn't matter; Numbskulls came and went.

He shook his head then; no, that wasn't true.

There were some he remembered and still cared about.

Chapter Three: Hooked

Ethan banged the bullseye on the top of his dartboard alarm clock, yet it kept ringing. Only after he sent it flying did he realize it was his phone that was ringing; his dartboard alarm clock hadn't worked in years.

"Hello?" His voice was raspy, rough with sleep, and he cleared his throat.

"Ethan! So glad you answered. How are you?"

As much as he liked Caroline, it was too early for pleasantries. "Fine. What's up?"

"We believe a suspect in the death of Rachel Steward, a flower-shop owner here in Jasper Springs, has just fled across the border into Canada."

"Solid lead?"

"Eyewitness confirmed the plate number, make, and model of his vehicle."

"Details?"

"Email should be there…. now. A separate informant overheard the suspect, Miller Renfrew, suggest they might go 'A middlin' fishing in BC,' if that means anything to you. We also have reason to believe Miller may have known Debra McGown."

"We'll jump right on it, Caroline."

"Thanks. Be careful. Guilty of the crime or not, consider Renfrew armed and dangerous."

"Understood."

After rubbing the sleep out of his eyes, Ethan read the email and called Bert. Predictably, Bert was on board, so after downing a cup of coffee and inhaling a slice of cold pizza, Ethan made his way to the station.

As Bert drove them south, Ethan read out the particulars.

"This 'Miller Renfrew' has an extensive wrap-sheet."

Ethan thumbed through the pages he'd printed out. "Juvey record, though of course we can't see that. Married twice, despite spending half of his adult life in jail. Assaulting a Peace Officer, Resisting Arrest, threats, assault, drunk and disorderly...it goes on. Domestic abuse, including stalking/harassing women. Somehow, between jail sentences, he parlayed his collegiate wrestling skills into becoming a professional wrestler under the name 'Tubby Tubman.' He gave that up after his last stint in jail, one year for violating his patrol agreement, and got a job working in a flower shop. Apparently, on his last hitch, he took up flower arranging, and was trying to get his life in order."

"I suppose stranger things have happened, boss."

"Caroline said something about Renfew expressing an interest in 'Middlin' fishing.' I've heard of 'noodlin,' but not 'middlin.' That said, I do know there is a Middling Road off Forestry Road 12."

"Whoa, Middling? That's a long way out there! Most people don't venture that far up FR12, let alone try pounding up the Middling."

"Ya, and as far as I know, it's a dead-end road, Bert."

"I've only been there once. Good trout fishing in a lake tucked into the hills."

"Now why in the heck would somebody try to escape on a dead-end dirt road?"

Bert pulled off his toque and scratched his curly brown hair. "Search me, Ethan. Furthermore, who would even make the ID so far from Jasper Springs?"

Ethan had wondered the same thing, but in his haste to track down anyone that might've been involved in Debra McGown's disappearance, he had parked his skepticism.

"Hard to say; some people that live near the border are pretty curious, and vigilant — especially if they're Outfitters."

"Yes — Outfitters do guard their territory and camps like rottweilers."

"Yep. Ah, that lake up the Middling Road. Isn't it part of a remote park?"

"Hey, that's right, boss. Fish Lake Wilderness!"

"Original name." He winked at Bert before continuing. "So, what are the odds of Renfew *just* going fishing? If he did some research, he would know a camping permit *and* a fishing license would be required."

"That's right! I'll call my friend Don at the Parks Service. He might know."

They pulled off the road at the crest of a hill just shy of the Farm Road 12 turnoff. Beyond this point, they would venture into the hills, and communication would be iffy.

As Bert reached out for more information, Ethan sent a text to Reggie at HQ. The second-year officer, who was a first-order jokester, said he had things under control.

Ethan got out to stretch his legs, and with Bert on hold, he decided to take a stroll. He walked across the ditch, stepped over an old fence, navigated some rusty, old, barbed wire strewn through the grass, and sat on a blowdown. While he chewed on a granola bar, he looked down the gravel road they would soon be travelling on. A warm wind was pushing waves of grass toward the road, threatening to claim it as their own. Above, a red-tail hawk was suspended in the sky, waiting for a mouse or rabbit to break cover. *Or perhaps it just liked hanging out?* Behind the hawk, a blue sky made cobalt by the occasional puffy, white cloud. Further into the distance, blueish-green mountains with grey and/or rusty tops. On the highest of them, patches of snow were perched like skullcaps. It was beautiful.

He heard Bert crunch through the grass behind him.

"Picturesque, isn't it, Ethan?"

"Sure is."

"I'm still waiting for a call-back."

As Bert snapped a few photos, Ethan gobbled down the rest of the granola bar. It might've been in his glove box for a year, but under the circumstances, it tasted divine.

Bert's phone rang and after a short back-and-forth, he turned to Ethan. "Turns out, Renfew got himself a park pass and fishing permit."

Reluctantly, Ethan got up. *Back to business.*

"The strangeness continues, Bert. Normally, bad guys and murderers aren't too bright, and when panic mode sets in, they ratchet up the *idiot*. Getting a permit doesn't sound like something a person on the lam would do."

Bert nodded. "Right. Do you want to continue?"

"Yep, let's go."

Back in their 4x4, they turned down the Farm Road. Thirty-minutes on, they had to carefully skirt a washout that had wrecked half the road. It was clear that several vehicles had turned around at this point.

"What do you think, Ethan?"

"I reckon we'll continue. There's no telling if Renfrew might've turned back. If he did, he's long gone. If he kept going, we'll find him."

"Understood."

Ten minutes later they came to where the Midling Road branched off from the Farm Road. The road was greasy *and* rocky, and thus, nasty. It was probably why more vehicles had elected to pull U-turns and go back to the highway. The only fresh set of tracks went up the Middling.

"Sempre avanti, mio capitano?"

"Who the watta?"

Bert chuckled.

"It's Latin for 'always ahead', as in we continue to follow the tracks."

Bert often surprised him with his bits of arcane knowledge.

"Ah, 'I see' said the blind man to his deaf dog. I'm just glad you weren't asking for pizza. By all means, let's, ah, sempray away."

"Follow the tracks?"

"Yes, please follow the tracks, Bert."

After three miles of steady altitude gain and sketchy conditions even for a four-wheel drive, they arrived at the western edge of Fish Lake. Just a few feet into the trees was a campsite with a tarp stretched between three large conifers protecting a tent underneath.

"Lights, siren?"

"Just lights, Bert."

They rolled up slowly to find two men, both asleep.

One, a rangy guy, was fast asleep in a lawn chair with his feet dangling in the water, empty beer cans rattling against the chair's aluminum frame. The other, a rotund individual, was laying in a hammock between two pine trees farther back from the shore. There was a fishing rod positioned in his belly button and a Jack Russell Terrier perched on his voluminous hairy gut, holding the fishing rod in its mouth.

Both men were snoring loudly.

"Not even noon, and already passed out."

"I wish Reggie was here to see this, Ethan."

"He would certainly make friends with the Terrier; he loves little dogs. I don't see any weapons, Bert, do you?"

"The tall one has a knife on his belt."

"Roger." Ethan walked a few steps closer to the man in the hammock. "Based on the mugshot and physical description, this must be Miller Renfrew."

"Threat assessment, boss?"

"The suspect appears unarmed." He noticed a book entitled *Mastering Your Emotions: A Practical Guide to Overcoming Negativity and Better Managing Your Feelings* sitting on a beer cooler next to the hammock. He couldn't resist picking it up and showing it to Bert.

"Doesn't exactly cry, 'Murderer evading justice.'"

"Nope." Ethan sat the book back on the cooler and was about to announce himself, when suddenly, the fishing rod twitched, and the bobber thirty feet out in the lake plunged down.

The Jack Russel growled and instantly pulled the rod backward. A good size trout jumped at the end of the line. The big man groaned...and farted. Without opening his eyes, Miller Renfrew said, "Just drag it on in, Doop."

19

Rod in mouth, Doop jumped from Renfrew's belly. The leap set the hammock to rocking and as Doop 'reeled in' the fish, the man at the shore's edge woke up, grabbed the line, and, holding the sixteen-inch fish aloft, announced, "*Doop*, there it is!"

"A good catch," Ethan commented.

The man turned around so fast that his nylon lawn chair folded up like a pretzel, and both he and the trout floundered at the shoreline.

Doop had raced back to the water and was snarling and barking at the fish. As 'lawn-chair man' took the fish off the hook and added it to a fish chain, he stammered, "What's the frickin' Fuzz doing here, Miller?"

Miller Renfrew, surprised, and not a little inebriated, jerked up; the movement was not accommodated by the hammock, and a second later he was unceremoniously flipped out and onto his back. He groaned and rolled slowly downhill to the water's edge.

Both men were now looking up at Ethan and Bert. Miller rubbed his meaty face with both hands, did a head shake that a bear would've been proud of, and then squeaked, "What gives, Mounties?"

Bert and Ethan exchanged glances. Not only had Ethan not expected to find Miller fishing with a friend, but the high-octave of his voice contrasted sharply with his 5'11", 300-pound frame.

"Can I please see your IDs, Gentlemen?"

"Sure, it's in my tackle box," Miller answered.

"And we both have our fishing licenses," the slim man chimed in.

"We're not Fish & Game or Natural Resources. We're RCMP officers."

"What's the diff?"

Ethan shot Bert a nod; the lanky guy had an attitude. The taller man rose to his knees then, as he clutched his hands to his lower back, unfolded his 6'8" frame.

Miller quickly interjected. "They're RCMP, Bill, like State Troopers and City Cops all rolled into one."

"Oh, yuck."

"Is your ID also in the tackle box, sir?"

The man named Bill glared at Ethan and started reaching into his pockets.

Reaching up from the ground, Miller grabbed Bill's hand. "Don't go into your pockets, Bill. They don't know if you're packing heat."

"That bulge is my home-made dick, Miller. Just thought my ID might be in my pocket, but I guess it's probably in the truck."

Bill pointed at a dented, heavily-bondo'd green suburban parked beside a picnic table.

Ethan nodded toward Bert and said, "Tackle Box."

Bert moved over to the tackle box, and Doop started growling. When Bert touched it, the dog raced over and menaced his pant leg.

"Doop, Doop! No, it's okay, boy. Here, Doop." To Ethan, Miller's 'here' came out as a piercing 'eer.' Doop let go of Bert's leg, but only moved a few feet from the tackle box.

Miller looked apologetically at Ethan. "Doop's very protective of his fishing gear."

"And he doesn't even have a license!" Bill added.

Miller looked at Bill, laughing loudly. The big man then stroked and slapped his belly. "Holy fuck, Bill, that was good!"

Bert opened the tackle box and pulled out some folded papers and a wallet. He examined both. "Miller's ID and Fishing License and the other Fishing License says Bill, uh, de Vanden...brog..."

"It's de Vandenbrough, 'bro'...hear the similarity."

"So, you're Mr. de Vandenbrough?" Ethan asked the tall man.

"Duh."

Ethan furrowed his brow and gave the man a hard look, which prompted a more civil response.

"Yes, I'm Bill de Vandenbrough, though back when Miller and I were tag-team wrestlers, I went by Slim Vice, because my grip was crushing, dude."

"Mr. de Vandenbrough, please go over to your truck with Officer Dawton and retrieve your ID."

Bill's head and shoulders both slumped forward, and he kicked a beer can. "Ohh...kay..."

Bert stayed well back from the grumpy Gumby and watched him open the door and then the jam-packed glove box. He pulled out a wallet, and, in so doing, dislodged a revolver.

Bill went to pick it up, but Bert cautioned him not to, adding, "You have paperwork for that weapon?"

"No."

With Miller Renfrew prohibited from leaving his state and his friend in possession of an unregistered firearm, Ethan decided that he'd seen enough.

"Gentlemen, you're going to have to come with us."

"Can't you just confiscate his gun and let us enjoy our camping trip?" Miller whined plaintively.

"You're not taking my fucking gun, I'll tell you that! My grandpa gave me that gun!"

Ethan held up his hands and attempted to diffuse the situation. "We have two issues here. An unregistered handgun, which is illegal in Canada, and your friend here isn't supposed to be out of state — let alone out of country."

"I'm so damn..." Miller paused, as if to collect himself, before continuing, "I'm so tired of people saying I had anything to do with Rachel's disappearance or murder. I mean, fuck..." Again, he paused. "Can you please pass me my book?"

Ethan picked up the book that had been thrown from the hammock, flipped through it to ensure it wasn't concealing a weapon, and passed it to Miller.

Miller pawed through it. "Damn! Nothing in here about how to control your temper when pigs ruin your outdoor outing!"

"Look, if you had nothing to do with it, Mr. Renfrew, then you'll have an opportunity to prove it in court — but as a suspect, you were also instructed by authorities not to leave Montana. Fishing trip or not, it doesn't look good, so we need to take you in... peacefully."

"I never killed Rachel. She helped me when everybody else had given up on me, even myself."

Ethan wasn't about to argue on points he knew nothing about. The law was the law, and if he believed everybody that said they were innocent, the courthouse would be mothballed and the jail empty.

"Can we help you get your things together and into your rig? We'll make sure no one messes with any of your stuff."

Miller looked at Ethan sideways. "How did you know we were here?"

"Not important; let's go."

"It was that fucking Leadshat bitch, wasn't it? She's been on my ass ever since I came to Jasper Springs. Plus, she killed Asner, and he was my alibi for Rachel!"

Asner must've been the man that tried to kill Caroline recently.

Ethan was getting frustrated. "Bert, lock Mr. de Vandenbrough's weapon in the trunk. Gents, I'm giving you fifteen minutes to put whatever you want safeguarded into your vehicle. Your dog can ride in the back seat with you."

"I'm getting my gun back, right?"

"Sir, we'll give you every chance to provide the paperwork to get your gun back."

Bill stepped right into Ethan's face; the former wrestler towered over him.

"Well, I tell ya one thing, Mr. RCMP man, I'm not leaving Canada unless I get it back."

Ethan braced himself.

"*Step back*, sir."

"Bill, calm down. Chances are I'll be going back to the States in a police car, so you need to take care of Doop and the truck."

"I don't know, Miller. These guys are being assholes."

"Bill, enough!" Renfrew screeched before bringing his hands together and pleading in a softer tone, "Please, Bill."

"Your friend is right. Now, let's please make this quick." Ethan coaxed more tersely than he would've liked.

Bert stepped forward to help diffuse the situation and inadvertently kicked the tackle box, which spilled its contents onto the ground, including one bag containing a suspicious-looking white substance. Doop again attacked Bert's leg.

"Call off your dog!"

Bert was standing on one leg, with his other leg extended, trying to shake off the terrier.

Bill's eyes flashed to the bag, and then to Ethan. Meanwhile, Bert had grabbed Doop by the collar and was trying to pull the dog off his leg. Doop yelped as the collar bit into its neck.

Bill rushed forward, linebacker-style, and crashed into Bert's midsection.

Ethan grabbed for his taser, but somehow, in the commotion, fishing line had looped around the holster and his leg.

"Miller, off the top rope!" Bill encouraged his partner.

With balance belying beers and bulk, Miller walked along the edge of the truck box. Bill had Bert's shoulders pinned down, and Doop was tearing into Bert's pant leg.

Ethan freed himself from the tangle of fishing line and ran over to Bill, kicking him in the head, before he, too, tripped over the tackle box. Bert rolled away just before Miller's bulk belly-flopped to the earth.

Bill had grabbed his revolver and was frantically trying to load a clip.

On his knees, Ethan fired a shot into the air. "Drop it! Drop it *now,* or I'll have to shoot you!"

Bert had scrambled over to Miller, who had knocked the wind out of himself; judging from his groans, he'd probably cracked some ribs. Bert was cuffing him, while Doop had a mouthful of Bert's ear.

Bill looked at Ethan, then back at Miller and Bert. He slammed the clip in the gun.

Ethan shot him twice in the chest, sending the man down to the ground, dead.

Miller was now sobbing *and* groaning. Doop had let go of Bert's ear and gone to sniff at Bill. The terrier barked at him several times, probably trying to wake him up, but as blood spread out from Bill's body, Doop slumped to the ground, chin on his front paws.

"He should've died in the ring," Miller moaned.

Ethan knew better than most that Death didn't give a shit about time, purpose, place, or karma.

He also knew that this marked only the third time he had killed someone. Despite de Vandenbrough's reckless antics and nasty demeanour, Ethan knew he would be feeling shitty about it for a while.

Ethan looked over at Bert, who was kneeling on Miller.

"He's handcuffed?"

"Yeah."

"You okay to drive their rig? I figure once we load Bill's body into the back, Doop will jump in with him."

"Probably, but likely he'll saw off half my leg just getting there." They both looked down at what was left of Bert's pantlegs.

"I hope not. Oh, wait, I have some of Twix's doggie treats in the back of the car!"

"Hey, good idea!" Bert gave him a double-thumbs up.

Sure enough, Ethan's breadcrumb trail of doggy delights got Doop into the back of Miller's truck. They installed Bill and another portion of dog treats in the back before closing the tailgate.

They pulled Miller to his feet. The man smelled of beer and barf, but at least he went quietly and calmly into the back of the police truck.

By now, Ethan was gassed, and Bert didn't look too good. Both had fishhooks stuck in their clothes, and Ethan had a spinner with a small treble hook, complete with fake fly wings, stuck over his eye. He reached up and twiddled it with his finger, which caused him to grimace.

"Can't say I care for my new piercing."

"I definitely wouldn't go for matching earrings."

Ethan grinned. It was hard to find levity in such a situation, but he did manage to clap the shoulder of the big man.

"Good job out there, Bert."

"Thanks, you too."

Ethan looked around at the scene. It had all gone wrong so fast, and so lethally. His mind flashed to Doop sniffing at his fallen friend. Poor dog deserved better, but he wouldn't tell Bert that, at least not just yet.

"I don't want to do it, Bert, but let's gather up their stuff, and put it in the back of our truck. If you can get the crime scene tape up and focus on their gear, I will take some photos and measurements."

"Roger." Bert limped to the task and Ethan went back to the truck to grab his camera, measuring tape, and Tylenol.

He saw Miller Renfrew in the back, sobbing and hammer-fisting his thighs. For some reason, Ethan felt sorry for the guy. He shouldn't, because it wouldn't have taken much to have flipped the script, and it be Bert or himself, or both, dead on the ground. Nevertheless, sorry for him, he did feel.

Ethan opened the back door and Miller looked at him, his eyes a sea of despair.

"You took a hard fall, Mr. Renfrew. You want a couple Tylenol?"

"Will they bring back my friend?"

"No."

Miller just looked down and replied, "Then you can shove 'em up your ass."

With Bert driving Miller's truck and following Ethan, they rolled out.

Just before they got to the Farm Road, which coincided with Miller Renfrew no longer crying, Ethan caught the man looking at him in the rearview mirror.

After reading him his rights, he asked, "Ever hear of Debra McGown?"

Renfrew just shook his head.

Chapter Four: Walkabout

As was often the case, Twix picked up his spirits. This morning it was just her resting her chin on his knee and looking up at him in a way that seemed to say, "I know life can be hard, but at least you still got me."

"You're absolutely right, my friend." He patted Twix on the head and then topped up her food bowl, which he suspicioned might've been part of the reason she was being so empathetic. The way she wolfed the food down indicated Ethan was right, but he shelved his doubts when she returned from chowing down to lick his hand and then playfully tug at his pant leg.

"Oh, I haven't forgotten, Twix. Today's your day with Bert and Terran D. Bonaparte."

The mention of Bert's rescue dog, a Corgi Boxer mix, caused Twix to issue a few sharp, enthusiastic barks.

"Just let me finish my coffee."

Twix looked at him expectantly as Ethan downed the last of his java. Both knew what was coming.

"So, are you ready…"

Twix took off at warp nine and was back, leash in mouth, in mere seconds.

Thirty minutes later, Twix and Terran D. Bonaparte were racing around the green space behind the cop shop, loving and smelling life.

Ethan and Bert grinned at the dogs and one another.

"Without a doubt, those two absolutely *live* for the day you take the 4WD down the backroads between here and Elk Point."

"Too bad you can't come today, Ethan."

"It's alright. Have to get a tetanus shot and some bloodwork."

"For the…" Bert pointed at Ethan's forehead.

"Yep, that's right."

Ethan pulled off his sunglasses and ran his index finger above his right eye, which no longer had an eyebrow. It also no longer contained a lure called a "Mepps Spinner."

Twix and Terran were now standing at the back of the truck, waiting to be let in.

"There's your signal, Bert."

"Copy that. I'll let you know when I get back."

Bert and his doggie deputies drove off and Ethan made his way to the clinic. It was quick and painless, so rather than return to the office and bother Reggie, he decided to stroll around the neighborhood.

Today, Ethan was plain-clothed, but his small-town location, stature, gait, and RCMP-issue sunglasses still made him an easy mark.

A 4x4 pickup crawled by, and a fellah he knew by the name of Frank, who worked at the sawmill, leaned out the window and called, "Good morning!"

Mr. Archfield — a *delightful old curmudgeon*,' as Reggie defined him — passed Ethan on his scooter, looked over his shoulder and said, "You're one plow short of a furrow, Officer."

Jasmin, the aged mail lady, stopped him to thank him for all he did for the community. Ethan thanked her for not *'mailing it in.'*

Mertle Blackdurn, who Ethan swore spent twenty-three hours a day tending to the lilacs, roses, and caragana's that fenced in her yard, ambushed him with a cup of Earl Grey and a tea biscuit.

The tea and biscuit were good; her attempts to fix him up with her Chatty Cathy Doll of a daughter, however, were not.

Two ten-year-old boys tried to hit a roadside puddle with their bikes and splash him. One hit the curb and cut his forearm on a pair of pruners Mertle had left laying by the sidewalk instead.

Ethan used his undershirt to stop the bleeding and called the boy's mother. She got there in less than five minutes, told her son to be more careful, and apologized on his behalf. She then cuffed her young'un on the head and her son, Kenny, knowing what was good for him, dutifully mumbled, "Sorry, Mr. Birchom, it won't happen again. We were just funnin' around."

In the interim, Mrs. Blackdurn had sent her daughter out with another cup of tea. After Ethan darn near burned himself gulping it down, a teenager in an old Chevy Nova did a break-stand and threw up an f-bomb. The boy's father owned the tire shop, and Ethan decided he would have a word with him.

Ethan pried himself away from Blanche Blackburn and hung a right at the next intersection. It would be a circuitous route back home, but it got him off the main drag and ran next to a green space. He rubbed his face with his hands, took a deep breath, and resolved to walk slowly.

Seven white-tailed deer, seemingly without a care in the world, strolled across the road in front of him. As beautiful as the ungulates were, they were presenting issues to the flower and gardening community and drawing predators, like cougars, too close to town. There was talk of a cull, and those opposed were already planning a protest.

Of course, gardeners and Outfitters would be involved in a counter-protest, and Ethan would have to be there as Devil's Advocate, AKA the RCMP, to keep the peace. Altercations were unlikely but given recent events and that humanity in general was becoming angrier, less tolerant, and more entrenched in their positions — political or otherwise — with every passing day, he would have to be watchful.

Ethan spotted a red fox and its four adorable kits eyeballing him from a sand hill that had once been a jump for a motocross track. The fox was another critter drawn to "civilization." People meant excess, and often that excess came as food. One species' garbage was another species' deli.

Owls, hawks, and weasels, which could all prey upon young pups, seemed averse to living in town, which meant foxes felt safe. There were few things Ethan enjoyed more than watching fox kits play on the sand hill, and while it was unfortunate that few youths were stepping away from their game consoles, he preferred the foxes raspy bark to the relentless roars and *reears* of dirt bikes.

Turning a corner, which lead to the end of the road and a walking trail that snaked back toward Main Street, Ethan saw a woman on a park bench looking at the activity at the birdbath. Too late, he recognized her as a former classmate of Chelsea's.

"Hi, Mr. Birchom."

"Ethan's good, Kimberly. Nice to see you."

"You're just saying that."

Ethan always knew Kim was perceptive. Of course, as one of Chelsea's best friends, he'd always cared for her; however, Ethan had to admit he didn't do a great job of staying in touch, which he felt guilty about.

"No, Kimberly, it really is nice to see you." He paused and decided to come clean. "In all honesty, and it's my bad, but I struggle with people that used to know Chelsea. It's a reminder of how much I loved her...After eighteen years, I guess I've never really healed from her loss."

Ethan stood there by the park bench and they both looked at the birds.

Finally, he decided to sit down and nervously brought his hands together.

Kimberly reached over and softly tapped his forearm.

"I loved her too, you know, Mr. Birchom. We used to come here, before Fox Sandhill, before the Motocross, back when there was a swing set and a merry-go-round."

"Good memory, Kim...if it's okay to call you that?"

"It is."

"What brings you here? I thought you moved away."

"You really want to know?"

He sensed she wanted to tell him, so he rested his hand on her right shoulder.

"Husband ditched me. Two kids. Nowhere to go... so we're back at Mom's until I can figure out what to do and where we can go."

Ethan knew Kim and her mother had often been at odds, and it must've rough returning to that environment.

"I've been thinking about renting out the basement; there's lots of room, but the place needs work to make it comfortable. Still, if you were okay with roughing it, I would be happy with you and yours living downstairs, at least until I get it fixed up or you find a better place."

Her face lit up. "Are you serious?"

By this time, he had taken his left hand off her shoulder, and rested it on the park bench. Kim scooped it up and squeezed his hand with both of hers.

"You would do that for us?" Tears were shining in her eyes.

"Any day and every day, Kim. You know I love you."

She threw both of her arms around his shoulders and kissed him on the cheek.

"When can we move in?"

"Anytime you like. I've the day off tomorrow *and* a pickup, so if you want —"

"Hell, yeah, Mr. B! I love you!"

"I love you too."

"Don't mean to be rude, but I would love to go and start packing."

"Sure, go for it. Oh, one thing: Obviously, I'm a police officer, so that comes with some inherent risk, but I'll do whatever I can to keep you out of harm's way."

"It's all good. We'll be fine." She hugged him again and was half-skipping, half-running as she left.

Heart gladdened, Ethan allowed himself some time to smell the roses of the quaint and natural place he lived. Finches and warblers were taking turns splashing off in a birdbath fed by the cool waters of an artesian well. A frog jumped onto his boot, and they had a brief conversation. Ethan couldn't speak for the frog, but that it hopped away when he started talking about the weather suggested it found him dull.

When Ethan looked back to the birdbath, a Spotted Towhee had splashed down to join the other birds. Ethan couldn't recall the last time he'd seen one. With a black head, white spots on its black wings, white chest, and a rufous flank, the bird was a many-colored jewel. It was a good-sized sparrow and, in some respects, resembled a small robin — only, one that had good taste in clothing and wasn't perpetually incontinent.

Seeing the bird felt like a reward for doing something good. Ethan wasn't a spiritual man, but he did feel a connection to the web of life. Before Chelsea, he might've considered himself an atheist, though perhaps an agnostic one. After Chelsea was born, it was hard to not have faith in a benevolent deity; after she disappeared, he found it difficult not to believe in demons.

The birds exited the birdbath, and Ethan took that as a sign. His three-day-old leftovers wouldn't warm themselves, though they might crawl out of the fridge. With Kim moving in, he was going to have to buy more groceries — and actually *cook* them — and get the BBQ working.

Emerging from the narrow walking trail close to Main Street, Ethan noticed that there weren't any cars parked out front of "Drop the Needle!", a Vinyl Record and music collectibles shop.

It was owned by a young man named Mitch Craig, who was the nephew of Ethan's longtime friend, Angela Craig, who lived in nearby Elk Point. Frequented by both the young and old, Drop the Needle was nearly always busy.

"Maybe today you can unwind a little, you old bugger," he quipped to himself, and smiled — a sincere smile. With a hop in his step, he walked into the store and was quickly greeted by Mitch.

After exchanging small talk, Ethan asked Mitch if one of the store's two music rooms was available to listen to a record or two.

"Yes, Room thirty-three is. Any preferences, or should I surprise you with something?"

"Hmm...how about some Spanish guitar, followed by Pink Floyd?"

Mitch nodded, apparently satisfied with Ethan's request. "Excellent choice! Consider it done. I'll cue up Room thirty-three for twenty-five minutes of uninterrupted music. Buzz me if you want a beverage or the flip sides."

"Thanks, Mitch." Ethan gave him a thumbs up – and twenty bucks, which was more than what the young man would charge for the allotted time. When Mitch protested, Ethan insisted he accept the tip. Owning a small business had never been easy, but during COVID and the corporate restructuring that flowed from it, staying afloat was increasingly challenging.

The young store owner had designed *amazing* sound rooms. You could choose your lighting scheme and what was displayed on the wall panels, but like most, Ethan went with the default. Mitch had proved genius at gauging what his clients wanted.

Ethan let the chords, both visual and sonic, wash over him. He'd not visited Spain, but images of Spanish beaches, countryside, and architecture blended with the six nylon strings, and he felt suspended in time and place. Immediately, he was glad he'd dropped in, while also being upset with himself for not coming more often. Ethan realized that he was becoming an automaton. He had to start making a real attempt to find meaning — even happiness — outside of work.

The Spanish Guitar transitioned seamlessly to some of Pink Floyd's best. Images of their live performances and, for lack of a better term, "psychedelic imagery," cascaded around him. As the music played, he sensed his happier self: the man he most often was when his little girl was still alive. The last song was *Learning to Fly*. Chelsea had liked that song just as much as he did, and it was her that told him that the song was "a metaphor for a spiritual journey." That factoid surprised him, as did her knowledge, and use of the word, 'metaphor.' Normally such a memory would make him sad, but not today. Maybe Chelsea or the Universe were trying to tell him something? Maybe good things could *still* happen in his life? Ethan felt less a robot when he left the room yet with a desire to leap over tall buildings in a single bound.

He nodded at Mitch on his way out and surreptitiously left him a gift card for the town's bakery.

Getting home, Ethan snagged himself an ice cream treat and sat on his veranda.

He bit the top off his Drumstick, closed his eyes, and felt even more stress seep out of his shoulders, down his arms, and out his fingertips. From down the street, there was a loud popping noise. Ethan's eyes snapped open to see his neighbour had fired up his old Chevy pickup. The popping was simply its engine backfiring. When he closed his eyes again, Bill de Vandenbrough appeared, in black and white, and two more popping sounds produced two red holes in his torso.

Ethan got up, went to the kitchen, tossed his ice cream into the garbage, and poured himself a stiff drink. An hour later, he still hadn't touched his drink, and he couldn't stop seeing the expression on Bill de Vandenbrough's face as the bullets tore into him.

Chapter Five: SinglePass

Online dating. Ethan wasn't sure if an eyeroll accompanied his exhale of resignation, but as he hit 'Submit Your Profile,' he felt a twinge of hope — or maybe it was indigestion.

How bad can it be? The agreement said one could opt out at any time. It wouldn't hurt; well, at least not physically. Ethan reached up to ensure the bandage on his recently-shaved eyebrow was staying stuck. It was, and the three-pronged Mepps fishing lure was now in his own tackle box.

Miller Renfrew had been expeditiously extradited to the US, all the while profusely and profanely proclaiming his innocence. Doop was quickly adopted by a fishing fanatic, and de Vandenbrough cremated according to his American family's wishes.

That collective nasty bit of business done and dusted, save for the occasional bad dream, Ethan was ready to face another epic challenge: dating. "The barbed hook of social interaction," he said aloud, grimacing.

It had taken two months to work up the courage or embrace insanity — or both — to do as Bert, Angela, and Reggie unanimously recommended.

Late into one of their bi-weekly 'Darts Night's', Reggie had been particularly adamant.

"C'mon man, you're not, like, a *hundred*! I'm sure you must still have some lead in your pencil." He'd smiled and nudged Ethan with his elbow.

"Reggie..."

"Oh, sorry, boss, I mean the desire to *boom-chick-a-wow-wow*!" Reggie waggled his eyebrows suggestively, as if his phraseology wasn't enough, causing Angela to chuckle.

"Ya, that's *way* better, Reggie." Ethan tried, in vain, to contain a grin. "Let's just say I might not be as good once as I once was, but I'm probably as good once as I ever was."

Angela and Bert laughed.

"Well, I suggest you make good on that, boss."

"I second that," Angela added with her patented impish grin.

"I'm with Reggie and Angela."

"*Et tu*, Bertus? Well, maybe, but given my job, I don't even know where to start. I mean, I don't even think it would be appropriate to use a photo."

"Trust me, Ethan, many of us ladies believe in mystery and a 'less is more' approach."

"Well, except for the less part, you know, the, ah, 'Junk in the trunk.'" Reggie made another hand gesture that made his meaning abundantly clear.

"Reggie, you do know there is a lady present, right?"

"Who? You mean Angela? Heck, she's one of the guys!"

There was no sanitizing Reggie, nor denying that Ethan needed some action.

Fortunately, the jukebox had stopped, and they were eager to seize upon the opportunity to play something other than the creative stylings of William Shatner.

"C'mon, Ethan, you need to pick something too!" Angela beckoned.

"No, you guys go ahead. I'm good with whatever you choose."

As his friends and dart partners walked away, Ethan stared into his beer mug, hoping it would provide answers; it might've, had the barmaid not topped it up with clamato juice.

His shoulders sagged.

"You did ask for clamato juice, didn't you?"

"Yes, I did, Giselle. Thanks."

"Then why so glum?

"Long story, and a boring one."

She winked at him. "I'm all ears — well, mostly."

Giselle bent low and reached forward to retrieve an empty glass.

Ethan caught both her intent and an eyeful of her cleavage, which she noticed.

"You don't need online dating, Ethan. *I'm* available."

He'd crossed that bridge before, 'round about the Trump administration; as much fun as they'd had, they both knew they weren't compatible.

"Thanks, Giselle. I appreciate that, but I'm looking for something serious. Plus, aren't you seeing someone?"

"Not anymore. Sent that guy packing when he kicked my dog."

"Kicked your dog? What a jerk! How could anyone not like Winkles?"

"I don't know, but Dennis didn't like him, and Winkles couldn't stand *him*. In fact, he would start barking whenever... you know."

"Winkles, or Dennis would start barking?" Ethan smiled and his face started to turn red.

"Sometimes both!" They shared a chuckle, then Giselle became somewhat serious — which was as serious as she ever got.

"Anyway, I'm not proposing we get married, at least not in the official sense."

"Thanks, Giselle. I'll just consider myself lucky to have been with you before, and that neither of us barked."

"Ha! But we did make quite a racket." She smiled before continuing, "Anyway, it's a standing offer, Ethan. You know I care about you."

"I know you do, and the feeling is mutual."

She bent down again and gave him a peck on the cheek.

"Some gal will be lucky enough to snag you one of these days."

"Thanks, Giselle."

As Giselle left, the gang was returning to the table...and, as was Reggie's way, he'd played The Hooters' *And We Danced*.

They'd enjoyed the rest of the evening, even though they lost most of their darts games to other teams.

Ironically, Ethan had looked at Giselle's phone number several times that night after he got home, and a few more times before finally submitting his profile to SinglePass.

Ethan dreaded the thought of Angela, Bert, and Reggie finding his profile.

It was 11:30 p.m., and he walked outside to look at the stars. How his daughter Chelsea had loved Orion! In fact, she could name all the stars. She even taught him their names, and he felt bad that he couldn't remember some of the main ones. It prompted Ethan to return to his laptop and look them up.

Moments later, he received a notification from SinglePass. His profile was active. Ethan viewed it again to see how bad it turned out.

First, there was no picture, which necessitated him having to state his hair and eye colors, salt-and-pepper and blue, respectively. The interface allowed users to click on the generic male avatar and select 'Ask me for a photo.'

He didn't envision accommodating any such requests.

When Ethan perused the site, he saw few profiles with pictures. That made him think people might be trying to have affairs. Fortunately, he had the resources to check people out. Did he feel bad about that? *No, not really.*

Age: Fortunately, SinglePass used an age range, to help allay privacy or stalking concerns, so his fifty-five fell in the "50-55" bracket.

Where do you live? Again, since SinglePass was for the 'responsible adult that values privacy and honesty in their pursuit of a meaningful relationship,' one only had to use their region or electoral district. His location was Kootenay East. In a way, it felt like he was joining a glossy version of Craig's List Personal Classifieds, but at $65/month.

How many days of the year do you work? Ethan honestly didn't know. He knew he had several months of holiday time banked that he was supposed to use or lose. He received that note every year. Ethan guessed 310 days. Having to think about it made him question exactly what he was doing with his life.

How much time ya got? he asked himself.

Ethan imagined Chelsea saying, '*So, you work eighty percent of the time? That can't be healthy! What about fishing and looking at the stars, like we used to do, Papa?*'

A lump formed in his throat, and he raced back outside, hoping that Orion was still visible, and it was. "Alnilam, Alnitak, Bellatrix, Betelgeuse, Hatysa, Meissa, Mintaka, Rigel, Saiph, and Tabit." *Whew!*

Satisfied, Ethan went back in to continue reviewing his profile.

Occupation? After some thought, he went with 'Security Alarms.'

Interests? Darts, fishing, reading, true crime. He reckoned best not include, 'Hunt down the person who took my daughter and kill them twenty times over.'

Turn-ons? Ethan thought about submitting 'Willing and able,' but since he'd already turned down Giselle, who met those criteria, that would've been bogus. The qualities he admired, such as dependable, funny, fit, kind, professional, weren't really 'turn-ons,' per se... Well, 'fit' could be, so he added that. He thought someone who was into martial arts, or perhaps an adrenaline junkie, might turn his dial, so he added those. It was enough for starters.

Three deal-breakers. He really had to think about that. As a fifty-five-year-old man who was still wondering how he might be happy in a relationship, let alone even be *happy* at all, he probably shouldn't have a deal-breaker other than 'Meth addict' or 'Belly-button lint collector.'

Ethan admitted he could be with someone that smoked the occasional joint or cigarette, but not a chain smoker, so he put 'Heavy Smoker.' *Liar?* Yes, his upbringing and work meant he disliked the dishonest, so he typed in 'Dishonesty.' Serial-Killer would also be a deal-breaker, but... *Nah.* Chances were, it went unsaid that most people would be averse to dating mass murderers.

A third deal-breaker? Hmm. He had watched an episode of Seinfeld recently about a 'Close talker.' That might not be too bad, but a loud talker? Yes, he found them annoying, so he went with 'Noisy.'

A risk you would consider now, but not ten years ago? This one was easy: 'Online dating.'

Children? 'One.' Yes, he would always be Chelsea's papa.

Marital status: 'Divorced.'

Open to more children? 'No.'

Who are you looking for? This one took him a while. He finally settled on, 'I'm not sure, but I hope they're honest, outdoorsy, funny, and passionate (about something)'.

Ethan decided his profile was decent and then clicked on the other notifications. He already had two 'Interests.' Unfortunately, the first one was a non-starter; not only was the woman from Glyph's Gulch, but there was a picture, and he knew the, *ahem*, 'Lady.'

Judith was the only woman he'd met that suffered from a Napoleon Complex. She was overly chatty, abrasive, and aggressive. He'd arrested her for drunk and disorderly at least twice, which was ironic since she said, 'Heavy Drinkers' and 'Heavy Smokers' were turnoffs. Maybe she'd turned over a new leaf, but he still wasn't interested in barking up that particular tree.

Ethan moved on to the second expression of interest, expecting another hard '*Nope!*'

There was no picture, but the avatar showed a dark-haired woman, with a label that said, 'You won't be disappointed.'

Maybe he should've thought of doing something like that? People said he was good-looking, but they might've just been polite or blind. *I'm certainly no Brad Pitt, or that Clooney fellah.* Heck, he wasn't even a Sam Elliot, though Angela said he resembled Sam's character in the movie *Road House.* Ethan had taken that as a compliment. Coincidentally, Angela looked a fair bit like Kelly Lynch, who starred across Elliott and Patrick Swayze.

Ethan opened 'Becca's' profile.

Age? '40-45.' So, she could be as much as fifteen years his junior. It was surprising she could be interested in him! This could be his first time dating a woman over ten years younger than him, except for Giselle. *Then again, Giselle and I never actually dated; we only hooked up.*

Where from? 'Flathead, Montana.' That was comfortably far enough away, though both his region in BC and Montana's Flathead were quite large geographically, so they could be within 45 minutes of one another or several hours distant.

How many days of the year do you work? '366.' *I like that.* It showed him she was busy, if not ambitious, and would understand him being a workaholic. Plus, she had a sense of humor.

Occupation? 'Guidance counselor.' *Oh boy.* If she had serious sociology or psychology skills, she might see him as a case study. On the upside, she would probably be a considerate, empathetic person.

Interests? 'Chess, billiards, fitness, martial arts, true crime, skydiving.' *Interesting!* Chess suggested *smart*; Billiards, like darts, showed she wasn't socially inept and liked games, and might also be competitive. 'Fitness equaled 'in good shape,' or at least someone that tried to take care of themselves. And *cha-ching!* a common interest in true crime.

Turn-ons? 'Off switches.' *Good one!*

3 Deal-breakers: 'Lazy, Complicated, Heavy drinking.' That was all good.

A risk you would consider now, but not ten years ago? 'Online dating.' *Yes!*

Children? 'Yes.'

Want more? 'No comment.' He would've preferred a 'No,' but maybe 'No comment' just meant 'None of your business.'

Marital Status: 'N/A.' Ethan could respect not answering that question.

Who are you looking for? 'Someone who likes me but loves who I can become.' *Deep!*

An 'Expression of Interest,' could come as a thumbs-up, wink, or a flame. Hers was a wink, which he rated pretty good. If he was going to do this, he was going to do it right. No half-measures. *Ugh.*

He winked back.

His phone vibrated. *Surely, not another return wink or something?*

Rather, it was a message from Bert. *They found Miller Renfrew dead in his cell; seems he hung himself.*

Ethan let out a labored sigh. He hadn't expected Miller Renfrew to throw away his life.

Chapter Six: Kayak Kid

Ethan got off his quad, slapped a thick layer of dust off his uniform, and walked to where Bert was standing. He followed Bert's eyes down a steep, rocky embankment to a stream, glistening and rapid.

"What do we have?"

Bert put away his vape pipe pen and, as a vanilla strawberry scent ebbed away, responded,

"Kayakers spotted an orange lifejacket in the willows near the shore, and as they went by, they thought they saw an arm looped over it. They put in down there." Bert pointed at a backwater eddy with a small strip of beach. "They walked back, thinking someone might need to be rescued, or worse, that a fellow adventurer had drowned. Turns out, there was an arm in the lifejacket... an arm, and *only* an arm."

"Yeesh. The rest of, ah..." Ethan looked at the slender arm, mostly devoid of hair, and the lifejacket Bert had on the seat of his quad. "...them?"

Bert shook his head as his radio went off.

"Bert, this is Ernie. Nothing on Sesame Street. Oscar the Grouch show up yet?" Reggie was famous for teasing Bert and Ethan, incorporating the Muppets, Sesame Street, Looney Tunes, and even Archie Comics into his radio transmissions.

Ethan had largely given up trying to instill in Reggie a higher level of professionalism. However, with other searchers around, he had to keep him on the straight and narrow.

Ethan motioned for Bert to hand him his radio. "This is Ethan. A Search Team will be here momentarily. This is not comedy hour, you jughead!"

Bert tried to hold in a snicker, but it was no use. He started laughing.

Ethan looked at him with incredulity, and then he realized what he'd said. "Oh, fuck me!" He had the radio button down.

Reggie replied, "Only if I get a *big* raise, Officer McGinty."

Clancy McGinty was a police officer in Archie Comics, hence the connection. Despite efforts to the contrary, Ethan ended up enjoying, and even sometimes encouraging — willingly or not — Reggie's silliness.

"*Hardy har har*, Reggie. Search Team arriving now, so from this point forward, let's keep this professional."

"Roger, sir."

All of them, including Ethan, would occasionally make fun in situations that were weird or dark, but it was almost always about maintaining their sanity more than anything else. Still, when the public was around, a proper code of conduct had to be observed.

The search team rolled up in a four-passenger Gator. Two volunteer firemen, Mitch from the record store, and the driver, Mitch's aunt, Angela Craig. Angela was a librarian who also served as a data analyst and assistant at the RCMP detachment in the neighbouring town of Elk Point. She was the same age as Ethan, and they had been friends for decades.

"Thanks for coming, everyone; it's really appreciated."

Angela nodded politely and, ever an enthusiastic and proactive participant, asked, "What do we have?"

Ethan clued the searchers into the gruesome discovery and what they needed to do. Few had experience with a violent crime, but they all knew the drill.

Together, volunteers and professionals scoured the area. Twix couldn't find a victim-related scent upstream or down, and the searchers were equally unsuccessful.

It was approaching 4 p.m., and to ensure everyone's safety, Ethan ordered them to halt the search. Since the waters upstream were swifter, and the valley narrower, they would bring in a heli to fly the area. If they spotted something from the air, a physical inspection would follow.

The arm would go to forensics in Vancouver, but before that, Ethan presented it to a doctor-turned-veterinarian in town who was always willing to help.

"What can you tell me about the scene and scenario, Officer?"

"The arm was in a lifejacket, tangled up in some branches along a river. We don't know about the rest of them, nor the mechanism of, ah, injury."

"Let's have a look." The man put on his gloves, removed the arm from the evidence bag, and carefully examined the appendage.

"Curious." The veterinarian everybody called Hopper took off his gloves and stroked his grey goatee. He then put on a new set of gloves and re-examined the arm, paying close attention to the bicep end.

"Definitely curious." The veterinarian furrowed his brow, making his two-toned, long rebellious eyebrows look even more like those of a Rockhopper Penguin, for which the man was nicknamed.

Ethan fidgeted "How so, Hopper?"

"The arm appears to belong to a young man, small-boned, probably between sixteen and twenty-one. It hasn't been in the water for more than a week or two. The cut is very clean, so that rules out a circular or chainsaw, nor was it torn, as often occurs in a vehicular accident. I would say someone hacked it off with a blade, perhaps a sword or clever."

"So, probably foul play?"

"That would be my bet." Hopper than added a 'tsk-tsk'.

"I see your 'tsk-tsk' and add a 'damn'! It never fails to astonish me what people will do to one another."

The doctor took off his gloves and flung them angrily into the garbage can.

"Some bipedal beasts make the most vicious animal look tame! It's been a long time since I've seen something like this."

"I haven't seen something like this since my younger days when I was training in Regina."

Hopper rested his hands on his stainless-steel examination table.

"For me, it was July 2006."

"I don't recall that." Ethan furrowed his eyebrows, well, one of them.

44

"You wouldn't. I was in Wyoming, and in that case, it was the severed fibula of a young female."

"Did they ever find the rest of her, or solve the crime, if there was one?"

"Not that I know of. I was only there for another year-plus after that."

They exchanged some small talk with Hopper giving him a special dog treat to pass on to Twix. Ethan thanked him for that and his time before he returned, not empty-handed, to the office.

#

Two days and a helicopter ride later, Ethan joined Bert and Angela at Scaler's & Suds. Sawmill-related items and logging paraphernalia adorned the walls of the pub, as did some stuffed trout and a few animal heads, which Twix occasionally growled at, and people increasingly frowned upon.

Ethan didn't foresee decorating his home with an animal head; though, upon reflection, he thought that maybe the cranium of the person who took Chelsea would be fine in the garage.

A drone flight — conducted by Reggie in his free time — and a heli recon of the river found nothing that warranted further investigation. It could be weeks before forensics, including DNA information, would help illuminate the presumably-wrongful death of the young man.

Regardless, Ethan would not let this case get buried in bureaucracy. He'd already approved Reggie to obtain a better drone that could fly farther and gather better imagery. In the coming days, Reggie would launch more missions, and if he saw anything, Ethan would get someone to rope him up so he could repel down and investigate the potential clue.

Someone had lost a son or brother, and while Ethan had failed to find out what happened to Chelsea, he *would* find out what happened to this young man.

Tonight, though, another challenge faced him, Angela, and Bert. Their darts team, the one-win, four-loss *Legally Blind* was going up against the five and nil *Tina and the Tree-Beards*. As an outfitter with her own hunting and guide service, Tina was every bit as tough as her two logging teammates.

Ethan was sure they would get trounced, but it didn't matter that much; a friendly game of darts was a great way to de-stress. Plus, Angela had already nominated herself as designated driver, so for he and Bert, 'wobbly pops' would accompany their wobbly darts.

Predictably, Legally Blind lost the first two games, and while Bert looked bummed, Ethan couldn't help but feel a tad out of it. He wasn't sure if it was the beer or the beatings. The next game would be a formality.

Thankfully, Angela remained chipper. "C'mon, you pair of turkeys, we have them just where we want them!"

"How's that?" Bert asked.

"*Overconfident.* Plus, see, they're getting into shots."

They all glanced over to see Tina, who was now sporting a fake beard, and her male friends laughing loudly as they picked up another round of shots.

"Let's buy them more!" Angela giggled.

Bert slapped her shoulder. "I like it when you're evil, Angela."

"What do you think, Ethan?"

"Heck, why not? I heard Giselle said she would drive them home."

Ethan caught Giselle's attention.

"Oh, Bodacious Barmaid, can you please get Tina and the Tree-Beards another round of shots?"

"And I'll buy them one after that!" Angela beamed.

"Will do, folks."

After the first round of gifted shots were consumed, Tina walked over.

"Thanks for the drinks, Wobbly Cop and, uh, accop-lices."

Ethan grinned. "Our pleasure, Tina. I like your chin lettuce."

"Thanks. Now don't think that just because y'all bought us some drinks that we won't kick your sorry asses in the last game — and if we do, please don't catch us on our ride home...you know...*entrapment*." Tina air-quoted 'entrapment' to add gravitas to her statement.

"Oh, not to worry. I've instructed Reggie not to pull anyone over that looks like Gimli's wife or her cousins. Plus, Giselle said she would see you all safely home."

In the next game, Bert, Angela, and he all played unusually well and beat Tina and the Tree-Beards. Ethan even managed the double-12 that closed out the game.

"I don't know when I've been more surprised; you making that shot or when I saw that pasty-looking skinny guy thumbing up the Swatfly, carrying a kayak."

Ethan smiled at the backhanded compliment, then what Tree-Beard Derek said fully registered in his head.

"Sorry, 'pasty-looking skinny guy thumbing up the Swatfly, carrying a kayak?'"

"Yep. Some of these eco-tourists make me laugh."

Ecotourism was gaining in popularity, but Ethan knew there were no such attractions up the mountain road and associated, rugged region locals termed the Swatfly.

"Did you talk to the guy?"

"No, I was coming down, loaded. Dusted his ass pretty good though, to give him some color."

"How long ago was this? Can you describe him? Did you see him again?"

"Whoa, whoa, what is this, Twenty Questions? I'm half-gunned here, man."

"This could be very important, Derek. Come sit down, please." Ethan motioned to an empty table toward the back of the pub.

"Will you buy me another drink?"

"Beer yes, shooter no."

"Oh, okay..." Derek looked deflated, but complied.

Giselle brought Derek a beer, which picked up his spirits, and Ethan an ice-water.

"When did you see this young man?"

"I don't know; about a month ago?"

"Time of day?"

"I think it was mid-morning, maybe noon...not sure."

Derek guzzled down half his beer.

"What did he look like?"

"Skinny-assed white kid, about twenty; I think he was wearing a bug vest, but Lordy, the horseflies would've been having a field day on his scrawny legs."

"Do you know if anyone else might have seen him?"

"Probably not."

"Why do you say that?"

"I remember radioing out, saying, '*Coming down, one mile on the Swatfly,*' and nobody else radioing in. We had just finished hauling from a log-cut we had way up the mountain, and I was probably the last run of the day."

"That's great information, Derek, thanks. Did you see any other vehicles on the Swatfly that day?"

"Only Hampstead the Harvester, but he left a couple of hours before me. I loaded myself."

"Nobody else? No vehicles?"

"Not that I can think of. That's rough country, and that road — not sure if you've been up there lately, but the washboard is enough to shake the teeth out of your head."

"Do me a favor, Derek. Give this a think and pop by my office tomorrow. Maybe you'll have remembered something else, and I can get a statement from you."

"A statement? Am I in trouble here, Ethan?" Suddenly, Derek looked sober.

"No, Derek. I could just really use your help; it's a missing persons case."

"Okay, but it won't be early. Tomorrow's Sunday, and I can tell I'll be nursing one *hell* of a hangover."

"Understood. I appreciate it, Derek."

"For sure. Hey, I'm tapped out. Can you get me another brewski?"

Ethan went to the bar and bought Derek another drink. He hoped that when Derek wasn't inebriated, he might provide even more useful information. Regardless, what the Tree-Beard shared was welcome and valuable.

Legally Blind left shortly thereafter. After dropping off Bert, they were heading to Ethan's place when he spoke up.

"Turn right here, please, and thanks, Angela. I want to visit Chelsea."

Angela did as Ethan asked, pulling up to Pineview Cemetery.

"It's late, and dark. Are you *sure* you want to visit her tonight?"

"Yes; I've been to see her so many times I'm sure I could find her grave blindfolded."

"I bet you could too, Ethan."

"Anyway, thanks for a fun evening and the ride, Angela. It was so nice to unwind *and* win a game."

"No problem."

Once they arrived, Ethan opened the door to get out, but Angela gently tugged on his shirt sleeve, which caused him to look at her curiously.

Her face was serious.

"Ethan, we've known each other forever, so can I offer you some advice?"

"Sure."

She patted his hand and, looking into her soft brown eyes, wizened with years, tears, and much laughter, Ethan knew she would in fact do anything to help, well, anyone. Her good-hearted nature probably explained why, despite having prematurely grey hair mixed in with blonde, her face was perpetually like that of a wide-eyed child, treasuring a fresh experience. Her husband, a former friend of Ethan's, had been a damn fool to leave her.

"I say this respectfully, Ethan, but you're a workaholic. While your dedication is admirable, I sometimes wonder if you would benefit from a break. I think if you got away for two or three days, you would come back more clear-headed, maybe even inspired. Perhaps you could go on a fishing or rock-hounding trip?"

Ethan couldn't help but not and agree. "You're right, Angela, but there are so many things that need my attention."

"Like the kayak kid case? How's that going, anyway?"

"Not much to go on. DNA's not back yet, though analysis suggests the arm is from a young man between eighteen and twenty-one years old. The heli spotted nothing, but we're going to do some more flying."

Angela smiled affectionately. "No doubt you will figure this out, Ethan. Any help you need, you just ask."

"Thanks for that, Angela. Have a good night."

"You, too."

As he walked toward Chelsea's grave, Ethan brought his hand up to his coat pocket, where he kept his horse memento. Even though he kept a small piece of orange flagging around one of its legs, he was always worried he might lose it. Yes, he kept a picture of Chelsea in his wallet, and how he adored it and her, but when he held the horse, one of his fondest memories, outside of Chelsea's birth, came to mind.

#

Despite its wobbly legs, the dark foal was quick.

"Papa, it's heading toward the road!" Chelsea exited the truck before his pickup came to a stop and he could say, "Be careful."

He saw Chelsea stumble and tumble, and right herself on all fours before her sneakers chewed up dirt racing toward the small, dark, gangly equine.

Ethan scrambled out his door and eyeballed the westbound traffic. A semi, hard on the bumper of a compact car, was motoring toward them.

The horse crested the shoulder with Chelsea in hot pursuit, and the big rig, its driver's vision undoubtedly obscured by the dust kicked up by the car motoring down the shoulder and the setting sun, was moving into the eastbound lane to avoid the car.

Ethan threw his arms into the air and yelled, "Stop!"

It was too late.

Dust cascaded over him, and the squealing rubber reverberated in his eardrums and echoed in his heart. His hand brushed against the bumper of the big rig as it skidded by.

"Chelsea!" he exclaimed as he found himself draped across the hood of a Honda Civic.

For a horrible eternity, or fifteen seconds, dust and fear choked Ethan's senses.

He rolled off the hood and tasted dirt. Not knowing which way to go, he moved his head to the left and then the right... and then a tongue slopped the side of his face.

Ethan looked up to see the foal, and then, from out of the waning dust, like an angel that had gathered sunlight about herself, Chelsea.

"You're bleeding, Papa," she said as she caressed his cheek.

He sat down, and she pressed a band-aid over his minor abrasion. "As you usually tell me, you should be more careful."

Too dazed and happy to say anything, he allowed the foal to lick a big fat tear that was rolling down his cheek.

#

Reaching Chelsea's headstone, Ethan knelt in front of it. Since they'd never found her, all that was buried there was a small box with a few of her favorite possessions.

To his knowledge, April, Chelsea's mother, hadn't been here in a decade. April had remarried. Ethan said he didn't care, but truthfully, since part of Alice was in Chelsea, he hoped she was happy. The last thing April said to him before moving away was, '*I can't even grieve here.*'

Ethan understood that. *Closure seldom comes without a corpse.* Even thinking that made him shudder and reprimand himself, *Don't you ever use that term again as it applies to your child!* Ethan swallowed hard.

He wouldn't.

When graveside, most of the time he just thought of Chelsea. Occasionally he prayed. Today, he talked.

"Angela figures I should take some time off. I probably should. You remember Angela? Yes, of course you do. You shared a love of horses. She still rides. Great gal, even a better friend. Why don't I ask her out? Probably all those years of her being married to one of my best friends is the main reason. Or perhaps it's that I've only ever thought of her as a friend. Plus, she knows I'm a working fool, and that cops often make for poor life partners. Ah, anyway, I just consider myself lucky to still have her in my life, especially since April, ah, your mom buggered off."

He noticed the chill in his voice, so he softened. "I'm sure your mom misses you. How could one not miss the delight that is you?" Ethan fought off the emotion that his voice was testifying to. "That's a rhetorical question." He paused, stifling a sob.

"We played darts tonight and actually won a game! And get this, yours truly got the double-double to best Tina and the Tree-Beards. You would remember Tina too...strange lady, cusses enough to make a prison inmate blush. I remember you saying to me, *'Dad, is it normal for a lady to swear like that? Seems she likes it so much she even doubles them up and inserts them into other words!'*"

Ethan laughed at the memory. "To repeat, *it is not normal for a woman to use so many expletives.* Her Tree-Beard partners don't seem to mind. They're good guys; the one even provided a good clue to a missing...." He stopped, feeling foolish for bringing it up. "Anyway, they're good people, like most around here."

Ethan looked down at the grave, then skyward. It was pitch black, but he always looked upward at least once when they were talking. It wasn't a planned thing. Maybe he thought they would somehow make eye contact, that through the vastness of space, or time, or realm, a fissure would open, even for a split second.

It never did.

"Hard to think of you not being here, Chelsea...

"You remember when you asked me if there was such a thing as Heaven and Hell? I said I didn't really know, but that surely there must be a special place where good people go after they die... Umm...So, what is it like?" Ethan gave her time to reply.

"Your very own horse and grandpa and grandma get to see you ride it? Sweet! Plus, you probably never have to clean out the stall, right?"

He smiled at that and thought of how Chelsea's smile had reminded him of the rising sun. You would get a hint of its coming, and then it gathered until it was so full and radiant that you were lost in its glory.

Ethan pulled the horse out of his pocket and folded his hands over it, and, he imagined, her hands and her own horse replica, as he had done so many years ago.

"Can you feel that, Chelsea? Good. As I said before, I'm never letting go of your hands or your memory, my sweet, smart, funny, kind-hearted, adorable little girl."

Ethan fumbled with his horse figurine and wondered if whoever took Chelsea had hers in a collection, or if they buried it with her, or just threw it away. The thought made him so mad that he couldn't speak for several minutes. He clenched his fists until they hurt and then he relaxed. *Positive thoughts, Ethan, positive thoughts.*

"Oh, I can't believe I almost forgot to tell you! Your old friend Kim Shockley has moved in for a while! She has two children and unfortunately, the father of her kids is a jerk, and you might remember her mom was *very* difficult to live with. Anyway, she and her young'uns have installed themselves in the basement, and she found a part-time job at the record store. I've a hunch she and the owner, Angela's nephew, might fancy one another.

"Kim's kids are very well behaved. They play so well together. You would adore them. I hope you don't mind, but I even made them some of my world-famous pancakes.

"It's been good. Kim's already made me a couple of delicious meals, and the place is cleaner than it's been in years. She bought a Swiffer-thingy to dust off the furniture; probably wishes she would've bought a small shovel instead." He chuckled weakly. "But in some ways, it makes me sad too. I'll hear a sound in the night, like her or one of her children getting up for something, and for a split-second, I think it's you."

Ethan stopped talking then and just thought about how lives are so easily torn apart, but also that, if you're generous, maybe, just *maybe*, some goodness comes back your way.

He stood there, hands in his pockets, for a few minutes, unsure of what more to say, or how to be.

"Well, sweetie, I best be going. We'll visit again soon. I love you."

Ethan walked away, feeling his way along before encountering an old maple tree. He moved to the far side of the tree, and with his back against it, slowly slid down to the ground. Then, witnessed only by the black, he wept.

No matter how much time had passed, he couldn't get over losing Chelsea. Maybe, as long as he was an RCMP officer, looking for other people's children, he would never overcome his grief.

Gathering himself, he used his phone to light the way ahead. As he crossed the small footbridge that spanned Twisty Creek, he felt a crunch under his foot, which made him think he had squashed a big beetle. Then Ethan clutched his chest; no, not for a heart attack, something even worse: what if his horse ornament had fallen out and he'd stepped on it?

He breathed a sigh of relief when he felt the horse in his pocket. He bent down and shone his phone's flashlight on the shattered fragments of a broken fishing bobber. Ethan took it as a sign, and then childishly crooned one of Chelsea's favorites from The Farmer in the Dell.

"*Hi-Ho, the derry-o*, a-fishing, I will go."

Chapter Seven: Swatfly

"Penny from Dispatch said that Hampstead the Harvester was down two hours before me, and they didn't have any other company vehicles in or out that day. I also ran into a certain guy that does, ah...other 'business' in that area, and he said he's abandoned the Swatfly because of the sorry state of the road."

"Thanks a lot for doing that, Derek. You've some investigative talent."

"You think?"

Ethan smiled. If the guy could control his booze intake, he might be a good recruit. He recalled seeing Derek as valedictorian the year he graduated, so the young man had potential. The RCMP was always looking for help.

"If you remember anything else, please call or stop by the station."

"I will, Ethan — er, *sir*."

The hefty, bearded man stood up and paused. "Oh, one thing I remember, but it's probably nothing."

"Hard to say, Derek. Sometimes the seemingly smallest thing can be huge in an investigation."

"I don't recall *exactly*, but I think it was at Coleson's Creek bridge, about twenty-five or thirty miles up the Swatfly. I *want* to say there was an old camper van, maybe even one of the four-by-four kinds, sort of tucked off into the sticks. Just figured it was somebody fishing, or maybe an abandoned rig."

Ethan nodded his head, taking notes.

"Good memory, Derek. You're not just a dart-throwing Tree-Beardian wizard, after all."

"Dart-throwing... Tree-Beardian... wizard?" Derek said slowly, then grinned. "I really like the sound of that! Mind if I steal it?"

"Steal away; it's no crime."

"Thanks. So can I go now?"

"Certainly. Again, appreciate your help, Derek."

"My pleasure, Officer, Ethan, sir."

Ethan smiled, and after Derek walked out, he shook his head slightly. People would still be uncomfortable around him, even if he lived in Glyph's Gulch for 500 years. Despite having grown up on the outskirts of town, when he became a cop, people looked at him differently and had trouble distinguishing between the man and the Mounty, the person, and the police force. Invariably, when you had the RCMP uniform on, you became the most obvious individual one never saw.

People would avert their eyes, stumble on his name, buy him a coffee one day and curse him out for a speeding ticket the next. Needed, admired, trusted, respected, distrusted, and despised, all smooshed together in a red or blue-with-yellow-stripe uniform.

Periodically he embraced anonymity, but sometimes Ethan hated it. Still, the day they had the celebration of life for his little girl, he swore every single person in the East Kootenays showed up to offer their condolences, shake his hand, give him a hug, and say what an amazing girl Chelsea had been. Days later, he was back to being Officer Birchom: to some, a valued commodity; to others, a necessity, albeit a grating one; and to a handful, a damn power-tripping pig.

Ethan accepted all of it. He would do anything for the people of Glyph's Gulch. Like their surroundings, they could be rough, magnificent, and free-spirited. The people he valued respected him. It's why Ethan felt comfortable asking for their help on short notice.

Two hours later, seven such people were standing at the junction of the main highway and Swatfly Road.

"I can't thank you all enough for coming. It's hot out, so take extra water, and do the 'slip, slop, slap' thing."

Already he could see Derek put his t-shirt back on, Angela pull on her Tilley, and Reggie smear sunscreen on his freckled nose.

"Good. There are eight of us. Perfect. Reggie, Angela, Matt, and Wanda will take the north side of the road. Derek, Julie, Mitch, and I will check the south."

They found nothing at the turnoff, except for two dollars' worth of beer cans. Now, the searchers would hopscotch themselves and two vehicles up the road. They'd go as far as two coolers full of water and pop, volunteer stamina, and interest would last.

They walked along the road, and in banks or ditches when possible. After three hours and three miles, coolers and energy resources were exhausted.

They hadn't found a single item of interest.

Ethan gathered everyone together and thanked them for their efforts. As an additional thank you, Ethan raided the office slush fund to give each of the volunteers — and Reggie — a $20 gift card for the hardware store.

Ethan and Reggie watched the volunteers drive off, and Ethan put his hand on Reggie's shoulder.

"Thanks again for coming on your day off, Reggie. I thought Sundays were basically sacred to you."

"Well, they are, more or less, but since I bought the DVD set for *MAD TV* and all the *Sabrina the Teenage Witch* episodes and films, I can binge-watch afterwards."

"My daughter Chelsea loved Sabrina."

"Ah, cool. You're welcome to come over and watch some. My vintage popcorn machine is working, and I just got in a case of Pop Shoppe pop."

"Thanks for the invite, Reggie, but after we're done, I have to file a report, and when *that's* done, I plan to tumble my rocks."

"'Tumble my rocks'. Is that what they are calling *it* these days? Wocka wocka."

Ethan was perplexed for a moment, but then he caught on.

"I have a rock tumbler, and in my spare time I polish colorful stones...been doing it since I was a kid."

"Oh. Very retro!"

"I suppose we both have our retro interests."

"For sure."

"Anyway, let's drive up the road and see if we can get lucky."

"Uh, boss, I didn't bring a condom."

Reggie blurted out a laugh, ran over to the passenger side of the vehicle, and got in the police truck before Ethan could even reply.

They made their way slowly up the Swatfly, eyeballing the ditches for anything unusual. An hour later, with nothing to show for their eagle-eye efforts, they made it to Coleson's Creek bridge — the spot Derek said he'd seen the camper van.

In terms of sound, the relatively small stream punched above its weight. Water churned and foamed over a chorus of rocky chasms. Picturesque, yes, fish-friendly, no. Scarcely any flat ground existed on the lower side of the creek for parking. Plus, the bridge was on a corner.

There wasn't another parking spot within five-hundred feet of either side of the bridge. The road was steep enough that if you were a truck going up, you wouldn't stop for a look-see. If you were coming down, your focus would be making sure nobody was coming up and safely navigating the narrow crossing.

They drove up past the bridge, turned around at the wide spot that would've accommodated one-lane traffic and a parked vehicle, then parked at a wide spot a five-minute walk below the bridge.

Ethan and Reggie walked back uphill and scoured the area. Nothing was visible except for chopped bushes and faint wheel tracks.

Having given up, Reggie sat on a bridge rail waiting for Ethan. It had grown blustery and dusty; it was time to call it a day. As a gust of wind forced Ethan to pull down on his cap, he saw a fleck of white dancing through the weeds at the edge of the road. Instinctively, he went after it. Like most people in the Kootenays, he hated seeing plastic end up in watercourses.

Ethan snagged it deftly from the air and discovered it wasn't a piece of plastic from a chip bag or whatever, but a piece of an envelope. He turned it over. All he could make out were the letters 'NAERP.' Probably a whole lot of nothing — or in this case, a shred of nothing. Nevertheless, he tucked it into an evidence bag.

"Let's roll, Reggie. *Sabrina* and my stones await."

"Sorry, creek's loud! What's that?"

"Time for *Sabrina* and my stones!"

"Kinky."

#

Refreshingly cool air, the rustling of leaves, the smell of pines and wildflowers, bumble bees buzzing, and a fishing rod in hand. Regarding the simple pleasures of life, Ethan had once heard an Easterner say, 'That's all ya need there, boy, that's all ya need.' It was true; he needed a day like this to reconnect with himself and nature.

Ethan baited his hook about thirty inches below his bobber and tossed his line out into the back-eddy. The water was lower than normal this year, but he reckoned there would still be some nice cutthroat and the odd bull trout in the deeper, colder zones, and places where overhanging tree limbs afforded shade and protection.

As Ethan relaxed further, he fully realized how much he'd needed this getaway. His sleep was frequently disrupted by dreams of cases and missing people's names. He would have to thank Angela for coaxing him in this direction.

In fact, he could've just not tied on a hook and sacrificed an earthworm. Just watching the red and white bobber moving across the water, tilting to-and-fro like it was dancing to a song only it could hear, was relaxing.

Before he'd married, Ethan often went fishing. When Chelsea was old enough, they would go out together. She had a knack for it, though she refused to use earthworms; she said it was cruel. Her weapon of choice was a Royal Coachman fly. The red, brown, black, and white pattern didn't imitate any real winged insect, though it resembled a mayfly. It was simply an attractor. Fish loved it, at least when she used it.

After fifteen minutes of watching his bobber "bob", Ethan sat down his now-empty coffee mug and reeled in. He liberated the worm and replaced the #6 single hook with a Royal Coachman.

Casting out, he said, "Chelsea, let's see what your fly can do!"

He'd only just poured himself another coffee from his thermos when he saw his bobber skid sideways against the slow, swirling current, as if he might have a fish investigating his fly. Of course, the hook could just be caught on the bottom.

Ethan hurriedly sat his coffee cup down, grabbed his rod, and prepared to give it a yank if the bobber twitched. His bobber dropped partway under the water and Ethan jerked

59

his fishing rod upward. It felt like he had something big, and then, in an instant, it was gone. The excitement made him feel like a kid again.

Ethan's heart was beating like he was in a dark building, wondering if the person who had committed the B&E might still be present, hiding behind the door with a knife. He missed the feeling of bringing in a nice fish, so he quickly reeled in, checked his hook, and made a careful cast.

He stood at the ready in case the lunker struck again. Was it a bull trout or a large cutthroat? Either would be epic, even though this being a catch-and-release stream dictated that he would have to let the fish go.

The bobber tracked slowly from its upstream location, where the current was faster, to the place where Ethan had the bite. Again, the bobber stopped.

He waited.

The bobber sank, and Ethan brought the tip of his rod up sharply. He felt the weight of something on the end of his line and started to reel in, but whatever was on the other end of the line didn't budge.

Ethan shook his head. He'd probably snagged a big broken off tree limb that was caught in the stream and moved with the current, manifesting as a fish. Ethan tightened his line and released, hoping the recoil would free the hook. No dice.

Excitement now morphed into disappointment; not only had he lost a mythical lunker, but he would probably lose his fly and bobber. Tightening his line, he walked back slowly and waited for the line to snap.

Instead, it pulled free, and he felt a heavy drag on the line. As he brought his line in slowly, he expected to see a chunk of wood hanging off the hook. Instead, he saw a running shoe... with a foot inside. Ethan closed and reopened his eyes to make sure what he was seeing was real. It was real... and really gross.

After putting the size eight man's shoe and decomposed foot in the plastic bag he had brought to put fish in, Ethan pulled a roll of crime-scene tape from his backpack — and his sidearm.

Some habits were hard to break.

Stringing tape between trees, he cordoned off a wide area, all the while looking for anything that might point to a murder, probably linked to Kayak Kid's arm. Ideally, he would continue to scour the scene, but there was no cell coverage in the valley bottom, so he couldn't call Bert. Ethan needed to get back to the truck and get a diver in the water as soon as possible.

He went upstream and filled his water bottle, inhaled one of the two tuna sandwiches he had brought with him, holstered his gun, and started scrambling up the steep bank. There was no trail, and the footing was slick from a morning shower. It would take him no less than forty-five minutes to get back to his truck. Shortly thereafter, after sliding back eight feet from a twelve-foot gain, he adjusted his estimate; it would take him an hour to reach the road.

Fifteen minutes later and a hundred feet up, a blowing noise and the clacking of teeth made him look up. Fifty feet from him, a black bear, one of the biggest Ethan had ever seen, was on its way down. They had surprised one another, the sounds of their approaches masked by the stream below and the wind through the trees.

The wind had been coming down the valley, otherwise the bear would've smelled him, or the foot, or the tuna sandwich. After making eye contact for a split second, Ethan breathed, "It's okay, big fellah."

The bear stood up. It was easily six-and-a-half feet tall and probably weighed seven-hundred pounds. It extended its massive paws against a dead snag and, with a grunt, pushed a rotten tree over toward him.

Ethan jumped to the side and skidded fifteen feet downhill, narrowly avoiding being nailed by a one-foot-wide, twenty-foot-long section of deadfall that crashed and slid by him.

The bear was gone when Ethan got up, but he heard twigs snapping away.

"*Bearly* dodged that bullet." Ethan said out loud, half-jokingly.

Suddenly, a bullet tore through the top of his fishing cap. Had he not just bent forward to grab his hiking pole, he would be dead.

As he heard the echoing retort of a rifle, Ethan pressed himself flat to the ground and half slithered, half slid downhill. Then, suddenly, he was ass-over-teakettle off a moss-covered rocky outcrop; he hit the ground so hard it knocked the wind out of him and broke his fishing rod, which made him gasp twice as hard.

Once he got his breath again, Ethan moved up under the greenish-grey cornice he had just tumbled over. He pressed himself against rock and tree roots, gathered himself, checking his gun, and waited.

Yes, there were some people who didn't like him, but want him dead? Ethan couldn't even think of an ex-con who might do this. He reasoned that whoever just tried to kill him must've had something to do with the sneaker and foot in Ethan's backpack.

For ten minutes there wasn't a sound, not a bird flying or a squirrel chittering. It was eerie. Then Ethan heard a crunch, like a branch in the moss being depressed by a person's foot, and a big pinecone fell off a tree fifteen feet away.

Ethan stared at the pinecone; it was round, almost like a small pineapple, or ... *A hand grenade!* Instinctively, Ethan turned himself deeper into the twisted fingers of roots at his back.

The explosion was deafening, and he felt shards of shrapnel bite into his back and buttocks. Still, despite the pain, Ethan knew he had to move. He burst from his lair and scurried and clawed his way sideways through fading smoke and steam.

Bam!

A bullet hit him in the back. Ethan fell forward, then rolled and tumbled down all the way to the creek, where a rotting stump partially broke his fall before he splashed into the water. Standing up in waist-deep coldness, he looked down, expecting to see his guts hanging out and a lot of blood in the water. Instead, there was only a pink hue that the current quickly carried away.

He should be dead or dying. Ethan glanced upward, but he couldn't see anyone. The shooter must have realized their bullet hit its mark and wanted to ensure their target's death. Or, perhaps they thought he was already dead?

Regardless, Ethan moved onto the shore and sat down for a split second before the pain in his ass forced him to stand. He looked down at his backpack beside the smashed old stump. He grabbed it, saw the hole in the back, and then, inside, a shattered steel thermos and smashed multi-tool. The bullet, slowed by the thermos, had hit his Leatherman, and exited out the side of the backpack, along with some of his remaining tuna sandwich.

He had been lucky. Even thinking that, Ethan knew he was far from being out of the woods, literally *and* figuratively. What he didn't know was the full scope of his injuries, or if who blasted him might be about to deliver the kill shot. Nor did he know if there was only one attacker; there could be somebody on the other side of the creek about to put a bullet in his brain.

It made Ethan realize he was standing out in the open, shivering and bleeding from who-knows-what-wounds to his posterior. He felt as helpless as when he realized he'd probably never see his daughter again.

Ethan stepped back, rather painfully, behind a big cedar, and a bullet tore the bark off near his head. He quickly yanked a two-inch sliver of wood from his cheek. The angle of the shot told him that the shooter was indeed on the other side of the creek. If it was the first shooter, they must move like a goat *and* a fox! If two or more people were after him, they would staple him down to the creek. His demise would be inevitable.

He had to choose between going back uphill to his truck or following the stream. Ethan tightened the straps on his backpack, and with a running leap, hit the water. He felt a sharp pain in his leg, and it was all he could do to protect himself from being smashed against the rocks as the torrent carried him rapidly downstream. It took everything he had to push off rocky outcrops and glide under or over branches and trees that lay like hungry alligators in the stream. He was being scratched, sliced, and beaten.

After about fifteen minutes, he came to a sharp corner and barreled into a pile of driftwood at the stream's edge. He tried to grab onto a log, but it was too slick; he tore off a fingernail, and then the current had him again. This time, there was no angling to shore — the flow was too strong.

Then a waterfall flung him into something that was completely unforgiving. As he fought for air, he knew the impact had separated his right shoulder. Just as he became certain he was going to drown, his feet found purchase, and he used every ounce of energy he had left to push toward the shore.

As the current twisted him around, Ethan saw someone standing at the top of the waterfall, rifle aimed. He rolled into the water and kicked as best he could. Another wincing pain hit the same leg, and he breathed in some water. *Don't let them win! You still have to find Chelsea's killer!*

Then, he was back in the current, but it was only a short while until he was thrown over a slick green log. No, it was a half-submerged kayak! He grabbed onto one of the support lines of the kayak and pulled himself toward the shore.

In pain and possibly on the verge of hypothermia, Ethan took several deep breaths. It hurt like hell, but it was enough to clear his mind. He still had a long way to go the valley and possible rescue, and he was in no condition to walk or swim.

With his good arm, Ethan freed the kayak and crawled in. Moments later, he was floating downstream; the river had calmed, and he was away.

He just hoped he wouldn't bleed out.

Chapter Eight: Stones

The young man, clad in camo, moved cautiously westward down the slope, and crept to the meadow's edge. Once there, he scanned the area for ten minutes before cautiously emerging from the forest's protection. He walked slowly around the meadow, examining the trees. Then he stopped at an enormous maple, which was easily thirty inches in diameter. It was only ten feet from where he first arrived at the meadow.

He sat down at its base and, reaching into his backpack, pulled out two cloth pouches, each tied with a small strip of leather. He opened one sack; it contained a white stone. Then he opened another. It held a black stone. He held a stone in each hand and sat there for another five minutes before rising.

Returning the white stone to its pouch, he slipped it into his pocket. Standing, he reached up and partially tucked the pouch with its black stone into a hole in the maple. Then he stopped and sat back down again, shoulders slumped, pouches and stones in his hands. He had to squeeze his hands together to stop them from shaking. Having calmed himself, he held each stone at arms length until his hands and arms quivered. The hand that sunk first held the white stone, so he abruptly stood up, put it into a pouch, and deposited it into the maple. He marched away, not looking back.

Sixty minutes later, a horse and its rider gracefully entered the meadow from the south. Both the woman and liver chestnut Marwari were rare beauties. As the Marwari's ears were curled up almost to touching, so too was the woman's cowboy hat. The woman and horse almost seemed as one creature.

Dismounting with the ease of someone long accustomed to the saddle, the woman examined the scene. She poured water from her canteen into a bowl produced from a saddlebag and gave the horse a drink. She stroked its white blaze and then, too, took a sip of water. The woman took off her cowboy boots and donned moccasins. Finally, she reached into her saddlebag and pulled out a small sack. She then walked cautiously, but confidently, directly to the big maple.

She reached into the maple, pulled out the previously-installed pouch, and looked at the white rock inside. She hesitated a bit before she took that rock and added it to the sack with her stone, then placed it back into the tree. Then she strode back to her horse, climbed on, and rode away.

An hour passed before the next visitor showed up. The middle-aged man, dressed in black, came out of the west, and strode to the maple. He looked at the two stones it contained, promptly and decisively added his own, and tucked the bag back into the maple. He turned to face the meadow, and, eyes closed, swept his arms outward, and then inward, and side to side, as if conducting an orchestra. He took a quick look around and disappeared as fast as he'd come.

Then, not one, but two people approached the meadow on black-maned bay Morgans. They had come from the south but circled the meadow to enter from the north. The grey-haired old man helped his elderly female companion from her horse, and they both stretched slowly, each grabbing their lower backs and rubbing their behinds.

Holding hands, they walked to the old maple. Both touched the massive hardwood with seeming reverence before resting their backs against it. They exchanged a long look before she nodded. The old man removed his black felt bowler riding hat and, after reaching into the tree, removed the stones that were inside and put them into his bowler. They both looked at the stones, and then, lingeringly, at each other.

After a long look around, they each pulled a stone out of their riding jackets. They clinked their same-colored stones together and then he added them to those within the pouch in his bowler. The sack of stones then went back into the tree. After that, he took his mate's hand, and they danced in the meadow. A long hug ensued, and then they sauntered back to their horses. Sitting astride their Morgans, they admired the scene, and then turned away.

Because of their dalliance, the last balloter, who was at the whip of a team of Friesians, witnessed their departure from the crest of a hill. His wagon was covered by a canvas tarpaulin, but one could make out the footprint of an elongated wooden vessel. His steely countenance, as much as the movement of the reins, propelled the two 1300-pound horses forward with their relatively small load.

The horses were there as statements of tradition, pride, and power. The black-as-night Friesians were descendants of horses from the fourth century in the Netherlands. Over those seventeen-hundred-plus years, Friesians had carried knights in armor, pulled wagons, and starred in dressage events and in films. They had the muscularity of a draught horse combined with the agility of lighter breeds, and were, consequently, versatile. Friesians were intelligent, friendly, energetic, yet calm, and not spooky. A better all-around horse, suitable for a variety of riders, was nearly impossible to find.

As a gathering wind moved the horse's long, thick black manes and tails and caused the silky hairs on their lower legs and hooves to dance like feathers, the elderly man at the reins dabbed his brow with a black handkerchief.

The man stopped his team at the secluded meadow after a lengthy ride that had begun at dawn. Teeth clenched and brow furrowed, he stepped down from his seat — the picture of determination.

As he strode toward the vast maple, the speed and force of his pace increased, such that he was close to stomping on arrival. He pulled out the five stones. There should've only been four, but the couple had left two instead of one.

There were three white and two black stones. He hefted the black stones, feeling the full weight of them, while looking in the direction the couple had come. Then he did the same with the three white stones. Angrily, he thrust all five stones back into the sack. He looked at the sun and determined the time by using his hand and fingers to measure the distance from the sun to the horizon. From out of his long black jacket, he pulled out his own black and white stones, and with a shake of his head, deposited a white stone. Then he waited.

Twenty minutes later, a lean, somewhat frail old man, hiking poles in hand, stepped out of the woods. He walked up to the man holding the stone sack and gave it a hard look.

The man with the horses walked back to his wagon and grabbed a small wooden box. Then he walked back to the hiker, who looked to be about ten years his senior.

He sat the box on the ground, and they took a seat across from one another, the box in between them. One by one, the leader of the Friesians placed the round stones in the box.

At placing the sixth stone, the old man got up, turned south, and shook his fist in the air. Then, he calmed himself, sat back down, and opened his palms toward the man seated across from him. There was a slow, but unmistakable shaking of the head from the man in control of the box and the stone rounds.

They sat there for several minutes before the younger of the two stood up and, bringing his fingers to his mouth, made two piercing whistles. The horses immediately came forward, wagon in tow, to their position. Then the man made one very long whistle. The young man who initiated the vote arrived from the east five minutes later. The vote-counter walked to the back of the wagon and pulled back the canvas cover. He grabbed two hatchets and a large axe.

A hatchet was passed to each the old man and the young man, but he retained the axe. The edges of the hatchets gleamed in the light; their twenty-inch-long hickory handles stained nearly as dark as the horses that had delivered them.

Knowing what was to come, the tall old man hunched down, feet wide apart, hatchet held waist high and just behind his back. The young man stood tall; his hatchet held out in front of him in a defensive position. Then, as the two hatchet-wielding men's eyes moved to the arbiter, the man that ruled over the proceedings raised his axe high and then drove it into the ground.

The old man seized the initiative and swung his hatchet low, but the younger man was agile and skipped away. Had he not been so quick, or the old man a few years younger, his ankle would've been shattered, or Achilles severed. Instead, he only had a small cut on his shin.

They circled each other before the old man instigated a handshake. They both laid down their respective weapons and shook hands, the old man squeezing so hard it made the young man wince in pain. Then, it was back to the hatchets and the circling.

The young man feinted, once, then twice. The second time, the old man moved somewhat awkwardly over what appeared to be a bad hip.

This enticed the young man to circle in the other direction, forcing the old man to stagger over his bad leg, rather than move fluidly.

Then the young man jumped swiftly in the opposite direction, and using his long reach, swept his blade over the old man's left shin. It wasn't a heavy blow, but it was enough to put the elder on two bad legs.

After a brief pause, the young man pressed his advantage. Repeatedly, he ran towards the old man, and then, like a bear, weaved to the side before getting within distance of a strike. The actions tired the old man, and he sank to one knee, grabbing his chest, before standing again, sweating profusely.

The young man crept in close, and the old man swung his hatchet at shoulder height. The thrust missed, and as the old man's momentum took him around and off-balance, the young man moved quickly forward and, with an overhand chop, sank his hatchet deep into the old man's left trapezius.

The blow was a lethal one. The old man fell to his knees, then pitched forward.

His vanquisher knelt beside him, torn between elation and anguish. He reached down and stroked the old man's remaining wispy hair even as blood fanned out around them.

The Friesian captain strode over, grabbed the young man roughly by his shoulder, and marched him over to the wagon, pointing at the vessel in the back.

The flaxen-haired, handsome twenty-something young man climbed into the wagon and opened the coffin that was inside. A young, dark-haired woman wearing a blindfold got out. The young man stroked her hair affectionately, whispered in her ear, and led her to the dead senior. Removing her blindfold, the master of the Friesians passed her the axe.

She didn't hesitate to chop off the old man's head in two swings.

The young man feverously dug a grave and the remains, except for the head and voting stones, were installed, the grave hastily backfilled.

Clearly unimpressed, the elder pointed to the east, and the two young adults, hands entwined, walked in the appointed direction. The dark horseman produced an incense stick from out of his pocket and placed it on a chunk of charcoal on a small tin plate. This he started with a match and placed near the decapitated head.

For the next twenty minutes, the sweet aroma of the combined resins, herbs, and wood spread through the air. Silently, the man wafted the smoke over himself. Once the smoke dissipated, he retrieved the head, hatchets, and axe, and using some branches, swept up the area.

Chapter Nine: The Walking Wounded

Ethan stifled a groan as he stepped down. Walking was a pain in the ass, literally and figuratively, but stairs — well, they were utterly butt-hurt excruciating.

He looked around, glad that nobody had elected to trot down the two flights of stairs to the cafeteria. Despite the bad reputation hospital cafeterias often gained, Ethan had no complaints. Mind you, as Bert had pointed out, Ethan found supermarket deli subs tasty, so a cuisine expert, he was not.

Still, Chelsea had always said his pancakes were '*otherworldly yummy*,' and he clung to that praise, and her memory, with all his might.

Ethan had three more steps to go; then he would climb back up and hopefully be in his room before anybody was the wiser. Ethan rubbed the back of his thigh and his buttocks and held his shit together until he got down to the landing, beads of sweat running down his head and cheeks — all four of them. He let out a withering, "*Ow-ow-ow-ow...*"

"Serves you right!"

Oh, crap. Ethans head dropped in resignation.

He looked up to see Bert looking down at him and Angela wagging a disapproving finger.

His doctor joined them both, bushy eyebrows furrowed.

"Please help your friend back up the stairs, will you?"

Following the doctor's orders, Bert scampered down the stairs with an ease that pained Ethan's butt almost as much as his wounds.

Bert's shrug was an unspoken, *I feel you, man, but let's just do this*, so Ethan allowed Bert to help him back up the stairs. Thankfully, Bert had been mindful to help him on his left, for his right shoulder was still awfully sore. By the time they got back to his room, Ethan was glad for the help, albeit embarrassed.

The doctor asked Angela and Bert to look away from Ethan's exposed derriere. "Fortunately, you didn't tear any stitches. Do that again, and *I* might even kick your backside."

Ethan looked at the doctor, a Ukrainian immigrant; he reckoned the gruff old man might just follow through on the threat, so he said, "I'll be a good boy from now on."

"See that you do."

Angela stood with her hands on her hips; after the doctor left, she let out a chuckle, and added, "What do you have to say for yourself, not-so-bouncy-Birchom?"

"I may not have a bounce to my step, but I just can't wait to get the heck out of here." His head sank deeper into his pillow.

"We understand, Ethan, but we also know you can be, ah…." Bert looked down at his feet before continuing, "A stubborn jackass. I say that with all due respect."

"I second Bert's 'stubborn jackass' and raise you a 'dog-with-a-bone' determination." Angela looked Ethan square in the eye.

"Geez, thanks for the pep talk, guys," Ethan teased.

Bert and Angela smiled affectionately.

"But seriously, thanks a lot for visiting…it means a lot to this crippled, old cop."

"They cancelled the tiddlywink convention and we had nowhere else to go."

"Thanks, Angela…very touching."

At that, she came over and squeezed his good shoulder before giving him a kiss on the forehead. "You get better, okay? I'm off to help Mitch at his store. He might be a music maestro, but his bookkeeping skills…" Angela slapped herself on the forehead.

"See ya, Angela. Again, thanks for coming by."

As Angela left, Bert skidded a metal chair up beside Ethan's bed.

It was time to talk shop.

"We processed the crime scene. Whatever sign there might've been was probably wiped out by heavy rains. Sorry, Ethan."

"No need to apologize. What about shell casings?"

"No." Again, Bert looked apologetic.

"The hand grenade?"

"Only a few shards. Nothing that would point to a maker or point of purchase; probably old army surplus."

"Damn."

"Oh, some other non-news."

"What's that, Bert?"

"You had asked about friends of Miller Renfrew and Bill de Vandenbrough that might want revenge."

"Yes."

"From what I found out, if they had any friends, they're all in jail. Even their families weren't overly distraught to learn they were dead."

"So, we're at square one." Ethan bit his lip to avoid a curse and asked a question he expected another negative answer to. "Let me guess, nothing more on Kayak Kid either?"

"No, sir." Bert looked at his fitness watch.

"Am I keeping you from a workout?"

"No. But I do have some other police business to attend to."

"I understand. With me stuck in here, you are carrying the load."

Bert shrugged. "It's okay."

"Thankfully, they're going to let me out in a few days, so I can start earning my pay again. It feels like even my *bruises* have sores."

"I bet! And you are *sorely* needed. Reggie and I have spent so much time together that we're starting to get on each other's nerves."

Ethan thought about that and almost offered some sage advice, but he elected to take the low road.

Ethan mimicked Reggie's voice as best he could and used one of Reggie's favorite made-up expressions, one he often said, apropos of nothing: "The noble Cassius hath told me that you rubbed the Brutus the wrong way."

Bert's eyebrows went up, his face contorted; he blinked, and before Ethan knew it, Bert was on his knees, holding onto his chair and laughing hysterically.

Eventually, Bert regained his seat and, after another burst of laughter, calmed down.

"Boss, no disrespect intended, but in terms of funnies, you totally outdid yourself on that one!"

"No disrespect at all. Good to see you bust a *ha-ha*. Sorry to change the subject, but are the RCMP temps still coming in to ease some of the backlog?"

"Yes. Reggie and one of them will take turns being stationed at your house."

Ethan brought a weary hand to his forehead and sighed. "Ya, I feared this would happen… but with Kim and her children there, I suppose an abundance of caution is appropriate."

"Definitely — and it's the rules; after all, your life was threatened. It was that, a transfer, or extended leave. Given the RCMP's staffing demands, I think this is the best we could do. Plus, I'd hate to see you go."

Ethan put his hand on Bert's shoulder and gave it a firm squeeze. Ethan knew the RCMP wouldn't transfer him; he'd already told Bert he would retire if they even suggested it.

"Thanks for everything, Bert. You're an even better friend than you are an RCMP officer, and that's saying a lot."

Bert beamed. Ethan knew Bert to be a humble and underpaid man, but, like anyone, would be buoyed by a kind word at the right time.

"On that cheerful note, I best go, unless you have anything else for me?"

"Just one thing. How's Twix?"

"Every time someone enters the station, she jumps up, clearly expecting you to be walking in. When she discovers it's not you, she lays back down and looks like somebody stole her favorite bone."

That wound added to Ethan's other pains.

"I will make it up to her."

Bert nodded, and with a satisfied smile, excused himself.

Ethan was damn lucky to have people like Bert, Angela, Reggie, and Kim in his life.

With his shoulder and posterior physiotherapy not for another two hours and nothing to watch on TV, he opened SinglePass. He was admittedly eager to see if Becca, the woman he had exchanged winks and messages with, had pinged him; him operating under the name, *Blake*.

He smiled when he saw her latest communique. *I also love grilled cheese sandwiches, Blake, especially out in nature. It's like everything tastes better when you're outside having a picnic or even bouncing down a dirt road.*

I couldn't agree more, Becca, he replied, then feeling an elevated level of whimsy, added, *Perhaps, one day, we can do that together. Aside from pancakes, grilled-cheese sandwiches are the only thing I make reasonably well.*

That sounds inviting. Might have to have your people talk to my people?

Good idea. Then his practical side kicked in. *We should talk on the phone sometime, you know, so neither one of us finds the other's voice to be like fingernails on a blackboard, or maybe like the guy Billy Bob Thornton played in Sling Blade.*

Becca replied with a laugh-emoji and *LOL*, before adding, *It's probably a good idea. Hey, I must run, but we should discuss this another time.*

Roger. Take care, Becca.

You too, Blake.

Well, that was encouraging! Perhaps they'd have chemistry in person.

Ethan saw other notifications of interest and potential matches, but he resolved to be a 'one quasi-cyber-relationship at a time' sort of guy.

He had just turned on the TV to pass the time when his phone pulsed a text message.

I'm in town. Care for a visitor? It was Caroline.

They'd only met in person four or five times, and while the frequency of their text messages had increased over the years — especially since the encounter with Miller Renfrew and then the attempt on his life — he hadn't expected her to visit.

Definitely. I'm on the second floor.

See you in fifteen minutes.

Great.

Ethan raised himself up in his bed, finding that sweet spot where he was mostly upright without overtaxing his shoulder, while applying minimal pressure to his posterior.

Shortly thereafter, the RCMP trainee who was guarding his door poked her head in and said, "Caroline Leadshat here to see you, sir."

"Please let her in."

A woman that looked like Lena Headey, not from Game of Thrones, but from the Sarah Connor Chronicles, stepped in. He'd only ever seen Caroline in uniform, but today she was in denim jeans, a white t-shirt, and a brown suede jacket. In uniform, she was "officially" attractive; in casual wear, she looked downright pretty.

"So how are you doing, Ethan?"

"Pretty good; sore, but I'm well enough that I'll get out of here soon."

"I bet you can't wait!"

"Definitely. Ah, please, have a seat, Caroline."

Caroline grabbed the chair and slid it to his bedside.

He detected a subtle, but very nice perfume.

"Mandatory time off, I assume."

"Uh, ya, sadly. At least another week."

"Security detail at your house?"

"Yes, unfortunately."

"Probably for the best."

"I suppose."

"Any leads?"

"Nope. Anyway, what brings you to our neck of the woods?"

"Wanted to give you something in person."

At that she got up and stepped to the door, where his guard passed her a gift-wrapped box.

Returning, she sat it on the bed beside him.

Ethan looked at the box, then at Caroline.

"Well, aren't you going to open it?"

A gift from a woman — and a pretty one!

"Oh, Caroline, you shouldn't have..."

"Just open it."

With care, Ethan removed the wrapping and then the lid on the box to reveal, *drum roll please*, a set of astronomical binoculars!

"Wow! These are incredible, Caroline! I always wanted a pair. Thank you so much. But how did you know I enjoyed stargazing?"

"I have my sources."

Reggie! It was probably Reggie.

"You'll want to get a tripod for them at some point. Sorry, I didn't have time for that."

"Oh, don't apologize... this is..." He looked at her; the softness in her eyes was beguiling. He hadn't expected that, for previously, it was her resolve that shone through. "This is awesome. Thanks again, Caroline."

"Oh, and here's the card."

What have I done to deserve this?

The 'Get Well Soon' card was nice, and the note inside read:

Given the magnification levels, you might not see your neighbor's grilled-cheese sandwich, but you will get excellent views of the moon's cheesy craters. –Becca.

Ethan was sure his eyebrows raised several inches and his mouth hinged open like a giant grouper ready to swallow a turtle.

"Becca, you're Caroline — ah, I mean, Caroline, you're Becca?"

"Yes, *Blake*."

He was about to ask how she'd figured it out, but he was lost in surprise and her bright eyes.

Chapter Ten: Nearly Clueless

Ethan could tell by the look on Bert's face that the news wasn't great. "Okay, let's get started. Any DNA matches on the Kayak Kid?"

"No." Bert removed his toque and held it in his hand, almost apologetically. It always surprised Ethan that Bert could wear a toque even when it was hot outside.

"Not even for a probable relative, Bert?"

"Nothing close enough that we have the resources to narrow down."

"Shit! Tell me we had better luck with the ballistics on the bullets they pulled out of me."

"The rifling on the bullets suggest a Remington, but we've no idea of the model."

"And, of course, there are loads of Remington rifles out there, so it's a shot in the dark."

"Unfortunately, yes."

"How about the kayak itself?"

"Garden-variety, inexpensive model that you can buy at any number of hardware, department stores, and sports shops."

"Any other DNA in it that can link it to the missing young man?"

"No."

"Double shit!" Ethan paused, scowling. "Sorry, Bert, it's obviously not your fault. I'm just frustrated. All the sitting, the physio, the waiting, wanting to solve a crime, more physio, etcetera."

"Understandable, but we'll figure this out."

Then something occurred to Ethan. "Wait; when I was in the kayak, as I tumbled my sorry ass downstream, I ended up twisted around with my head toward the nose and my feet up on the seat. I want to say I remember seeing something — a sticker — wait, a flag, yes, a flag like a Union Jack, on the underside of the deck! Let's go have a look!"

They rushed to the evidence room, insofar as Ethan could "rush," and pulled the kayak off the wall. Once down, Ethan got down on his knees and gingerly contorted himself into a position where he could look up at the inside of the kayak, just forward of the seat.

Using the tiny flashlight on his keyring, he shone the light on it.

"It's a flag alright, but I can't quite make it out."

"Snap a photo with your phone. I bet it will show up better on flash."

"Good thinking!" Ethan snapped a few pictures using his mobile phone.

After he slowly — very slowly — got out of the kayak, he pulled up his photo gallery and zoomed in on the image. It was definitely a flag, but not the Union Jack. "It's the provincial flag of Manitoba!"

"Whoop, there it is! A lead!"

"Yes! Let's see if we can get forensics to check DNA matches for Manitoba. Start with Winnipeg. It has half the population of the province."

"Will do, Ethan. Great job!"

"Well, Bert, I do my best work upside down."

Bert clapped him on the back and together they stowed away the kayak.

Thank God we finally have something to go on!

It took much longer than planned to get a diver into the river. The rains that had followed the attempt on his life had left the water high, rough, and dirty. A piece of cement block, presumably used to hold the deceased foot to the bottom, and two small ropes, one with a chunk of chain attached, were all that they recovered.

Reggie was looking into those aspects of the investigation, so Ethan swung by his desk and caught him just before he was leaving.

"How are we doing with the concrete block and the rope that the young man strangled or dangled from, Reggie?"

"Nothing from the block, but we analyzed the rope; it's not made of nylon, polyester, and polypropylene, but hemp. You know what hemp is, boss?"

"Yes, Reggie, I know what hemp is."

"It's like the t-shirts Mitch sells at Drop the Needle. I mean, it has so little THC in it that you could smoke a whole shirt and not get high. Plus, the cost of all the Zig-Zag papers would be outrageous. And then there is..."

Ethan raised his hands in a 'please stop' motion which, mercifully, Reggie heeded, well, except for adding, "But, I digress."

"Thanks, Reggie. So, we have old-fashioned rope." Hemp rope was notoriously strong and durable, used for a range of things, including weight loading, climbing, and shipping. He even had a roll of it in his garage.

"Yes, but I did some digging and found out there is only one primary hemp rope manufacturer, Ravenox. They started in 2012, and after sending them a sample, they said it wasn't from one of their products. And they didn't know what smaller operation might've made it."

"Interesting. Good work, Reggie!"

"That's why they pay me the big bucks. It's not just because of my dart prowess!"

Ethan smiled; Reggie might be a bit weird, but he was capable, and a good soul.

"It suggests that the perpetrator or perps may well be making their own rope."

Reggie shrugged. "Could be."

"And the chain attached to the other piece of rope? Anything on that?"

"Not yet."

"Anyway, appreciate your efforts, Reggie. I'll see what I can dig up on the chain rope."

Ethan took the rope and chain back to his desk and sat them on top of the pile of papers he called 'Maybe tomorrow.'

Twix needed a walk, so man and canine exited the building and sauntered down the trail that snaked between the trees of their station and into a small dog park. The park was empty, and after tossing a tennis ball for Twix for fifteen minutes, Ethan said, "Well, girl, you know how it is; paperwork won't do itself."

Twix grabbed the tennis ball and together they walked back toward the office.

As they emerged from the trees, Angela stepped out of the detachment.

"*There* you are!"

"Indeed, here I am, mostly-mobile Mounty. How are you, Angela?"

"Right as rain. I stopped by your desk, left you some of my red velvet muffins."

"Oh, marvelous! Those are the best! Had I known you were bringing velvet muffins, I would've rolled out the red carpet."

"Funny. By the way, what's the chunk of hemp horse lead doing on your desk?"

"Horse lead? Is that what it is?"

"Yes, and it's for a mighty big horse. Not your average thoroughbred or trail horse."

"Really? Wow, that's so helpful, Angela, thank you!" He gave her a big hug and practically hopped up the steps.

"Hey, not too fast there, cowboy!"

"But I have to get to the muffins, ahem, I mean, hemp horse lead, before anyone else does!"

Angela smiled.

"Honestly, I'm just going to have one muffin before I probe into your horse lead, ah... lead."

"Would you like me to explore who might have such big horses?"

"That would be fantastic! Any initial thoughts?"

"There are a lot of people with big horses in southern BC, Alberta, and Montana. I think we start with the Kootenays and take it from there."

"Good thinking. Can Elk Point manage without you for a while?"

"I'm happy to help, plus I already bribed them with some muffins, knowing that I wanted to come and visit you." Angela smiled at Ethan. He smiled back, champing at the bit to grab a muffin.

"I'll pop by Stella's Stables; she may have some ideas."

"Excellent."

"I don't suppose you'd be up for a ride?"

"Oh, Angela, I haven't been on a horse in probably ten years."

"It's a bit like riding a bike. You'll pick it up fast."

"I also fell off bikes a lot."

Angela smirked. "I could ask Stella if any of her horses come with training wheels."

"Yes, please! This old guy is only one or two tumbles away from retirement."

"Oh, Ethan, you're far from old!"

Just then, his phone rang. It was a ringtone he had added specifically for Caroline.

"Sorry, Angela. I have to take this."

"No worries. I'll keep you posted."

"Thanks a lot."

Ethan didn't answer the phone fast enough to catch Caroline, but a beep alerted him to a text.

He answered Caroline's *Is it okay to call* with a *Yes, just give me a minute.*

Caroline called again just as Angela stepped out the door and he walked into the empty interrogation room.

"Hey, Caroline." Since they had been speaking regularly, he'd found that, occasionally, his voice rose an octave when he said her name.

"How are you, Mr. Survivor Superstar?"

Ethan cleared his throat and said, in a more manly voice, "Coming from someone that probably only wears a flack-jacket so her coworkers don't feel insecure — *and* apparently dodges bullets like Neo from the Matrix — I take that as a compliment."

Caroline giggled, and Ethan felt his face redden. *She really does fancy me!*

"Well, we'll definitely have to celebrate our ability to defy the dastardly deeds of delinquents this weekend, and it's on me, no arguments."

He swallowed hard and squeaked out, "Sounds good."

Chapter Eleven: Brickwallaby

Having Kim around had been a real blessing. No, they didn't talk a lot, but having someone to share the occasional meal and joke around with was uplifting. Kim was going above and beyond with meals and little errands, so Ethan could focus more on rest and recovery. She was saving up for an apartment, so he wasn't charging her anything.

This morning, after dropping off her children at her mom's, which she did occasionally to save on daycare, she stopped at the station to drop off some steaming-hot bran muffins.

"Thanks a lot, Kim. I'll get it the next time or five."

"No problem. It's the least I can do."

"I'm just happy to have y'all around."

"Thanks. The kids are calling you 'Grandpa Cop.'"

"That's sweet, though makes me feel old."

They exchanged a smile, and then she noticed his laptop screen.

"That girl looks familiar."

He should've closed his screen or not had a missing person's photo up.

"You probably wouldn't know her."

"Hmm...I was good friends with a girl from across the line, Leslie McGown. I met her in 4-H, and we used to hang around a fair bit. Haven't spoken with her in two years, but that picture sure looks like her little sister, Debra."

"You're right, Kim. That is Debra McGown. She went missing a while back. Though the authorities in Montana are probably all over it, I tend to take an interest in these cases, well, because, you know..."

"Of course. Still, I mean, wow! Debra is missing. I will definitely catch up with Leslie; I know she and Debra didn't get along all that well. Leslie always called her a phony; 'Miss Goodie Two-Shoes' one minute and a backstabber the next. Still, it's her little sister, and she must be sick over it."

"Yes, I know the family is pretty broken up over it; they even offered a sizeable reward for knowledge of her whereabouts."

"Geez, life is weird... so many nutcases out there!"

"Sad, but true."

"Well, Mr. B, I better get to Mitch's. I'm helping him design a third listening room."

"Oh, great! Pass a 'Howdy' to him from me."

"I will. Try to stop by later if you can. We could use another opinion."

"Err...that *sounds* good."

"Oh, *groan*." Kim rolled her eyes. "Your law enforcement shtick is always strong, but sometimes, Grandpa Cop, your pun game is weak."

They shared a giggle.

"Don't I know it, Kim."

"It's all good. Hope to see you later."

They exchanged a quick hug and Kim gave Twix a pat on the head before leaving.

Ethan reflected on what Kim had said about Debra and if she was a phony. He knew Debra had done nice things for people, especially seniors. Really, it didn't matter; she was a missing girl, and like any missing person, he was determined to find her and find who was responsible.

In that spirit, Ethan returned to his laptop and clicked on an icon that looked like a spider web with a robot stuck in it.

Angela had worked with one of her brainiac associates to design the program for him. Actually, Angela called it '*a creepy-crawler macro designed to deliver results tailored to his specific needs.*' All he had to do was insert a location, which could be anything from a county to a continent, a date range, and hit 'Execute.' Far from being a techie, he was totally good with that. He had only run the program once, and it had generated three results that were new to him.

However, just as he was to look into it further, Ethan had been called out to address the 'emergency' of a teen that stole some cigarettes from the 7-11. It was now 9am the following morning, and with fresh-brewed coffee and warm bran muffins, he was primed to scrutinize the three new unsolved cases that the program had generated the night before. Unfortunately, when he opened his laptop, he realized that he'd neglected to save the results, so he would have to run the program again. Oh well, it was still early on a Sunday morning and the program would quickly regenerate the previous results.

Sipping his coffee, Ethan used end date as today, keyed in 1998, which is the date he'd used before, and hit Execute. As he savored a bite of a muffin, he stared at the date range that said 1968 to 2023. *Wait, 1968!* He had entered 1968 instead of 1998. *D'oh!* Ethan then realized he had unwittingly left the location as "Default–Canada–USA" when he meant to select just a few provinces and states as he had done the first time.

Serves you right, Ethan, for operating before at least one cup of coffee!

The first time he ran the macro, it had taken about ten minutes. Now, he could only guess how long it would take. It caused him to wrap his head with his knuckles, which actually stung, and also caused Twix to lift her head off the floor in apparent concern.

"Sorry about that Twix. I got a bit carried away. Well, I guess all we can do at this point, is to sit and wait, right?" Twix responded with a disinterested, albeit polite, *urm*.

After a few minutes of impatiently twiddling his thumbs, Ethan pushed back from his desk and stood up.

"How about another walk, Twix?"

Twix's *ruff* was infinitely more inspired than her *urm* had been, so Ethan grabbed his coffee and then slyly pulled a frisbee from out of his desk and tucked it under the arm of his jacket. Twix tilted her head at him, likely aware of what he was hiding. With his 'DMI' — Daily muffin intake — at an all-time high and his exercise rate at a career low, Ethan needed the walk far more than Twix did.

Five minutes out and entering Pleasant Park, he dug out the frisbee. Twix did her impression of a whirlwind and then gave him a *Let's do this* look, which he obliged.

The frisbee soared away, but then the wind caught it, and it hung in the air long enough for Twix to catch up with it and snatch it about five feet off the ground.

"Ace snag, Twix!"

Twix trotted back, proud as can be, and received the reward of a chunk of bran muffin.

"Now, feel like a bigger challenge?"

Twix barked an affirmative and crouched, ready to spring after the pancake-shaped vermin projectile.

This time, Ethan put more spin and angle to his throw, aiming to have it cut the wind and then turn more sharply toward the ground.

The throw went as planned, and Twix, being the frisbee-snagging all-star that she was, plucked the disc out of the air about six inches from the ground.

Twix came back slowly and wouldn't let Ethan grab the frisbee, as if to say, *I knew what you were doing,* Human. *You're the one who needs to be baited now!*

After a few bluff passes, Twix let Ethan take the frisbee. They played for another ten minutes, then they both sat down, enjoying their surroundings. A brown, black, and white butterfly landed on Ethan's hand, and Twix looked at both it and him.

"I think that's a Painted Lady, Twix, but I can't be sure."

Twix cocked her head sideways as if debating the veracity of his claim and went back to chewing on the frisbee.

"This is such a special place to live — well, except for the dismembered bodies and attempted murders and such."

This time Twix ignored him, surely aware of it being a rhetorical statement.

Man and friend sauntered back to what Ethan and his colleagues called 'Brickwallaby.' The bricks of the building that served as the RCMP station in Glyph's Gulch resembled the color of Twix's favorite chewy toy, a red-necked wallaby.

Ethan opened Creepy Crawler and was astonished to see 1,178 results.

"Eleven-hundred and seventy-frickin'-eight!" *This is going to take a while.*

Thankfully, a map accompanied the document and spreadsheet, so he could visualize the results on Google Earth — one of the few programs he had taken the time to become

87

familiar with. That Ethan also used Google Earth to help him look for waterfalls and fishing holes was incidental. He loaded the Google Earth KML file.

Pin flags denoting locations where each missing person was last seen popped up over much of the United States, with a surprising amount over the northwestern US and the extreme southwestern corner of Canada. Given the population of that area was small when compared to California or the northeastern United States, the data was certainly noteworthy.

Ethan clicked on one pin, and an associated file popped up. Among other items, the spreadsheet included the person's name, age, sex, home location, date when they went missing, day they were last seen, etc.

"This is sick!"

Twix let out another *urm*, and Ethan immediately realized he'd used an expression far younger than he was. He really needed to stop trying to fit in with the crowd at the record shop.

The printer ran out of ink twice before he'd printed the last page. After sorting through the pages, he put the documents into folders and wedged them all into two boxes. Boxes in arm, he headed for the door. As Ethan reached for the doorknob, Bert opened it.

"Here, Ethan, let me help you out. You shouldn't be toting heavy stuff like that around." Bert grabbed the top box and held the door open.

"Thanks, *Mom* — I mean, Bert."

"You know, it's Sunday, right?"

"Yep."

"And you've been here half the day?" He could see concern etched on Bert's face.

Have I been here that long already?

"Uh, I guess."

"You fed Twix?"

"Ah, a bran muffin and some doggie treats."

Bert sighed. "I'll help you put these in your car, and while Twix is scarfing down a bowl of Kibble, I'll buy you a cold one."

There were no pubs open, so Ethan knew Bert meant a beer from the fridge they weren't supposed to have beer in.

"Sounds good." Ethan didn't feel bad that he'd been at the station so long on a purported day off, nor that he'd skipped lunch, but he *did* feel bad for not feeding Twix properly, and, relatedly, for disappointing Bert.

After securing the boxes in the back seat of his truck, he patted Twix on the head apologetically, and after licking Ethan's hand, Twix trotted after Bert.

As Twix wolfed down her meal, Bert grabbed two cold beers from the fridge tucked in the corner of their snack room. Reggie was doing patrols, which usually entailed sandwiching in the occasional speeding ticket or warning between micro-naps and newspaper cartoons.

Each man pulled a thinly-cushioned white metal chair back from the wobbly lunch table and, with a couple *oomphs*, sat down.

"Let me guess: leg day, Bert?"

"Yes."

"What are you squatting these days, big fellah?"

"Two hundred, comfortably."

"Whoa! Two hundred, that's impressive."

"I would've done more, but since I'm relieving Reggie in a few hours, I didn't want to overdo it."

"Good call." Ethan nodded at the man who he knew to be a gentle giant unless provoked.

"You should join me again sometime — you know, once you're healed up."

"I'm planning to, Bert, but I'm also eyebrows deep in… well, you know."

Bert nodded. They had discussed Ethan being consumed with missing persons cases enough times that 'you know' covered what they both knew: Ethan would never stop.

"How about those Canucks, eh?"

Ethan smiled at Bert. Generally, when one of them wanted to reset a conversation, the person asked about the status of BCs hockey team, the Vancouver Canucks. There was no hockey at this time of year, so it was an opportunity to change the subject, or do a 'cheers.' They clinked their half-empty bottles.

"But no way in hell's half-acre am I going to miss darts this Thursday, Bert!"

"Absolutely! We're going to wreck those tools!"

Bert was talking about their sister detachment in Elk Point; they cheered again and drained their beers.

"Sure, you say that, but if your heart-throb Donna throws another," — Ethan used his best-worst British accent — "'*One-hundred and forrrty*!' you might start clapping like a seal in heat."

Bert grinned. "I confess, she could probably miss the board twice and get a one with her last toss, and I'd still be her biggest fan."

"Yes, Donna is a Pixie, but tough too."

"Yes." Bert had a dreamy look about him.

"Well, my oh my, Bert. I think you're officially gaga over her."

"That obvious, eh?" Bert's face had turned red.

"You reckon you'll finally ask her out?"

"I think so."

"Good for you." Ethan clapped him on the shoulder.

"But that doesn't mean I don't still want to spank her and her teammates."

"'*Spank*'? Now there's a Freudian slip if I ever heard one!"

Bert chuckled. "Guilty as charged. Anyway, I better go home, clean up, eat, and come back."

"Copy that. I probably won't see you until tomorrow."

"Yes. Anyway, don't read that stuff all night, Ethan. You'll go nuts."

"My friend, *that* ship has sailed."

Chapter Twelve: First Date

Ethan saw Caroline's black Ford Bronco and let out an anxious sigh. He had hoped that, by arriving twenty minutes early at Stern's Salad and Steakhouse, he could limp in with some dignity, maybe even splash some cold water on his face before she arrived. *Nope.*

He should've known better; Caroline always seemed prepared. On the upside, at least she hadn't stood him up.

As he walked around the front, darn near tripping over his feet due to a sudden attack of nervousness, Caroline was suddenly there, arm extended, formal-like.

"Mighty kind of you, Caroline." He accepted her arm.

"Can't have you taking a tumble before our night even begins."

They made their way to a private table and agreed on a bottle of merlot.

Between the shine of the glasses and Caroline's sparkling dark brown eyes, Ethan was mesmerized. Caroline was five-foot-nine with long black hair, possessed a stately posture, and her classy dress did nothing to hide her lithe, but strong, frame. Ethan knew she was 42, but she could easily pass for 10 years younger.

Starting with the weather, they gradually advanced to talking about their respective communities, eventually becoming engaged in a thoughtful conversation that revolved around the challenges of their jobs and how police work impacted personal relationships.

Caroline made a good point about how stress, even if well managed, always seemed to accumulate and threaten to overwhelm a person at the worst possible time; Ethan, while agreeing, steered the conversation to something lighter.

"Well, I know a couple that has thrived under stress, and somehow their relationship just gets stronger."

"Oh, really? Do tell."

"You wouldn't know them; they're friends of mine, Becca and Blake. They're so happy together that it's practically a wink-athon when they go out on the town."

"Hmmm... Becka and Blake? Those names seem so contrived."

"I know, right? But let me tell you, the chemistry they share is very real, even if you've only witnessed it in bits and bytes."

Caroline smiled. "They must be lovely people."

"Well, he's *okay*. She, on the other hand, is in a league of her own."

The waiter came by and asked if they would like their glasses topped up, and they eagerly accepted.

"Becca's 'in a league of her own?' In what way?"

Without thinking, Ethan blurted out, "Please don't be jealous, but Becca is hotter than a firecracker." He felt his cheeks turn red. *Oh, Ethan, what are you thinking?!*

For a moment, Caroline seemed surprised, and then she giggled, causing him to smile, albeit sheepishly.

"Well, thanks for that, Ethan! I'm not sure who's more surprised: you for saying it or me hearing it."

"Oh, Caroline, I'm sure you and Becca both hear that fairly often."

"Maybe, but not from you, and certainly not from Blake!" Caroline gave him an air-smooch.

This is going swimmingly!

Easy banter followed, as did another glass of wine, before dinner arrived.

He had veggie lasagna and a salad, and Caroline, prime-rib steak with all the fixings.

"It's nice to see a man being careful with what he eats."

"Thanks, Caroline. I'm trying to cut back on the calories, you know, since I haven't been able to get much exercise."

"Makes sense."

"I admire how you're taking down that steak, though!"

"I was famished today — skipped lunch. You know how work can be."

"I sure do."

"On the subject of work, any leads on who tried to kill you or the deceased?"

"Nothing significant, though we may be on to something."

"Oh, good."

As the waiter gathered their now- empty dishes and then brought them Irish coffees, Caroline continued. "Do you want to talk about it?"

"It may be nothing; just some hemp rope that appears related to larger horses."

Caroline's eyes widened, and she sputtered, "Large... horses?"

"I confess, I don't know much about horses, particularly ones big enough to pull wagons, but my resident expert said the horse would be like a draught horse, perhaps a *little* smaller. I'm not sure how many *drafts* they can drink at one sitting — or pulling, as the case may be. Certainly not a keg."

Ethan expected a chuckle, even a groan, but Caroline was quiet, for several moments.

"Draught and draft, *ha*, that took me a minute. Sorry, sometimes I can wander off at the most inappropriate of times."

That she might already be getting bored with him caused him to take a double pull of his hot whisky dessert drink.

No sooner had he put his cup down than she reached across the table and grabbed his hand warmly.

"Please don't ever think it's you, Ethan. I'm having a wonderful time. You may not know this about me, but I'm not the most social person."

He rested his other hand on top of hers. "I know where you're coming from, Caroline."

She smiled affectionately and put her other hand on top of his. "It's so nice to be with someone who understands. Thanks for that, Ethan."

"The pleasure is all mine. I can't thank you enough for this evening."

She looked at him rather strangely. "The night is still young."

As they left the restaurant, a waxing moon poked out between pillowy clouds. The evening was warm and the weather wonderful.

"You know, there's this lovely lake about a mile off the road. Feel like sitting there for a while and seeing if we can spy some stars between the clouds?"

"Sounds great. We can take my truck."

"Super. And I have a wee bottle of apricot brandy in my Bronco that we can bring."

"Again, grand idea!"

They spent the next hour sipping brandy and stargazing. By the time Orion's belt had revealed itself, she had unbuckled his belt, and he had hiked up her dress.

If the successful dinner date hadn't fried Ethan's noodle, the ensuing sex on the tailgate of his truck would've blown his mind.

He got home at 2:30 a.m. Ethan couldn't remember the last time he stayed up that late for non-work-related reasons. He felt like he had just finished a huge workout; well, it was more like cardio, judging by the way his heart raced.

Ethan sat in his truck for fifteen minutes, savoring the experience. He could smell Caroline on his clothes and taste her on his lips. Not since his honeymoon with Alice had he experienced anything even remotely close. Even then, this was...

He shook his head and sighed, giggling like a kid. He had been wondering if his junk *should* be put in a trunk, but not now! Reggie would be proud of him. *And on the first date!*

Was the experience *merely* lust? Of course, some of it had to be that they were both peace officers and needed a release, but still, he felt like he was in his twenties.

Now, don't get ahead of yourself here, Ethan. It was one date; an awesome one, yes, but just a single date. *Maybe it was just a one-night stand?* No, it had been too powerful, and they had already planned their next get-together. *Not in my wildest dreams did I...*

His front door swung open, and Kim was standing there, trying to look past the light in the yard that his entry into the driveway had activated. It was then he realized his truck was still running and *Tragically Hip* was blaring out his half-rolled-down window. He felt like a teenager coming home too late, and with *lots* of explaining to do!

Ethan quickly turned off his stereo, rolled down his windows, and shut off the engine.

He winced as he made his way, somewhat sheepishly, to the front step.

"I know I have no right, but I was getting worried. Judging from your smile, though, you had a good time."

Ethan gulped. "Ah, yes, it was a good night."

Kim smiled at him knowingly.

"Well, I'm happy to hear that, Uncle Ethan. You deserve to have a good time. Not my business, but will you be seeing her again?"

"Oh, for sure!" His exuberance was as embarrassing as it was obvious.

Kim beamed. "Well, that's encouraging! Now that I know you're okay, *young man*, I'm going to tuck back into bed with the kids."

"So, I'm not grounded?"

Kim laughed. "No." She wagged a finger at him. "But you still have to get up in time for work."

"I will." He feigned sadness, which was summarily refuted by his permagrin.

Chapter Thirteen: Wagons Ho!

The Numbskull yelped as the whip bit through his shirt.

"Buckets! Oats!"

The half-wit scurried on all fours across the ground to the silo and filled two five-gallon pails of oats.

"Oats! Wagon!"

Obviously concerned he would suffer more pain, the Numbskull hustled over to the wagon and dumped the buckets in the back.

"Again!"

The whip snapped air, but it might as well have found purchase in flesh by the way the Numbskull flinched before accelerating.

It was just a snapshot of what was happening; all around, whips cracked, and hard labor, much of it by Numbskulls, was being performed.

The next few hours saw six wagons loaded with oats, weapons, people, and provisions. He remembered such a time, but then, he didn't have to toil, only keep up. Now it was his turn to be strong. It was two hours before dusk and both man and beast were now moving the wagons northward. He looked back to see only a handful of people and some stock staying behind.

They all struggled under the weight of things, not just the wagons, but memories, and the fact that home was being left behind.

The moon was but a sliver, and the light that flickered from the wagon's lamps served little more than to tease and tempt shadows. Night asks the hardest of questions, but all, except for the Numbskulls, knew what they were about and where they were going. If there was any doubt, the Hatchet leader and the oldest Friesian mare held the course.

Through the black of night, they walked over fields and seldom-used trails. They made many sharp turns and forded several streams. On one of the larger crossings, a Numbskull drowned; they had never learned to swim. A Hatchet directed two Numbskulls that *could* swim to retrieve the body and toss it onto a wagon.

When they were approaching a major road, or might be sky-lined, the Hatchets doused the lamps. Scouts on Marwari's fanned out and trickled in, ensuring safe passage. On one occasion, a scout returned with what the Hatchets called a 'Vagabond.' The homeless person would join the ranks of the Numbskulls.

Pounding out the miles through forest and field, they finally stopped for a break when the crescent moon reached its apex. The Numbskulls dashed back and forth with pre-made meals and invigorating drinks.

One Numbskull collapsed from exhaustion, and two others heaved it on top of the drowning victim. Another Numbskull tended to it, cold water reviving it enough such that it could sit up. It then pitched forward and broke its neck when it hit the ground.

Moves were difficult.

Death, whether mystical or mortal, came with moves. Their mother had not died during the last move, but shortly thereafter, the strain simply too much in her elder years.

And then, darkness enveloping them, they were on the march again. Horse sense and scents, as much as memory, kept them on track. Manure of Marwari and Friesian, laid down in advance, were road markers to the lead mare.

The elder Hatchets would've traveled the black road many times. He had long observed that Hatchets not only dressed in black but wore it as a cloak. Where others, even Numbskulls, took pleasure in the sun's warmth, the Hatchets seemed to draw comfort from the cold and the dark.

The pace slowed. At first, it was hardly perceptible, but with each passing moment, it felt like they might come to a grinding halt.

The Whipmaster that had previously flogged a Numbskull got off his horse and propped one arm against a wagon, put his other arm around the same Numbskull he had lashed, and pushed.

More Hatchets followed his lead. All were tired, but they found union in their condition; the sweat, the lamplight, the grunts, and groans made for an age-old orchestra of movement. Every entity had a place and a purpose — even the Numbskulls.

It was shocking and, for lack of a better word, heartening, to see a Hatchet throw an arm around a faltering Numbskull and give it a drink from its canteen. Others, witnessing it, did the same.

Never had he seen Numbskulls *almost* treated as friends or equals. It seemed time was their enemy and, from slave to senior, all must put forth every effort to vanquish the tick-tocking foe.

Energy renewed, momentum recaptured, pace quickened, until suddenly, they stopped. They were at the end of a trail, which became a road on the other side of a gate.

Moments later, the gate opened, and a huge, covered truck backed up and yoked to the first wagon. Timbers were used to join that wagon to the next, and so on and so forth. Most that had been walking, climbed into the back of the truck. Only the strongest stayed with the wagons.

The truck moved forward, and they went over a bridge and continued onward. This time, travel was easy. It was just a matter of putting one foot in front of the other, except for the former lead mare, who was now stumbling and had fallen to the rear.

Black gave way to steel grey and then streaking shadows. By the time the sun kissed them, they had arrived. A beautiful valley, their childhood home.

They gorged themselves on food and water but stopped when a team of Friesians and a stone-boat with the body of the old mare powered by.

Then, someone cracked a whip.

Chapter Fourteen: In Deep

Pulling up to Margie's Café, which was halfway between Glyph's Gulch and Jasper Springs, Ethan could see an elderly man in a wool hat sitting with Caroline.

A shift in the man's eyes suggested he had noticed Ethan.

Ethan didn't rush out of his rig, and by the time he got within twenty feet of the entryway, he heard the *clomp-clomp-clomp* of a person bounding down the steps. The man he'd just seen with Caroline had exited rather hurriedly and taken a sharp left away from Ethan, disappearing around the side of the building. Ethan only got a partial glance of a serious and chiseled face.

Caroline looked up at him and smiled.

"Right on time, as usual, *Mr. Right On Time.*" She added an air-smooch to her turn of phrase, both of which were quirks he was coming to adore about her.

"Thanks, Caroline. Seems I may have put the run on your visitor. Sorry about that."

"Oh, don't be. Just my uncle." She winced almost imperceptibly before continuing, "I mean, he's a tad fidgety and not very comfortable around strangers."

"Maybe he's my uncle, too!" Ethan smiled a wry smile.

Caroline snickered. He loved it when she snickered.

"I hope not. That would make us cousins and given what's happened at the end of our last three dates, we are doing something immoral, if not illegal."

Ethan felt like kissing her right then; instead, words fumbled out of his lips.

"Ah, I thought you said you didn't have any family around these parts."

Caroline stiffened. "I don't. He was just passing through and recognized my Bronco. I'm surprised he even stopped."

"I see."

"Do you, Officer Birchom?"

Caroline looked a bit flustered, and that made Ethan nauseous. He was being too nosey. *Do not fuck this up, Birchom!*

"Forgive me; just my stubborn old ways rising to the surface."

She softened. "It's okay, I probably could've explained it better."

"You don't owe me any explanation. Again, I'm sorry. Like I told you before, I date like organically-grown cauliflower."

She reached over and grabbed his hand. "It's okay, Ethan. A very minor speed bump on our road to happiness."

He grabbed her hand with both his hands and kissed it. "Shall we eat?"

"Yes, I'm ravenous." She bit her lip and winked at him. Yes, she was, and he already couldn't wait for dessert.

Today they flipped the script; Ethan went with a surf-and-turf and Caroline a salad, though she had them add a chopped-up chicken breast to hers.

"How is that you maintain such an incredible figure, given you eat so… well?"

"You mean when I eat like a pig?" She giggled. "I suppose it's because I'm a perpetual Energizer Bunny. I've always been like that — jogging, horseback riding, martial arts. I usually only sleep about five or six hours a night."

"You're a marvel, Caroline."

She smiled affectionately. "You're also anatomically blessed, and it's fair to say you're rocking my world most marvellously, especially, well, you know." This time she gave him a full-on double-eyebrow raise and an air smooch.

They shared a look that spoke of more than just mutual admiration. They held that look until the waiter came by to top up their wine glasses.

"But I suppose we should deal with the elephant in the room, Ethan."

Ethan was confused. *Didn't we just share a moment?*

Caroline pointed behind him. A large elephant balloon had floated away from a tween's birthday party and was about to crash into a vase full of flowers.

Like a cat — *perhaps a cougar*, Ethan thought — Caroline leapt from her chair and bounced the balloon back to the table of youngsters before it collided with the vase. She also snatched the vase from its precarious position on a ledge and sat it on their table.

"You might *actually* be Captain Marvel, Caroline."

"Oh no, there's no Kree in me." She wrangled a western accent and added, "Plus I got no quarrel with them Skrull folks."

Had Ethan not just watched Captain Marvel with Kim and her kids, that would've gone completely over his head.

Instead, he laughed and jumped out of his chair, going over to Caroline and kissing her lovingly.

The tweens let out a long "*Wooo!*"

Normally reserved, an open display of affection like that was something Ethan avoided, but not today; today *he* was marvelous.

They opted to share a tiramisu for dessert, and since neither had to work the following day, some coffee. There was also the unstated goal to make it a late night. *To his recollection, he'd taken more days off the past few weeks than the previous fifty-two!*

"What was your wife like?"

As they had both said they didn't much like to talk about previous relationships, the question surprised Ethan. However, if their relationship was to prosper, this topic would inevitably have to be discussed.

"She was kind, but..." He had to flip through his internal dictionary. "She was kind, but aloof. And 'buttoned-down,' if you know what I mean. April was hard-working and organized, but her pendulum swung a long way."

"As in, moody?"

"I suppose that's another word for it."

"And not especially good in bed?"

The question surprised him again, but he was learning that Caroline could be forthright, which was probably a function of her training.

"Well, I guess good enough that we could make a baby. Plus, I might not have, well, 'stirred her drink.'"

"Well, you sure stir the heck out of my inner daiquiri, Ethan."

"You bring out the best in me."

"Thanks, and you most definitely bring out the best in me...more than you'll ever know."

It was a compliment, but a curious one.

Perhaps sensing that her comment might be taken the wrong way, Caroline added, "I can be a bit emotionally distant. Maybe that's part of the reason Harrison cheated..." She trailed off, and for a moment Ethan sensed a fragility in her, which only made him care for her that much more.

"Go on, Caroline, if you're comfortable doing so."

"My ex cheated on me — a lot. I didn't learn about most of it until after we separated. Here I am, a cop, and I couldn't see that my husband was boning bimbos."

"Don't be too hard on yourself. You trusted him and were probably focused on your work. I've often heard that ace mechanics often don't take care of their own vehicles."

"That's a good analogy, Ethan. Perhaps my devotion to work also drove him to do what he did."

"Not your fault, Caroline. A man would have to be totally insane to cheat on you. I'm sorry you got hurt, but that Harrison fellah didn't deserve you. His loss is my gain."

"Thank you, Ethan. I only wish I didn't have to see him again —"

At that, she stopped abruptly. Ethan was sure she had just said something she hadn't meant to say. He cared enough about her to know now wasn't the time to pursue the issue.

"It's okay, Caroline. I felt the same when things fell apart between April and me. I read somewhere that an end is just a new beginning we haven't quite come to grips with. To new beginnings." He held up his glass.

Caroline smiled demurely and raised her glass to his. "To new beginnings."

103

That night, they had more than just great sex; they made love.

Chapter Fifteen: Horseplay

"The arm and foot are from the same person. Based on the flag in the kayak, we think that person came from Manitoba." Bert slid a folder across Ethan's desk.

Ethan grabbed the folder and tapped it repeatedly on the table, as if a clue would shake out.

"How about the shoe?"

"A type of hiker called an 'approach shoe' — not typically what a kayaker would wear. I tasked Reggie with looking into it further."

"And?"

Bert shrugged.

Ethan dialed Reggie's cell and put him on speakerphone.

"I'm at Buckley's Footwear right now. They say they don't carry those shoes. The manager here said you either had to order them over the internet or cross the line to buy a pair."

"As in the States?"

Ethan heard Reggie talking to someone.

"Yes, boss, that's affirmative."

"Could be that he bought them on eBay; regardless, it's a step in the right direction."

"Woo! Good pun, Sir!"

Ethan rubbed his temples. "Later, Reggie. Thanks for your help."

"No worries, the game is a*foot*!"

"Bye for now, Reggie."

"Onward and footward…"

Ethan let out a sigh and ended the call.

"We're not making much progress."

"Nope. We sure aren't, Bert." Ethan tossed the pen he was holding onto his desk.

"How about ballistics? We usually get something to go on there."

Ethan detected Bert's attempt to find optimism but had to shoot down that balloon.

"Angela conducted a widespread search and confirmed the bullet in my leg was from a Remington, but not linked to any other crimes."

"Well, poop."

"Shit, indeed. Hey, I better dangle, Bert. It's three and I'm supposed to meet up with Angela."

"Wow, one day it's Caroline, next day it's Angela. You've become quite the stud!"

"*Hardy har har.* You know Angela and I are just friends."

"I know, just teasing."

"Later, I'll look through missing persons — again — and see if there might be a connection. Plus, we need to follow up with the Outfitters and kayakers that haven't got back to us."

"Right; I'll jump on those contacts."

"Thanks, Bert."

As was often the case in situations like this, Ethan wasn't sure how to feel. On the one hand, they were making *some* progress; on the other, nothing conclusive, and no bodies — at least not full ones.

There remained the hope, faint as it may be, that they'd find Debra alive and well, or *well-enough* alive. Failing that, information leading to her remains, so the family could have a measure of closure.

Then there was the issue of justice; final closure, or at least as final as the law would allow. Additionally, they presumably had a murder on their hands and a murderer in their midst.

Thirty minutes later, Ethan pulled into a rest area which served as the halfway point between Glyph's Gulch and Elk Point.

Angela stepped out of her SUV. Her grey-blonde hair was up, and she was wearing cowboy boots. She looked at him in his uniform and RCMP-issue black boots.

"I see you didn't get my message."

Ethan looked at his phone, and there it was, an unread message from Angela: *Be ready to ride a horse.*

Oh, crap.

Angela opened up the trunk of her SUV and pulled out a plaid western shirt and a cowboy hat.

"You'll have to make do with your striped pants." She grinned widely and added, "Fortunately, the equine fashion police are out of town," which caused her to giggle behind her hand. Angela had this innocent and impish way about her, and Ethan wagered she had always been and would forever be a joy to be around.

"I hope the horse won't mind."

"Well, they can't see as many colors as we do, but given the clash between the yellow and black striped pants and the green and blue plaid shirt, you might throw her off her oats for a while."

Ethan couldn't help but laugh at that one.

"Here." Angela tossed him an apple. "You can use this to buy her off."

"Good thinking."

"Well, we should go. The stable owner's expecting us. Stella's short on words and patience — at least with humans — and only agreed to talk if we paid for two three-hour rides."

Stella was waiting for them, three horses saddled and ready to go, reins tied to a hitching post near the house, which also served as her office. Ethan only knew Stella to see her, though he had known the previous owner reasonably well as Chelsea had taken riding lessons with him. That man moved away a couple years after Chelsea vanished, and Ethan didn't have much cause to visit the

107

stables. Stella nodded approvingly at Angela and furrowed her brow at Ethan, but made no comment beyond, "Let's ride."

They plodded along, Stella up front, Angela in the middle, and Ethan, at the back on an old, stocky, black-and-brown Canadian.

Five minutes out, Angela perched atop her own light-grey Arabian, peeked over her shoulder. "Aww, it's a match made in heaven." She smiled at him and added, "And a color combination from hell." Again, she snickered behind her hand.

"Funny. At least she likes me; don't you, girl?" Ethan patted the old mare, and she promptly fluffed. Now he knew why they were pulling up the rear.

Stella slowed her horse, allowing Angela and Ethan to get closer to her. "Angela filled me in about what you're looking for, so pull on up, so I don't have to shout."

Ethan did as he was told, pulling his Canadian by Angela's Arabian.

Stella started talking, albeit slowly and with pauses long enough that Ethan was tempted to throw in the occasional, "and...?" and "Please continue," but restrained himself.

Stella may have been socially awkward, but Angela said she knew her horses *and* most of the people around that had them.

"Fewer people these days pulling wagons..."

Clip, clop, clip, clop.

"And riding carriages, well..."

Clip, clop, clip, clop.

"Save for some die-hard Mormons, like the Jensen's near the border..."

Clip, clop, clip, clop, clippity, clop.

"...that seem to fancy themselves as Amish..."

Clip, clop, clip, clop, clip, clop.

"You don't see many Percherons or Belgian..."

108

Clip, clop.

"...draught horses."

The minutes droned by before she started up again. "These days, people that have the draught horses tend toward the Clydesdale."

Clip, clop, clip, clop.

"But the rope in question is small for all those breeds. It's also..."

Clip, clop.

"...too big for a standardbred, like what you would use for pulling..."

Clip, clop.

"...a carriage, like for harness-racing."

They had reached the top of a knoll and were now snaking their way downward. The trail was rough and the footing uncertain, and consequently, Stella stopped talking.

Ethan relaxed and just tried to enjoy the experience — and not fall off. He let his mind wander, imagining what it must've been like for those who re-introduced the horse to Canada in the seventeenth century. Beyond that, to ride in spaces not tamed and tarnished by colonization. Ethan caught a glimpse of a stream through the pines below and imagined how excited people would be in "discovering" it, looking for color that spoke or riches, or maybe just an opportunity to catch some fishes. Then, nature could be friend or enemy, now it was more a medium, which was unfortunate. Still, it was a lovely day, and the trail, both that which the horse walked, and the one that he pursued to find answers, brought him back to the present. Moments later, they reached the bottom of a ravine to where a small brook snaked its way along.

Stella dismounted and tied up her brown and white horse to a tree, close enough to the stream that it could drink. Angela followed suit, and Stella helped Ethan with his horse.

"Thank you, Stella. Your horse is stunning, but I honestly don't know what kind it is."

His comment seemed to warm her demeanor. "It's a Haflinger. I have four of them, arguably the best trail riding horse there is."

"Forgive me for my conjecture, but would the hemp rope we found be something you would use on these horses? They seem about the right size for light draught work, as well as riding."

She pursed her lips. "Well, I can assure you neither me nor my horses were involved in any shenanigans."

"Oh, I'm not even remotely suggesting —"

"And I'm at my stables every single day, so that's my alibi."

"Miss Stella." Ethan found himself feeling and acting like a character in a western talking to a fine lady. "I mean, Stella, it would seem a horse breed *similar* to your lovely Haflinger's might be what we are looking for."

"Oh, yes, sorry, sometimes I take offense where there is none. You made a sound judgement. Coffee?"

Ethan looked at Angela.

She nodded. "We've time for that."

Stella started a small fire in a pit obviously dug here for just such occasions. Fifteen minutes later, they were all drinking black coffee from old tin mugs.

"Haflingers, Irish Cobs, Icelandics: all versatile breeds that are equally good to ride as they are for light draught work."

"Interesting."

"And not uncommon. Still, for our region, might only be twenty places that have them."

Twenty was quite a lot, but it was a start.

"Oh, I almost forgot: there's also Friesian. You probably haven't heard of them before but might've seen them in movies. Few around, but they're smart, easy to work with, and beautiful."

"Do they look like this?" Ethan pulled his horse ornament from his pocket.

"Why, isn't that something! May I?"

Ethan passed his keepsake to her.

"That is lovely — and, coincidentally, it *is* a Friesian."

"Wow, small world."

"It sure is. I only know of two or three places that had them. I think one was south of the border and the other tucked back into the hills. Haven't seen that lot in years. They were a peculiar bunch."

"Peculiar? How so?"

"Never smiled, very short on words, always paid in cash, and uniformly dressed in dark clothes, some of which looked like homespun wool. Think Amish, but not so religious."

At that, Stella walked to the creek and sat down on a big rock, looking about like she didn't have a care in the world. She downed her coffee and rinsed out her cup; this prompted Angela and Ethan to finish their coffee. Stella took their mugs and rinsed them out in the creek before dousing the fire.

Stella got on her horse. "Let's ride."

Angela hopped on her Arabian, Ethan crawled aboard his Canadian, and they sauntered slowly back to the stables.

Dismounting, Ethan felt like he had ridden for three *days*, not three hours. He arched his back and couldn't resist rubbing his tush, which was still quite sensitive.

Angela snickered again.

"Any other questions, Mr. Birchom?"

"Yes, one other thing, *Miss Stella*." This time Ethan said it on purpose, which conjured up a full smile from the stoic horsewoman.

"Have you ever heard of NAERP?"

"No... what's a nerp? Narpe?"

"N-A-E-R-P, it stands for 'North American Equine Rehabilitation Program.'"

111

"No, can't say I have. Oh, wait — I recall something about them from about twenty years ago. Heard it was a scam. People would send their money in and hear nothing back."

"Do you recall any names?"

"No, I brushed it off. I only commit to memory the important stuff. The old noggin" — Stella tapped her head — "is like the old mare you're riding; she ain't what she used to be."

"Well, I don't know about that, though I, too, feel like I might be slipping a cog."

"Slipping a cog?" Stella slapped her knee, laughing, and dust flew up. "I haven't heard that one in years!"

They talked for a few more minutes before Stella excused herself. "Do come again, you two. I thoroughly enjoyed the ride."

In unison, Angela and Ethan chimed, "We will."

As Stella walked away, Angela poked Ethan playfully in the ribs. "You got Stella to smile *and* talk, and occasionally at the same time! I don't even recall the last time I saw her laugh. Tell me we'll do this again, Ethan, and 'unofficial-like.'"

"I unofficially say that we will officially do this again."

Angela threw her arm around his shoulder. "You know, for a guy that dresses like a court jester, you're alright, Ethan Birchom."

#

Halfway back to Glyph's Gulch, it hit him: No, not a bullet or an asteroid, but a memory that was just as powerful. Chelsea had once donated money to a horse rehab outfit, and for the first time, the NAERP initials seemed hauntingly familiar.

Could it be? Ethan sped home and raced through the door. Thankfully, Kim had taken her kids out to a movie; otherwise, he surely would've startled them.

He pulled out a box that housed Chelsea's personal records and various letters. In an envelope were a handful of financial records. There weren't many, as she didn't have a bank account for that long. Could a statement have captured the details of the transaction?

Two minutes later, he had the answer, in black and white and dollar signs. Chelsea, with a donation of $500, was one of the first of a hundred five-hundred-dollar-plus donors to NAERP. He recalled that the money had been a quarter of her savings and that she wouldn't be talked out of it. '*It's my money to do with as I please, right?*'

'It is, Chelsea.'

'*It's for such a good cause. And perhaps, maybe, soon, my allowance will go up?*'

She'd raised her eyebrows meaningfully and batted her blue eyes at him, smiling. Ethan had melted like butter.

'Oh, most definitely. *I foresee a forty percent increase, effective immediately.*'

She'd wrapped her arms around his waist and squeezed. At eleven, she was getting strong... not to mention strong-willed, like her father.

'You know what, Chelsea, you've inspired me. I'm going to match your donation. Maybe they will also send me a horsey.'

'My heart says, "yeah," but their timeline says, "neigh."'

They had shared a chuckle, and if their bond could've become stronger, it did right then.

He found the wooden box that had come along with the commemorative letter. It was what had contained her pewter-and-crystal horse figurine. His own miniature horse statue came later, but without a pleasant letter.

Ethan dug the horse out of his pocket; chills went up and down his spine, and he started sweating profusely. He raced down the hall to the toilet and puked his guts out.

Splashing cold water on his face, he looked at himself in the mirror. Could it be that what happened to the Kayak Kid also happened to Chelsea?

He retched again and fell to his knees in front of the porcelain altar; he remained there until the dry heaves made it feel like someone had kicked him in the stomach while he was doing sit-ups.

He gargled some mouthwash and stuck his head directly under the cold-water tap. *Get it together, Ethan!*

It might be coincidence; then again, it might be the key to finding Chelsea — and others. Ethan guzzled a quart of water straight out of the tap and, weak but motivated beyond words, made his way to his home office.

He picked up his horse keepsake and turned it over. Ethan recalled there not being a maker's mark, not even a copyright symbol, which hadn't struck him as meaningful at the time; curious, yes, but not *suspicious*.

He plopped down in his torn-up old computer chair and typed 'NAERP' into a search engine. Beyond some semi-related acronyms, he found diddly squat. Then, he typed, in brackets, the full name: North American Equine Rehabilitation Program.

Again, nothing.

There *should* have been something. He lost the brackets, which would allow for an open search, and after spending two hours going down several rabbit holes, came up empty. The lack of *anything* was, in itself, significant.

Could NAERP be related to some — or many — of the missing persons?

He recalled that Debra also loved horses; he would have to look further into this possible connection. Ethan didn't know what to make of the fact that Chelsea was somewhere between six and ten years younger than most of the other missing individuals. Then again, his search parameters could be too narrow; were there other Chelsea's? The thought brought bile up into his mouth.

Once again, Ethan gargled mouthwash and brushed his teeth. He changed all his clothes too. Even as he pulled into Brickwallaby, he could smell vomit; some icky particles were probably trapped in his nostrils. He didn't care.

He had something *extremely* important to do.

While it had been a couple years since he had delved so far back into his own cold cases, Ethan knew the folder by its position and the wear on its marker. He pulled out Chelsea's file, removed the 'Unsolved' tag, and replaced it with 'Active Investigation.'

With shaking hands, he re-filed it with the folders related to Debra and the Kayak Kid.

Chapter Sixteen: Grave

"Uh."

"*Oomph!*"

"Oy vey..."

Ethan tried, in vain, to squeeze his truck between the next two potholes.

"Son of a bitch, this road —" Bert had one hand on the dash and the other on the assist grip above the door.

The two men weaved within the cab, almost knocking heads.

"Since Forestry decommissioned it, it's gone to hell in a handbasket."

"Could they have picked a worse time for 300-hour maintenance on the helicopter?!"

"Murphy's Law rears its ugly-as-a-shit-fence head again."

"Seems so. Jeezus, boss, some of these potholes are big enough to have their own ecosystem!"

"I know it. Last winter I came out here to do some ice-fishing and limited out on trout in just five potholes."

Bert laughed, then banged his head against the roof.

Removing his toque to rub his head, Bert blurted out, "Are we there yet?"

Ethan smiled and countered with, "I hope you peed before we left."

"I did, but we did drive awful slow past that last trickling brook, *and* while they *say* the wildfires are all out, some of those areas look like they could use a dampening-down."

Ethan took the hint. "Might as well lend my squirter to your firehose."

They stopped for a bathroom break. The smell of the recent fire lingered in the air.

"Ah, the 'new normal' raises its smoky head."

"We're burning down our own BBQ, Bert."

They had discussed how climate change was taking such a heavy toll on British Columbia but agreed to try and not let it ruin their day. Besides, as they conceded, what's the common man to do but try to consume less and give more?

They returned to the vehicle and resumed their drive down the seldom used 4x4 track.

Twenty minutes later, they came to a section of road washed out by a creek.

"Pilot said it was a half mile from here that he spotted what looked like a grave disturbed by animals, so let's hoof it down there, Bert."

They dug out their backpacks, complete with emergency kits, evidence bags, and thermoses of coffee. Each had a revolver, and Bert, always prepared to unleash hell on a bad guy, had a rifle slung over his shoulder.

As they rounded a bend in the track, they saw two turkey vultures scamper and then wing away.

"That must be it, Bert."

Ethan had stopped, but Bert made to step into the meadow.

"Hold up, Bert; let's not get too hasty, my bench-pressing buddy. Let's move in slowly. You go 'round to the left; I'll stay to the right. Ears open and eyes peeled."

"Right." Bert nodded. Ethan liked that he never had to explain things twice to him.

Fifteen cautious minutes later, they met at what indeed was a gravesite — or what remained of it — near a massive maple tree. It must've been hard to dig out an area between the big, sprawling roots of the hardwood tree, but someone had managed it.

"You see anything, Bert?"

"No. You?"

"Nothing."

They searched for human remains, or at least *some* remains of a human. The most noticeable omission: no head.

"Damn, boss."

"Pretty grisly."

"Animals have worked this one to the bone."

"Yep, appears every manner of critter might've taken part in taking him apart."

"Yes. Not nice."

"Judging from the size of that femur there, and the scapula over there, a tall guy."

"True, but I guess we can't discount more than one deceased. There are a lot of bones." Animals had excavated, chewed on, and transported the bones over quite an expanse.

"Yes, there are. Let's bag it all."

"Will do."

"Thanks. I'll check around."

Again, Ethan looked at the grave and the surrounding area, then at his phone. They had little time. Ideally, they would set up and work a grid, but today he would just work out from the grave in concentric circles, focusing on non-boney clues. He added a waypoint to his GPS to mark the location and began looking for clues.

Ethan saw canine tracks and even those of a bear. There had been so many animals at the grave that any human footprints that might've been present would have been obliterated. With time ticking, it was necessary to focus more on the meadow and its obvious entry point, the old trail.

Ethan affected a serpentine search pattern, moving out from his last circle in the meadow toward the trail. Fifteen feet from the trail, he spotted a relatively narrow, linear depression a few feet long and a couple of inches deep. There was also some manure. He was not an excrement expert, but the dried-out droppings were too lumpy and large to be that from an elk or a moose, and given the proximity to the straight, flat "track," he reasoned somebody may have been here with a horse and wagon, or carriage.

After having driven the road, Ethan wondered why anybody in their right mind would come all the way out here with a horse and wagon; well, unless it was to off someone.

Too bad they didn't bring a coffin. At least they'd brought a gravedigger. He took pictures and even put some of the horse-hockey in an evidence bag.

He ventured back to Bert, who was securing a body bag full of bones.

"Find anything?"

"A little. I'll tell you on the walk back. Did you find anything other than bones and scraps of clothes?"

"Nothing, boss."

"Figures. Another case big on nasty and short on clues."

"It sucks, man."

"Did you poke around under the bones?"

"Not really. I pulled a forked stick through it and found a couple more bones."

"I'll take another look; you know, just in case." Ethan climbed into the grave. "Pass me the shovel, will ya."

Bert pulled the collapsible shovel out of his pack and handed it to Ethan.

"Thanks." Ethan started digging around. He heard the hallmark clang of metal on rock, and then, as he moved the shovel deeper, a couple more clangs.

"Got something?"

"Probably just more rocks." Ethan gave the shovel back to Bert and dug around in the now-loose dirt with his fingers. One round stone, then another; after a few minutes, he'd found six round stones, which he held in his hand. Without success, he tried to rub them free of dirt.

"Not normal to see round stones like that here, is it Ethan?"

"Nope. It's a long way from a river, and these stones are almost perfectly round. Here, kindly wash them off, please."

Ethan passed Bert the stones, and after he rinsed them off with water from his camelback, Bert held them in his big, outstretched hands.

Ethan examined them. "Four white stones and two black ones, and all nearly perfect spheres. That is *strange*, and possibly significant."

"Should I bag them?"

"Definitely."

Clambering out of the hole, Ethan checked the time. "It'll be dark in less than two hours. We'd better hustle."

They snapped some more pictures then gathered up their gear, bones, and stones and made for the trail. As they walked back, they discussed what they had and hadn't found.

A mile on, they encountered more wagon tracks, this time across from one another, which gave them an opportunity to better determine the overall size of the wagon. They also found more poop and some hoofprints.

"Big horses, two of them, boss."

"Yes. Our resident horse expert, Angela, can give us an educated guess as to their overall size, maybe even type."

"Probably so. She's incredibly knowledgeable about horses."

"And most everything. She's quite the gal, our Angela."

The two men walked in silence, enjoying the beauty of their surroundings: the butterscotch-like smell of the ponderosa pines, the occasional *rap-rap-rap* of a woodpecker, and the squirrels, chipmunks and ruffed grouse that crossed their path.

Seemingly built for biking, fishing, kayaking, and hiking, the East Kootenays were magical. *About the best place a person could imagine for horseback riding.* The horses really made Ethan wonder, and he voiced his thoughts on the matter.

"Why would anyone come all the way out here with horses and a wagon, unless you were transporting something or someone, or the trip was special?"

Bert looked at him. "As in, more *special* that killing someone, chopping their head off, and burying them in an unmarked grave?"

"I'm thinking a different sort of special, like trying to make a statement, be it religious or ritualistic." Ethan pointed back toward the meadow. "Those stones mean something. It's also possible the murder didn't occur out here, just the burial."

"Seems labour-intensive; surely the body could've been more easily disposed of elsewhere."

"That's true, but it adds to the potential ritualistic element. Regardless, it's a puzzle pickled in a conundrum."

"Conundrum? Y'all been reading them fancy new paper books, boss?"

Ethan chuckled and responded with a dash of his own redneckian flavour. "'Spose I read it when I couldn't puzzle out what went whomperjawed with my TV's rabbit ears."

This time they giggled in concert, before a very different feeling came over Ethan: a sense of foreboding that made the hair on the back of his neck stand up.

Just then, a big black bear crossed the trail in front of them. The bear never paid them any mind.

From off the trail, behind a blowdown and a high-powered scope, a person watched the bear startle the men, and lowered their weapon.

Chapter Seventeen: Passion and Poison

Normally reserved, love or lust — or a mixture of the two — overcame Ethan. Even the guy in the next room pounding on the wall and yelling, "It's four AM, call it a night, Big Bull!" did nothing to dissuade him from continuing until their hotel room looked like a tornado had hit it.

Caroline bit his shoulder and ran her hand across his chest and up to his throat and then gave it a tight squeeze.

"Two can play at that game, missy!"

Thirty minutes later, it was all they could do to get themselves into the shower, together, and desalinate.

"I need pizza." Ethan moved his hands in a circle over his stomach.

"We ate it all, after round two."

Caroline giggled, and Ethan smiled so widely he thought the edges of his mouth might swallow his ears.

"I forgot."

'We could order in again. Oh wait — it's, like, morning!"

Ethan laughed. "I could handle bacon and eggs."

She hesitated, but then agreed. "Sure, the truck stop is open twenty-four hours."

"Do you think they have chocolate milk?"

Caroline laughed. "Are you sure you're not 18?!"

He gave her a bear-hug. "No, but you make me feel like it."

They dressed and fifteen minutes later were sitting at a table in a little diner.

They had no sooner ordered breakfast than Ethan's phone vibrated.

He looked at it and Caroline sighed. "Work?"

"It's Reggie. He wouldn't be texting me this early unless it was something important."

Caroline stabbed her fork into her breakfast sausage, clearly disappointed; he couldn't blame her because they hadn't been able to spend nearly enough time together. Nevertheless, he called Reggie.

"Go."

"There's been a break-in, and a kidnapping, of sorts."

"A kidnapping?"

"Yes."

"Who, when, where? The details, Reggie."

"Well, it's more of a smash and grab. I guess it's not *really* a kidnapping if it's a corpse, right?"

"Somebody stole a corpse? Slow down, Reggie, and tell me what happened."

"We found Debra — well, more accurately, she found us."

"Debra? Debra McGown?"

Caroline dropped her fork. "Debra McGown?" Ethan nodded and focused on what Reggie was saying.

"Well, Bert and I are pretty sure it was Debra."

"'Was?'"

"Yes; she looked just like the photo we have. Longer hair, though, and darker. Plus, she was wearing a backpack. A black cat's head was sticking out. We think it was Mr. Scruffles."

"So where is she? What did she say? And what does this have to do with the kidnapping?"

"Corpse-napping, you mean."

Ethan sat the phone down, rubbed his forehead to calm himself, and picked up the phone again.

"Where is Debra?"

"Not sure. At four-thirty am, video surveillance picked her up getting out of the passenger side of a big flatbed truck that had just backed into the evidence room."

Ethan only managed a "Wha —" before Reggie continued.

"She and the driver — looked to be a man with a full-face toque — raced into the evidence room and, about five minutes later, came out with a body bag. It was the headless dude from the gravesite."

"Where's Bert?"

"He's chasing them down the highway."

"Does he have backup?"

"No. Our volunteer is sick with the flu, Elk Point is too far away, and, well, you're there."

"Heli?"

"Ceiling is too low here for them to fly safely."

"I'll call Bert on the radio. You collect whatever evidence you can, Reggie. I'll call you back shortly."

"Okay, but there's more."

"More?"

"Seems somebody else is also chasing the flatbed. Not sure what they're about. Witness said it's a green Range Rover."

"Roger."

Ethan sat the phone down and shook his head in disbelief.

"What on Earth is going on, Ethan?"

"I have to go, Caroline. I'll explain later."

"Can we provide support?"

Ethan thought about that for a second. "Have US Border Patrol on the lookout and make sure they know I'm racing to the border. I'll radio Canada Customs." Ethan fished for his wallet.

"Don't worry about that. I'll take care of it."

"Thanks."

"God speed and be safe."

"Sorry about this, Caroline."

"It's okay; just *please* be careful."

Ethan raced to his truck and his tires squawked on the pavement as he was trying to raise Bert on the radio.

The radio crackled, but he couldn't make out anything Bert was saying. After finding no success with the cell phone, he went back to the radio. The only thing he could hear was "...in pursuit...truck."

Ethan keyed in and said, "I'm coming as fast as I can, Bert. Right now, I'm your only backup. Don't take any unnecessary risks."

Twenty-five minutes later, Customs waved him through the border crossing, and he tried Bert again. Nothing, but that wasn't surprising, given the highway snaked through a narrow defile in mountainous terrain.

Ethan started round a hairpin turn, and a three-quarter-ton flatbed truck skidded around the turn and halfway into his lane. In a desperate act of self-preservation. Ethan jerked the steering wheel to the right and forced his vehicle toward the guardrail.

The truck continued to skid, and Ethan pinned the gas, attempting to squeeze past the oncoming rig. As the passenger side of his truck scraped along the guardrail, he actually thought that he'd made it — that was, until the back end of the rig clipped his bumper.

Ethan skidded sharply counterclockwise and an RCMP patrol car was upon him. He saw the whites of Bert's eyes as he narrowly missed crashing into the oncoming squad-car. As

Ethan spun to a stop, all he could see in his mirrors was the three-quarter ton tilting over the edge of the guardrail, and ever so slowly, go over the bank. Ethan knew it was a steep three-hundred-foot drop to the river; the rig wouldn't come to rest until it hit the bottom.

He looked up at Bert, and another vehicle — a Range Rover — came flying around the corner. The driver, a young man, hit the brakes, but there wasn't enough room to stop; he smashed into Bert's car, causing Bert's car to launch into Ethan's truck. Bert's airbags deployed, which probably, *hopefully*, saved him from severe injury.

Ethan tried to open his door. It wouldn't budge. He threw his shoulder into it twice, hard enough to make his opposite, injured shoulder hurt like hell, but the door remained stuck. He kicked out the windshield since the passenger door was against the guardrail. Scrambling out the window and off the hood, he was relieved to see Bert already out of his car.

"You okay, Bert?"

"Yes. You?"

"Better than *that* guy." Ethan pointed at the Range Rover. They looked at the driver sprawled on the vehicle's hood, his face a mask of blood.

A middle-aged woman hurried forward. "I'm a doctor. What can I do to help?"

"Check on him, please."

By then, other vehicles, from both north and southbound lanes, had blocked the highway. Ethan quickly tasked some bystanders with helping keep other people back. It would be a while before other emergency personnel arrived.

Meanwhile, the woman had checked the man's vitals.

"He's alive, but in bad shape."

"Okay, we'll see if we can get —"

The *chop-chop-chop* of an approaching helicopter interrupted them. Looking up, Ethan saw a US Sheriff support heli, and could just make out Caroline sitting up front beside the pilot. His cell phone rang; it was Caroline.

"This is awful, Ethan. We need to set down to help."

Ethan and Bert got vehicles on the south side of the crash site to move back and a team of off-duty teachers to cordon off the area. The landing spot no sooner cleared away than the heli set down.

Caroline exited, and in a crouch, rushed over to Ethan. She grabbed him by both shoulders and, while looking past him toward the Range Rover, yelled out, "Tell me you're alright!"

"Yes, but we need to get that man —"

A deputy and EMT rushed past with a gurney to aid the injured man.

"Yes, I know. We'll get him to the hospital."

Face ashen, Caroline stepped past Ethan and looked at the man strapped into the gurney. It struck Ethan as odd; Caroline would've seen all sorts of blood and gore.

"Are *you* okay, Caroline?"

Caroline's eyes flickered; then, just as she seemed about to say something, she shook her head, turned on her heel, and raced back to the heli.

It was what it was. Everybody processed things differently, and Ethan had a crash and a crime scene to deal with. Plus, Caroline and her American counterparts were helping them, and it might save lives.

Bert joined him, and they walked to the guardrail to watch the 206L LongRanger helicopter orbit down and land near the crashed truck. Incredibly, the truck had vaulted mostly across the river and lay in a foot of water.

He watched Caroline join her team and extract two people from the wreck. Ethan knew the 206 could only carry a pilot and five or six passengers, so with Caroline, a deputy, an EMT, and now three victims, the heli would be maxed out for weight. Caroline and her deputy hastily collected enough evidence to fill up a duffel bag. Back in the chopper, they slowly climbed out of the ravine and headed toward the American border.

It took him three tries to reach Caroline. "Where are you going, Caroline? Our hospital is fifteen minutes closer."

"Sorry, Ethan. My information tells me this crime originated on the US side with a stolen flatbed, and ID has the victims as US citizens. There's one more body down there. Deceased male. Your heli can scoop him up when it arrives. We were limited out."

Ethan was exasperated. *The crime happened on our side.* He stammered, "I — I don't know about this..."

"Trust me, Ethan; I know what I'm doing."

Caroline was always right about these things, but it still bugged him.

"You could've at least taken me down there."

"I couldn't. Trust me."

"Is Debra McGown one of the perpetrators? Is she alive?"

"That's a positive and a negative."

The line went dead before he could reply. "For fuck's sakes!"

Bert raised his eyebrows. "Let me guess, Ethan. She's taking them, evidence, and all, back to Montana?"

"Seems so, Bert — and apparently Debra is dead."

"Sorry to say, but that shit ain't right."

Ethan only nodded. No, it wasn't right, but they still had a crash and crime scene to control. The other *shit* would have to be sorted out later. And since it was a cross-border crime, there would be a lot of shit to deal with.

"Let's get this cleaned up."

Over the next two-plus hours, they opened a lane for traffic, got the wrecked vehicles towed away, and collected witness reports and evidence. Despite the squad car taking a pretty good hit, they could limp it back to town.

Minutes after they got traffic slowly moving again, it ground to a halt. A woman had stopped her vehicle and was laying on the asphalt, presumably trying to retrieve something from under Ethan's pickup.

"Here Kitty, Kitty, here Kitty, Kitty." The woman pursed her lips and made numerous high-pitched smoochy-squeaky noises and repeated, "Kitty, Kitty."

"Ma'am, what are you doing?"

Without looking up, the senior said, "There's a frightened cat under there. I almost hit the poor thing. We must save it!"

Oh, brother! If only Twix was here. The dog was a cat magnet.

Thankfully, Bert had the energy to get down on his knees. He joined the woman, mouse-squeaking, and in a minute, a black cat came to Bert.

Bert looked at the tag. "You're not going to believe this!"

"What?"

"It's Mr. Scruffles."

"Mr. Scruffles — Debra's Mr. Scruffles?"

"Yes, sir."

"So that was definitely Debra down there."

"What are we going to do with her cat?"

Ethan took off his RCMP cap and scratched his head. "Hey, Angela adores cats, so she should be happy to take care of Mr. Scruffles until we can get in touch with Debra or her family."

"Twix better not see him, or she'll be jealous."

"Definitely. That dog will viciously run down a thug, but melts like butter in the hot sun around a cat."

By then, Reggie had arrived, and they performed a last look for evidence.

Sure enough, near the guardrail where the Range Rover had smashed into Bert's car, Ethan spotted a small rectangular object about the size of a credit card.

It was a driver's license. The name: Aaron Leadshat.

Chapter Eighteen: Identification

If Ethan had to fill out any more paperwork, he was going to commit harikari with a pen! He still hadn't had a second cup of coffee, and he was manhandling his mouse and keyboard like they'd stolen something from him. However, if he was to get a new patrol car and compensation for his truck, it had to be done. This was in addition to all the bureaucratic red tape associated with crimes that spanned the border.

Since his Dodge pickup was irreparable, Ethan picked himself up a used Toyota Tacoma. A truck was a necessity in an area that could see a foot of snow drop on a winter's night. He almost wished it was winter so he could hibernate and skip all the damn paperwork!

"Any word from Caroline, Ethan?"

Bert's question jogged him from his stupor, and he responded in a slow, robotic fashion.

"Confirmation that Debra McGown died from massive head trauma, and the bag of bones we recovered from the gravesite are to be returned."

Ethan neglected to mention that he'd gotten the information from an official communique from the Jasper Spring's Sheriff's Office and not Caroline herself.

His phone vibrated with a message: *DNA match to two of your cases, file sent.*

The news prompted him to take a drink of his now-cold coffee and pretend to be alive.

He opened his laptop and, sure enough, the information was there. Two hits, one for 'Kayak Kid' and the other for 'Flatbed 4x4 Dead Guy.'

Bert exchanged Ethan's cold cup of coffee for a hot one.

"Good news?"

"Yes. And thanks, Bert."

"No worries. Do you think you can finally eat something?"

"Yes."

"Good. I'll have Reggie grab us some breakfast sandwiches from Molly's Bakery."

"Okay."

Ethan was eager to find out who the Kayak Kid was, so he clicked on that file first.

The young man was Rudy Ingersson.

Orphaned at nine, Rudy had been shunted from foster home to foster home. His listed address was for a Winnipeg homeless shelter where he volunteered. He also worked part-time at a gas station. No next of kin, no contacts. Ethan only had the name and number of the shelter. He dialed it directly.

"Hello, this is Officer Ethan Birchom of the RCMP detachment in Glyph's Gulch, British Columbia. Can I speak to the manager?"

"This is Josh. I'm what passes for the person in charge at this fine establishment."

"I've some unfortunate news for you, Josh."

"Let me guess: Kootenay Joe McCantry broke into one of your town's shops, and you nabbed him trying to swipe a sleeping bag?"

"This is regarding Rudy Ingersson, a former resident and volunteer."

"Rudy! Oh my God, please tell me he's okay!"

This is going to be difficult. "The case is still under investigation, but we've reason to believe that Rudy may have been a victim of foul play."

He heard a loud clattering, as if the man had dropped the phone; just as Ethan was about to redial, the man's voice returned.

"You mean... You think Rudy is dead?"

"I can't say."

"Please give it to me straight, Officer. I've been running this place for ten years — I'm sure you can imagine what I've seen."

"We've enough evidence to suggest that Rudy may no longer be alive."

"Dear God... Damn it! Why does God always take the best at such a young age?" His voice was tight, and Ethan imagined tears in his eyes.

The pit of Ethan's stomach registered the truth, reinforced by the foul bile that forced its way up his throat. With effort, he swallowed it and continued. "What can you tell me about Rudy?"

He heard the man take a deep, ragged breath. "Rudy was…a gem." Again, his halting breaths spoke of shock and grief.

"Perhaps you can start with the last time you saw him. Do you know what his plans were? Was anyone informed of his destination or his plans to travel to BC?"

"Rudy worked every day. He cared for people so much, too much, more than he cared for himself. I'm to blame for this…"

"I'm sure you did nothing wrong, Mr.…?"

"Font, Josh Font. I urged him to take some time off, travel, have some fun. Now he's dead — because of me!"

"Seems like you cared for Rudy a lot, Mr. Font, and just wanted him to enjoy life."

"Yes, but now he's gone."

Ethan heard the phone drop again and a cough or retch. After a minute, the man returned to the call.

"Sorry about that."

"No need to apologize."

"Well, about Rudy. He didn't have any family, which I'm sure you know otherwise you wouldn't have called here. He told me he was going to thumb to Vancouver, maybe even visit Vancouver Island. I asked him to stay in touch, even bought him a pay-and-talk cell so he could text occasionally, which he did. Then — suddenly — nothing."

"Any idea if he met someone, or perhaps he mentioned that he was going to visit someone in particular?"

"No, he was just winging it. As much as a giver as he was, Rudy was an introvert. I'm pretty sure I was the only one he stayed in contact with. Man, everyone's going to be devastated!"

"Well, we can't say for certain he is —"

"He's gone. I feel it, and you know it."

"Well, let's be optimistic until we have conclusive evidence."

"Yeah, you're right. I'll keep a lid on it. "

"Thanks, Mr. Font."

"You're welcome. Please let me know...you know..."

"I will. If anything should come to mind, my number is —"

"I have it on my display here. Good luck, Officer."

Next, Ethan rang the gas station where Rudy worked part time.

The person who answered the phone cried and passed the phone to another person, who could barely keep it together.

"He hadn't worked here long, but" — the person sobbed — "they just made things so much better. Rudy was one of those rare individuals who had a glow about them — you know — like, you wanted to be a better person when they were around. I'm gutted."

Ethan asked the usual questions and received the same answers. No, they didn't know Rudy's plan, where he was going, who he might meet, or even when he would return.

Only at the end did the first person who answered the phone return, providing a clue.

"Now Rudy won't ever ride horses, like he dreamed. This world *sucks!*"

At that, the line went dead. When Ethan called back, the manager said they were closing the gas station for the rest of the day, and if anybody thought of anything, they would call.

That Rudy was a volunteer and clearly a great person made Ethan wonder. The good did indeed die young. *The good die young...* The words tumbled over and over in his mind. *There's something in that...*

Ethan opened his Missing Persons files and began looking over some of the background information of other missing people. Thirty minutes later, as Bert sat down for coffee and sandwiches, Ethan let out a "Whoa —"

"Smells great, right?"

"Ah, yes, they do — but I think I've found something that may have us cooking with gas."

Bert perked up. "A lead?"

"Yes. A high percentage of missing were homeless and volunteers, whether at hostels, soup kitchens, even animal rescue centers — and sometimes, equine rescue."

"Wow! Maybe we can build a profile on the killer, or killers?"

Ethan rested his thumbs under his chin and began staring off into space. The phone rang, and thankfully Bert answered it, for Ethan was in a trance.

The homeless and those who didn't fall into society's acceptable boxes had long been easy targets for predators. Few people noticed or missed the 'invisible,' but people *would* miss those who volunteered. Combining the two represented something highly unusual — and despicable. If the goal was to kill someone, to satiate whatever sick desire the individual had, the aged shut-in, homeless, or sex worker was their huckleberry.

The sex or sexual orientation of the targets didn't seem important, which added an element of weirdness and removed an important variable. Typically, mass murderers were men, and sex or arousal played a role in choosing their victim. A female suspect was *possible*, albeit statistically improbable.

The killer seemed to aim for those who would go unnoticed, but there were exceptions — like Debra. Rudy was *technically* homeless but was also a much-appreciated worker and volunteer. Though missed, the person may not have any relatives searching for them.

That so many missing and apparent victims were good Samaritan's introduced a major wrinkle, but one that was potentially telling. *Why target the good? Out of resentment?* That was insane in ways Ethan could not fathom or measure. If they desired quality human beings, how would they identify them? By mining data from charities and NGOs? The thought was sickening.

However, before he could delve deeper into that maelstrom of morality, Ethan needed to learn the identity of the dead guy at the ravine crash site.

DNA analysis and subsequent follow-up by American authorities determined that the man at the ravine crash site was Petr Grenk, and unlike Rudy Ingersson, there was plenty of information about him. From breaking and entering to armed robbery, Petr was a career criminal — and judging by the number of arrests and convictions, not a skilled one. Then again, he had somehow evaded stiff sentences. Say what one might about Petr Grenk, the guy must've had an excellent lawyer.

After appraising Bert of the findings, Ethan left Bert to poke further into Grenk's recent activities and investigate any possible connection to Rudy.

Physiotherapy and relentless paperwork chewed up the rest of the day, and it was 8 p.m. before he hauled his tired ass into the house and plopped down at the kitchen table.

Kim peeked her head around the corner. "There are leftovers in the fridge. Hamburger steak and mixed veggies; nothing spectacular, but it will fill the void."

"Thanks, Kim, I really appreciate it. If not for you, I'd be eating a nuked pizza and washing it down with warm beer."

She winked. "I put two beers in the fridge for you. Oh, I think Caroline called; probably a message on the answering machine."

"Thanks."

To his recollection, Caroline had only ever called his house number twice. He checked the answering machine but found no message. *Caroline, what gives?*

Even though *she* should've called *him*, Ethan rung her cell. It rang and rang, and when it got to the answering service, he heard, "This person's mailbox is full."

I guess I'll just have to call her office number and have someone pass the damn phone to her.

A second later, he changed his mind. He'd already traced Aaron Leadshat to the same town in Wyoming where Caroline said she lived before moving to Montana. 'Leadshat' was not a common name; in fact, he'd never heard it before he met Caroline. He was all but certain that Caroline and Aaron were related, and given their ages, their relationship could be auntie to nephew, or even mother to son. And given the look on Caroline's face at the crash site, Ethan judged the latter option to be the most likely.

Ethan wasn't hungry, but he still managed to eat half of what Kim had left for him. Plus, he wanted to save room for a beer. No sooner had he cracked the can that his phone rang. *Ugh...*

"Hello."

"You don't sound good."

"Oh, hi, Angela. It's just been a long day."

"I got your message about the Kayak Kid. Bert filled me in on the details. So sad."

"Definitely, but at least now we know."

"Yes, that's right. Not to pry, but any word from Caroline?"

Ah...Caroline rears her ugly, pretty head again!

"I've only spoken to her once since the highway incident, and that call lasted about five seconds."

"Huh. That's strange. I hope she's okay...you're both okay, right?"

"Honestly, right now, it's clear as mud."

"Sorry to hear that, Ethan. Who knows; people's lives can get awfully messed up. Maybe just give her some time."

"True that, Angela. I guess we'll just have to see…" He trailed off, not knowing what else to say.

Angela probably sensed his discomfort with the topic, as she quickly interjected, "I know this is a tough time; one of the hardest things in life is not knowing. It can really sap your spirit."

"That's for certain."

"Well, buddy, just wanted to see if you were okay. Didn't mean to bother you when you are trying to relax."

"There's one thing I know to be true, Angela, and it's that you're never a bother."

"Thanks, Ethan."

"Talk to you in the next day or two."

"Nighty night."

The first beer went down smoothly, as did the second and third. The last two as he lay in a semi-vegetative state in bed were warm as piss.

Waking up, he saw that Caroline had messaged him, and his heart skipped a beat — or maybe ten.

You're in my thoughts. I will call you soon.

He frowned. *Enough of this relationship by text!* He called her.

"Very busy right now, Ethan."

"Understandable. The deceased is your son, isn't he, Caroline?"

She sighed.

"It's not what it looks like, but I can't say more because it's part —"

"— of an ongoing investigation."

There was a long pause. "Yes. I'm sorry, Ethan."

"I'm sorry you lost your son, Caroline, whatever the circumstances."

"Now both my children are gone."

Ethan was stunned. *Both?*

Before Ethan could inquire, Caroline said, "My little girl died almost nineteen years ago."

"God, I had no idea, Caroline. Sorry to hear that. If you want to talk, anything, you know —"

"I know. Rain check, okay?"

"Yes, for sure."

"Have to go."

136

Chapter Nineteen: Hal Stead

"One-hundred and forty!" Reggie said in a British accent, before adding in his normal voice, "Less a hundred."

Ethan, trying in vain to stifle a snigger, deducted his forty points off his team's total. They were behind in the rubber match with *The Shafty Barrels*.

"In my defense, I hit the twenty twice, Reggie. I think my other dart is wonky."

Ethan checked his one dart that had bounced off the board to the floor. "See, the flight was loose on the shaft! It was two turns short of tight."

Again, Reggie pretended he was from England. "Not since Boris Johnson and Brexit have we been witness to two full turns short of tight."

Angela spewed beer, laughing so hard Ethan had to hold on to her and her chair lest they both tumble to the floor.

Reggie joined in the guffawing, which got Ethan chortling as he took his seat beside Angela.

It's so good being around them! Alas, for Ethan, good times sometimes conjured up wonderful memories, which could simultaneously suck.

#

Chelsea was eleven-and-a-half, no longer a little girl. Yes, her hair was still in pigtails, but she was, as much as he hated to admit it, on the fast track to adolescence. Chelsea had remarkable hand-eye coordination and such grace. She was especially good at darts. By age ten, she would occasionally beat him in 501.

He was thankful she enjoyed some sports. Her mother, Alice, wasn't into sports. However, Chelsea was a natural at most everything.

Today, they were at two games apiece. Gone were the days he could fool her into thinking he hadn't played well. Now he had to try his best, or she would bust him.

"Now, no wobblies or 'that one slipped out of my fingers,' Dad!"

"Oh, trust me, I have no intention of letting you beat me in a best-of-five until you are *twenty*-one, not ten-and-one."

Chelsea giggled and held her hand over her mouth, much as Angela did, then quipped, "You asked for it!"

Fifteen minutes later, she had doubled on a 19 and won the game. Ethan was still at 106. He feigned dejection, and she immediately looked sad and gave him a big hug.

"I'm sorry, papa."

His jiggling clued her into the fact he was trying ever so hard to, and failing at, holding back a laugh. "Oh, you got me. You really got me, you wascally wabbit!"

Ethan laughed, and Elmer Fudd'ed an "Even though you, you are now the better da da, darts da player, I can still be de-la-be the ma ma, master of tease."

Chelsea laughed her golden laugh. "You will always be 'Master of Tease!'"

It was the last time they ever played darts.

#

Ethan looked at Angela after feeling an elbow nudge his side. "You were thinking about Chelsea."

"Can't get much by you, Angela."

"It's your shot, Ethan. *The Shafty Barrels* missed their opportunity. You only need double-19 to win us the match."

Ethan gathered himself, toed the line, and promptly tossed a double-19. *That one's for you, my little girl.*

#

In all his years in law enforcement, Ethan had never directly contacted Interpol; however, if what he was seeing in the missing persons data pointed to a serial killer, they could be helpful. Plus, his superior in Kelowna had given him an affirmative to proceed with his line of inquiry. Interpol had computational power and analytical abilities that dwarfed what the RCMP could apply, so it was a no-brainer.

Interpol's Manchester branch got back to him immediately, but he thought it might just be a 'We received your request and will respond as soon as possible' or some equally robotic response. Instead, the communication was from an *actual* person named Sherry-Anne Lexsmith.

Ms. Lexsmith said they were happy to provide as much information as they could and sincerely hoped this would further his investigation. In addition, she asked him to provide any insights he may have on their pile of cold case files — and a pile it was, for the embedded link took him to hundreds of images and associated documents.

He owed Sherry and crew a case of beer, or maybe an epic box of Earl Grey. From what he'd heard, Guinness was expensive.

Ms. Lexsmith also said that she d be happy to populate a program they had with his data and findings and work on profiling the killer. Ethan couldn't ask for more than that.

The files Interpol sent him were sorted chronologically, and while it made sense to start with something from the past thirty years, Ethan was curious about the older ones. He opened one file to see a scanned microfiche created from a much older source record.

Ethan zoomed in on the image, headlined by 'London Metropolitan Police, Scotland Yard, January 2, 1828. Officers in attendance: Myles Blackworth and Aldridge Pennington.'

After hours of intensive interrogation, the suspect had finally made a statement:

Eight murders? Pfft. Yes, but have some respect. I've slain-saved sixty-six and my goal, like my father before me and his father before him, is one hundred! Arrest me? You should thank me, exalt me.

Since time immemorial, Slayers have been the deity's dagger and nature's knife. Cut off an alder, ten fresh shoots spring forth. Extinguish a tender, innocent, and beautiful life, ten shining souls are born. It's a law before laws were laid down. Eight, sixty-six, one hundred, all bloody drops in the pan! We Slayers are a family of enrichers, and tens of thousands, perhaps hundreds of thousands, lay in our wake.

You think you understand; you think you know, but you know nothing of the most ancient of ways of the Ancient of Days. The great you see around us, those that have elevated humankind, have been spawned by our swords and born by our bullets! These hands – at this the man clenched his fists and then slammed them on the table - *have punched, choked, strangled, shivved, slashed, skewered, gutted, shot, hatcheted, and hung!* Ethan was surprised to see that the transcription of the interview contained supplemental commentary. Clearly, whomever documented the proceedings had felt it necessary to add comments about the suspects actions and demeanor, not just his words. In most cases, the commentary was tagged with 'MB,' which Ethan reasoned had to be Myles Blackworth's initials. The next line confirmed Ethan's hunch.

Showing his hands to those questioning him, including yours truly, Detective Constable, Myles Blackworth, he then added, *These are the hands of horror and the Ten Commandments. You think you know...*

At that, the suspect, Hal Stead, shook his head at the shocked and stupefied investigative unit and never spoke another word. *Was it madness? Manifesto? Both?*

The last part of the account read, *Two days before he was to be hanged from the gallows, Hal Stead escaped from jail, and was never seen or heard from again.*

It was a remarkable account. Was this 'Hal Stead' truly a serial killer, or just a whacko wanting attention? On a whim, Ethan looked at more of the files with metadata — a fancy-schmancy term that Angela had clued him into — relating to Hal Stead, Myles Blackworth, and Aldridge Pennington. Ethan would be the first to admit that sometimes he went down rabbit holes that led to China, but this was perversely exhilarating.

In a few minutes, he found three more files. The first was a death report.

June 21: Inspector Myles Blackworth was found dead at the Liverpool docks. You may note this as unusual, as Inspector Blackworth was from London. He was last seen alive at London's Saint Katharine Docks, shortly before the General Steam Navigation Company ship, the Belfast, departed for Liverpool. There were no witnesses to his demise, though it was reported that he appeared to have been strangled. In addition to Myles Blackworth being one of London's finest, he was a strongman of some repute, so his being strangled suggests he was felled by a formidable foe. No witnesses have come forward, though inquiries will be made of those who departed the ship in Dublin.

The second file documented the failure to track down Hal Stead or any of his family members. Efforts to locate them in London and Liverpool were stymied by the necessity to investigate a rash of other murders that took place over a ten-day period in the middle of June. Myles Blackworth's colleague, Aldridge Pennington, was put in charge of capturing Hal Stead and finding who murdered Myles Blackworth.

The third, and presumably last, metadata file was short, and not so sweet.

Constable Aldridge Pennington is under investigation for the wrongful death of numerous residents of Liverpool and London. Mr. Pennington has not been seen in several weeks.

Ethan knew there were probably more productive things he could be doing, but the story held a morbid fascination. Plus, there was something in the name, Hal Stead, that stuck in his mind, like the name of someone you believe you'd met, but don't recall where.

Chapter Twenty: h

Women had their intuition; Ethan had his hunches. Today, those subtle gut feelings and cerebral signals told him to be careful; danger was lurking.

As he walked in the light rain, closer and closer to the small gathering at Aronia Cemetery, his Spidey-senses were registering off the charts. *This is just a funeral, man; calm down. You're here to support Caroline, even if she's been giving you the cold shoulder.*

Still, the niggle persisted, so he slowed his pace and casually tucked himself behind an elm tree to compose himself and adjust his hat. Ethan hadn't loved anyone since April, and now here he was, sticking his nose into Caroline's business.

You're a moron, Ethan Birchom! He would've walked back to the car then if it wasn't for the ominous feeling in his gut.

He really needed to get more rest. Since Chelsea had died and April left, Ethan seldom slept for more than two hours without waking up. Case details and clues would reverberate in his mind, to the point that he would often get up and either do some research or fire up his rock polisher.

Ethan looked down at his boots. He couldn't recall if he'd taken them off last night. He knew he'd fallen asleep at the computer; his neck felt like it was a truck spring fused to the end of a slinky.

He rubbed his chin. He hadn't even shaved. *How disrespectful is that?*

Tired, ashamed, and confused, Ethan started ambling back toward his truck, but he only made it ten feet. Something was compelling him to turn around, so he finally yielded to it.

Ethan strode back to the elm and casually over to some flowering wisterias. Then he resumed angling toward the small gathering in the cemetery. There were only ten or so people, and despite the drizzle and the uniform black attire worn by all in attendance, he recognized Caroline in her black trench coat.

The tall man standing beside her turned his head slightly, enough for Ethan to see the corner of his eye, which suggested the man's peripheral vision had picked him up on approach. The elderly man sported the same old-fashioned, wide-brimmed black wool hat that Caroline's uncle had been wearing the day they nearly crossed paths at Margie's Café.

Seconds later, the people began walking away in different directions, but none, including Caroline, went toward Ethan. Only the man in the hat, presumably Caroline's uncle, was at the gravesite when Ethan arrived.

The man turned his head and tilted it slightly toward Ethan, but it was enough for Ethan to see his chiseled cheeks and confirm it was Caroline's uncle. Ethan gauged him to be about 6'3", roughly one-eighty, in his late sixties or early seventies. Thin black hair covered his neck and ears, poking out from under the front of his hat.

"Twenty-two is too young to die."

The man spoke softly, but his words sent a chill up Ethan's spine. The voice appeared to emanate from the air or the buried grave, not the man. Ethan also detected a very slight British accent. Before Ethan could reply, the old man continued.

"How did you know my grandson?"

Grandson. So, this was Caroline's father, not her uncle. She had lied to him. *Why?*

"Sadly, I never had the pleasure. I only knew Aaron was Caroline's son and wanted to be here to pay my respects."

The old man turned toward Ethan, yet looked past him before turning back toward the backfilled grave. Ethan looked over his shoulder to see Caroline's Bronco driving out of the cemetery, leaving only two vehicles in the parking lot.

They had not made eye contact, but Ethan noticed the man's eyes. They were like pools of ink. As Caroline's truck turned right and traveled down the main road and out of view, Ethan couldn't help but feel confused and slighted, even *wronged*.

Seeming to read his mind, her father said, "It was my idea to move the funeral ahead an hour and a half. You see…" He looked Ethan straight in the eye.

Long accustomed to owning a stern look that could force many a man to back down, Ethan was surprised by the willpower he had to exert to hold the man's gaze.

After glancing down toward Ethan's RCMP issue boots, then back up to hold eye contact, Caroline's father continued. "You see, we're a private family, and pride ourselves on continuity and longevity. Police officers aren't particularly good at longevity. I don't approve of you, Mr. Birchom, but Caroline has earned the right to make — and *own* — her decisions."

At that, the man righted his hat, glanced at the grave and, after briefly resting a hand on the headstone, walked away.

Ethan watched Caroline's father — whatever his name was — get into a late 1980s Mercedes-Benz and leave the cemetery, going in the direction opposite to that of Caroline.

Ethan looked at Aaron "Mars" Leadshat's headstone and started back to the car. Halfway back, something forced him to retrace his steps and reexamine the headstone.

This time, he noticed it right away: the curled shape of the 'h' in Leadshat. While the other letters were a uniform font, the 'h' was stylistically different.

He remembered something. When Caroline's father had tilted his head down to look at Ethan's shoes, Ethan had noticed the same curved 'h' on the brim. Its shape resembled a hatchet. Initially, Ethan had thought it was just a brand symbol, but now he wasn't so sure.

Ethan pulled out his phone and zoomed in on the 'h,' then snapped a photo of the headstone. He typed, *Does this stylized 'h' remind you of a hatchet?*

He felt his phone vibrate in his hands moments after hitting send. It was an incoming call, not a text.

"How's it going today, Reggie?"

"Good, I think. I spotted a camper van — an old one — and judging by all the dirt and mud on it, it looks like it's been over some rough back roads. I'd like to check it out, if that's okay."

"Did you get a license plate or see the driver?"

"No, but I'm staying quite a way back."

"So you're following them?"

"Yes, heading north towards Canada."

"I don't know Reggie; something tells me you should back off."

"Oh, c'mon, Ethan. I've been stuck chasing down shoplifters, treed cats, and issuing speeding tickets. Sometimes I wonder if I have it in me to be a real cop, like you."

"You are a *real* cop, Reggie, hence the badge and uniform."

"I know, boss; I just feel like I'm not contributing anything much to a *proper* investigation, let alone trying to find out who tried to kill one of my faves — that being you, big guy."

Ethan paused before answering. "I understand where you're coming from, Reggie, and thanks. It's against my better judgement, but should you continue, do stay back, and don't follow that van off the highway. Use your field glasses to grab a license plate number, and if they should pull over, snap a pic. Got it?"

"Yeah, *Dad*, I'll be careful."

"I mean it, Reggie."

"Yes, yes, okay. I will be very, very careful." Reggie said it like Elmer Fudd.

"Good. Drop me a line to let me know you're okay, or if you've found out something material."

"Will do."

Ethan was about to tuck the phone into his pocket when Bert texted him.

You were on the right track with the 'h' looking like a hatchet. I poked around and apparently 'h' owes its origin to the Norman's who brought their letter 'hache' with them when they invaded Britain in 1066. 'Hache' is the source word for 'hatchet.' As an aside, the Normans were descendants of pagan Vikings from Denmark and Norway that settled in the Normandy region of France.

While Ethan admired Bert's ability to bench press 250, he was even more impressed that his number one sidekick was passionate about history.

Chapter Twenty-One: Rammed

After messaging Bert, *Thanks a lot, I owe you one*, Ethan sat there, tapping his fingers on the steering wheel, thinking, and repeating "*hache*, hatchet, *hache*, hatchet" over and over until he ended up with sweet 'hat-shit.' He slammed the truck into gear and burnt some rubber as he came off the gravel and onto the asphalt.

Minutes later, he was slamming on the brakes and making another screech on the pavement. The mental image of the microfiche article on the early 19th-century accused killer, Hal Stead, had popped into his brain and filled his vision.

A car flew by him, honking, and he realized he had stopped only partially on the shoulder. Once again, Ethan pulled off the road; this time he backed onto an old logging road. Coming to a stop, he recalled Hal Stead's chilling words:

These hands have punched, choked, strangled, shivved, slashed, skewered, gutted, shot, hatcheted, and hung! How curious to use the word 'hatcheted.' Ethan didn't know if 'hatcheted' was even an actual word, but there it was, stuck in his mind.

Was there a connection between the 'h,' Hal Stead, Caroline's dad, and the investigation? Ethan couldn't say, but he suspected he would be up half the night thinking about it.

Too late, he heard a vehicle accelerating. When he looked up, all he saw was the grill of a Kenworth and the upper torsos of two men in its cab.

Ethan rammed his Toyota into reverse and pinned it, but the big rig smashed into him.

He was barely able to steer his truck around a gentle corner, then the semi was angling him to the left and toward a steep drop-off. Ethan strained to keep his truck to the high side of the road, but it was a losing battle, for as he did, his pickup turned sideways.

He looked to his left to see a sharp corner coming and heard the Kenworth shift down for more power. It was going to send him over the bank.

Ethan grabbed his 9mm Smith & Wesson from the holster behind his seat and tucked it into his boot. His faller's hat fell off where it hung from his gun rack and landed in his lap just as he was about to go over the side of the road. He jammed it on his head, then saw the orange Kenworth tandem axle wrecker disappear. Then it was smash, crash, broken glass, the smell of cedar and pine, and the sound of cascading water, and — once again — pain.

Ethan was hanging upside-down in the semi-collapsed roof of his truck. How far he had tumbled, he didn't know, but he knew there shouldn't be a one-inch-thick branch jammed into, maybe *through*, his shoulder. The limb was sticking through the windshield downward into him. He reasoned that if he unbuckled, it might slide out — or a branch of said limb might tear a bigger hole.

Moments later, the truck dropped a few inches and icy water started rushing in. As the water backed up against the one side window that was miraculously not broken, the cab started filling up. If he didn't do something, he would drown in minutes.

His seatbelt was stuck. *Don't panic!* Ethan pulled a multi-tool out of its pouch on his belt, unfolded the knife, and cut the seatbelt.

Slowly, painfully, he slid from the branch. Ethan sweated profusely, and when he hit the cold water, it was shocking. He collected his thoughts and squeezed himself out the side window.

Partway out, the torrent grabbed him and sent him tumbling downstream, where a blow to the head made him see stars. Ethan bounced along for another twenty feet before he scrambled out of the creek. As he did, a stab of pain accompanied the retort of a rifle, and pieces of shattered rock blasted his face.

Ethan clutched a hand to where he felt they had shot him and found the hole in his shoulder left by the branch. It seemed the bullet might've passed through the same hole — a stroke of luck. After he felt a round strike his right calf, Ethan didn't feel *quite* so fortunate.

Grabbing scrub and weeds with his right hand and pushing against slimed-covered rocks with his left leg, he got behind a boulder. A splinter of rock gouged into his skull as his safety boulder took a direct hit. He ripped off his shirt, tore off a decent chunk, and stuffed it in the hole in his shoulder. Most of the rest he wrapped around his calf.

How on Earth am I going to survive this time? Ethan had only just recovered from the last attempt on his life! Surely this time, those who wanted him dead were going to see their job done or die trying.

Again, it was Chelsea, as much as survival instinct, that fueled Ethan's desire to get away, and to see his pursuers die trying to stop him. He suddenly realized the horse was in his shirt pocket. *God, no!* He checked his shoulder; it wasn't there. He checked his bound calf; not there either. "No, no!" he said, muffled. Then, Ethan realized he had

147

popped the figurine between his teeth. "Oh, thank God!" He tucked it deep into his pants pocket.

Ethan took a few deep breaths to calm himself. Would his assailants come down, or perch themselves on the edge of the road and wait for a kill shot? In their shoes, he would stay on top, while trying to flush his victim out. His enemies had a rifle or two, and probably handguns — and grenades. He shuddered at the thought.

Ethan had only his revolver and multitool. He was outmanned, outgunned, and in an awful position. *Think, think! Upstream, you're dead. Downstream, deceased.* There was only one way to go, and that was up the bank. He knew full well he would, at one time or another, be exposed. Fortunately, the steep slope was blanketed by heavy conifers so he could — maybe — scramble and dart from one tree to another. *'Dart,' with a shot-up calf? Not likely!*

Another blast sent rock fragments flying his way, this time from the rock across from him. He wiped some bloody rock specks from his cheeks. His assailants seemed to be banking on a ricochet to inflict injury or death, or perhaps simply pry him from cover for an ensuing kill shot.

Knowing they had him pinned down, and would want to finish what they started, it was a foregone conclusion that at least one person would work down the bank to help flush him out. They would probably be taking the upper bank for an easier descent and better shooting angle. Given that most people were right-handed, the person would want to shoot with their left leg planted. Ethan reasoned they would be approaching from upstream, to his right; he was backed against a boulder on the northwest side of the stream. He needed to get that guy and his rifle, and he might only get one shot. Even as he thought it, Ethan heard rock clattering on rock, and a soft curse. Chances are his enemy was already within 150 feet of him.

Ethan was going to have to give up his pants, or at least part of them. He cut off his pant legs and quickly stretched them over a two-foot-long broken limb at his feet. He took a deep breath, said to himself, *"Fuck the pain,"* and tossed the pant-leg-laden limb up and to his left, simultaneously using his good leg to launch himself toward the boulder across from him.

Pant-leg-stick drew the fire from two rifles, and Ethan rolled sideways, right arm outstretched, and gun cocked. A burly, bearded man in camo was across the creek and upstream by thirty feet. His attacker brought up his rifle, but too slowly.

Ethan squeezed the trigger and shot him between the eyes. Another rifle barked, but the bullet pinged off a rock to his right. The shooter must not have been able to see Ethan...yet. Ethan played salamander, wriggling across the stream to the dead man, who had crumpled against a deadfall.

Just in time, Ethan brought the bulk man up to use as a shield, though the bullet passed through the dead guy and hit him on his left forearm. Fortunately, it only *just* penetrated the skin. He grabbed the dead man's rifle and, using the deceased and the deadwood as his defensive wall, fired upward in the general direction of his attacker.

He heard the truck's engine start, but the vehicle was just idling. Was the man going to shoot from the rig? Perhaps he was radioing for help? Regardless, Ethan seized the opportunity, threw the rifle over his good shoulder, and limped his way upstream, pulling the bullet from his left forearm as he did so.

There!

Across from him was a narrow defile, where a trickle of water had eaten a narrow channel upwards. Unless his attacker was directly across from it, Ethan would be at least partially protected, and the rocks and trees would give him hand and footholds. The rifle he could use as leverage.

Ethan made for the defile and started climbing. It was a slow, brutal, and painful ascent. He still heard the truck, and once, heard it move up the road. The man was probably trying to spot him through the trees. *Maybe you should concern yourself with retrieving your dead friend, asshole?*

Perhaps halfway up, feeling confident he wouldn't get shot at, Ethan stopped at a spot where the trickling water had formed a small basin to deal with his wounds. Despite his exertions, his calf wasn't bleeding badly. He had bandaged himself in such haste that he never examined the wound, but he elected to just splash cold water on it and leave it be.

Gingerly, he stood up and transferred more weight to that leg. It hurt, but it wasn't excruciating. As for his shoulder... well, once again, it appeared he had been very fortunate. He couldn't move his arm without shots of pain coursing through his body, but overall, it wasn't *too* bad. It seemed somebody upstairs liked him.

Once again, his thoughts went to Chelsea. Was she, his Guardian Angel? Or was it one of his parents? Ethan had lost both of them within two months of one another four years previously. Cancer was as much a remorseless predator as Hal Stead had been.

As he continued onward and upward, Ethan hoped climbing would become easier. *Nope.* From below, he could see that, while the slope had become less pronounced, it was choked with small trees that formed a nearly impenetrable barrier. Having driven down many back roads and hiked many a trail, he knew that areas where humans had manipulated the earth, whether to make a road or create a log landing, frequently became choked with alders, willows, birch, canes, or spiky blackberry bushes. All provided cover for other trees, generally conifers, to grow, and eventually the needle and cone-bearing trees mostly replace the deciduous units. Ethan elected to angle right to skirt the veritable fence of trees.

He heard it before he saw it: a culvert with water spilling out of it. *A road!* As was often the case, heavy rock buttressed the area around and below the culvert. Not much water was spilling out of the culvert, but Ethan stuck his head under it anyway to revive himself before taking a drink.

Now, to get to the road, and be ever so careful going down it! Ultimately, it would take him to safety, unless truck-driver-assassin-guy had found his way up this side of the valley. Whatever the case, the road was Ethan's best chance for survival.

Ethan clambered up the rocks until he neared the road's edge. Alas, some larger boulders lay there, and he had to lean his rifle against one of them before reaching up and over the rock. As he pulled himself onto the road surface and got to his hands and knees, he exclaimed, "Yes!"

A boot crashed into his head.

Chapter Twenty-Two: Bacon, Beans, and Beaver

Bacon and beans. Ethan inhaled again. Yes, bacon and beans, and what else? Warm honey on toast. He loved warm honey on toast.

Through the fog and low *thrum* of a headache, Ethan saw a plateful of food to his left. He focused harder and saw the bacon, beans, honey-covered toast, and a plop of jelly. Then a fork turned the mound of jelly over, and Ethan realized it *wasn't* jelly; it was a squished eyeball.

Ethan tried in vain to open his right eye. "Fuck." His throat was parched, and he would've recoiled in shock, anger, and disgust had his head — and the rest of him — not been bound to a high-backed wooden chair.

"Not to worry; you can still see your future, what's left of it, through one eye. The tip of my cowboy boot took out your other one. 'Sorry, not sorry,' as they say nowadays."

Ethan raised his eye up to see a woman with a tanned face in her mid-60's, with grey-black hair and dark brown eyes that reminded him of a falcon. She pulled a wooden chair up close to him, took off the grey and white scarf wrapped around her neck, and looked him straight in the eye as she started eating her breakfast.

"You know I'm —"

His sentence was cut off as he coughed, then his captor stuck duct tape over his mouth. She ate a few more bites of her breakfast, and when he coughed more, she shook her head and got up. After she sat her plate on a table, she grabbed a plastic bottle with a squirt lid, like a soap dispenser.

Pulling a long hunting knife out of her belt, she strode up to Ethan. He figured this might be the end, so he desperately tried to tip over his chair. It was fastened to the floor.

He wasn't going anywhere.

The woman guffawed. "I'm only going to punch a wee hole in the duct tape and squirt in some water. Move just a little and I might accidentally cut off one of your lips. Understand? Blink twice if you do."

Ethan blinked twice and was rewarded with an air hole and squirts of water.

"And yes, I know who — and *what* — you are."

With that, she turned her back on him and returned to the table to eat her breakfast.

Ethan scanned the cabin. The floor was planked, and the log walls chinked with backer rod. Light spilled in via two small windows. Animal traps hung on the wall, and between two pictures of horses, the brown-black fur of what was probably an American mink.

The woman interrupted his mental notetaking, scraping up the last of the food on her plate. "Well, I guess there's no time like the present."

She got up and walked over to him with only the eyeball left on her plate.

Ethan looked at it, and then at her.

She stick-handled the eyeball around the plate with her fork and laughed. It wasn't a pleasant laugh, but neither was it a witch's cackle; it was a mischievous laugh, imbued with supreme confidence.

"Oh my, you thought I was serious!"

Ethan was confused. In a flash, she was sitting astride him, her blade at his throat, hissing into his ear. "I've no need for those sorts of trophies."

Ethan felt the blade slide past his throat, then the tip of the blade eased along his cheek toward his right eye. He heard the cut, and then could see, albeit faintly, out of his right eye.

Thank God, he thought to himself, but the blade continued slicing, along his forehead and scalp, and he again lost the sight from his right eye as blood ran into it.

He looked at her face. It was serene, as if she was merely cutting a birthday cake. Meeting a monster was a new experience for Ethan. And yet, she was familiar.

"Not to worry, it's just a flesh wound with my signature, so others will know, should you ever be discovered."

He wondered about 'the others' and what comprised the 'knowing.'

After pulling an apron off a hook by the door, she stepped out to drag in a large beaver with one eye gouged out.

The monster flopped the beaver onto the table, and in less than ten minutes, had it fleshed out. As twisted as it all was, Ethan couldn't help but admire her skill. One didn't attain that ability with a hatchet and a blade without many years of practice. What Ethan knew to be castor sacs and anal glands were set aside in a bowl, presumably to be used for baiting traps.

She took the beaver's body outside, perhaps to hang it? Beaver was supposed to be good for eating, but he'd not tried it. Chances are, if she lived out here, she would make use of everything.

Was this mad trapper in cahoots with the men who tried to kill him? It seemed a reasonable assumption.

Two minutes later, she returned with an oval board, which she placed on the table. This she used to stretch the beaver pelt over. It only took her about five minutes.

She rinsed her hands off in a bowl of water and cleaned her tools. Then she took off her apron; it didn't look like she had got a speck of blood on it.

It was impressive, albeit rather morbid, to witness.

"It's not you, you understand. It's just that you're in the way, which has often been the case with badge-wearing bots like yourself. Anyway, without further ado, let's wrap this up, shall we?"

His captor grabbed a ratchet and started unbolting his chair from the floor. "Don't bother trying to rock and wriggle." She showed him a Taser. "You know what these do."

Yes, Ethan knew.

Instinctively, Ethan glanced down at his pants — well, shorts — pocket and saw the shape of his horse keepsake. The woman also noticed.

"Why, is that a bulge in your pocket, or are you just happy to see me?" She sliced out the bottom of the pocket and looked at the horse effigy.

"How interesting."

She turned the precious ornament over and held it up to the light that came in through the open doorway.

"I always admired how the craftsman so exquisitely blended the pewter for the horse and the crystal of the saddle, or vice versa. Artists like him don't come around every day. Where did you get it? Ah, never mind; I think I know." She winked at him.

153

"Obviously, its value to you far exceeds its price in dollars, otherwise it wouldn't be in your pocket. A fine remembrance. It's not a boy's toy, so it stands to reason it belonged to your daughter or granddaughter and you lug it around with you everywhere; it's like a keepsake and talisman at the same time. The girl's probably dead. Touching."

Through it all, Ethan watched her eyes. He expected them to be demonic pools of black, but there was a lively spirit there, a childish wonder, and curiosity, but then the monster reemerged.

"I know I said I'm not into trophies, but this little beauty will complement my modest collection." She walked over to the mantle set above the woodstove, which would serve as cooking and warming station for this cabin. She placed his ornament beside a team of black horses that were pulling a wagon.

Behind the wagon were other small horses, much like the one he had, only the pewter and crystal configurations were different. Above that were several hatchets, arranged to make a cross. Ethan also noticed the now familiar stylized 'h' burnt into their handles.

Before she finished unbolting his chair, she brought in a furniture dolly and slid it under the back of the chair. Then, she slung more ropes around him and the chair and around the dolly itself. Sinister, yes, professional and organized, absolutely.

Ethan noticed her hands were like the oil-stained hemp rope she worked with and the dark knots she tied. They were working hands, yet with an elegant quality he'd only seen in some women, particularly ranchers and horse-lovers like Angela and Caroline. Her heavy, long-sleeved western shirt appeared to be homespun. Like her skin, it too was tanned. Perhaps the shirt was also made of hemp.

Only after she had pulled on every rope and checked every knot did she fully loosen off the bolts on his chair. Then she wheeled him out the door and, via a ramp, into the back of a van that was quite high off the ground; probably it had a post-manufacture lift kit. Ethan only heard the slightest grunt at what should've required substantial effort. The woman had uncommon strength, but he wagered she wasn't over 150 pounds.

Once in the van, she bolted down the chair and applied fresh tape over his lips. She was thorough about it; the duct tape wrapped fully round Ethan's head. She'd tucked some plastic around the back of his head, presumably so that, when the duct tape was removed, it wouldn't yank out half a head of hair. He was sure she didn't do this to spare her victim discomfort, but to expedite the process.

A few minutes later, she tucked a bag of beaver parts into the camper van's small fridge. The van's interior had been modified to allow for a wheelchair. A cot was there, but underneath it, he could see coils of rope, tools, and gun cases — and what looked to be drops of blood.

She rested one of her hands on his shoulder. "We've a long and uncomfortable journey ahead of us. But here at, ah, 'End of the Road Enterprises,' we're devoted to singularly spectacular dispatches. I expect yours to be among the very best." She ruffled his hair and hopped outside.

Ethan was facing forward, but a bang, clang, rattle, and screech suggested she had closed and locked the van's back double doors. Then, not two minutes later, a screech and rattle, and light and fresh air poured in. That was, until a hood went over his head.

"I don't know how many times this has occurred to me at the last moment! Maybe, deep down, I'm an anti- Hooderite."

She cackled at that, and when he didn't respond, his head fell sharply forward from a stiff blow.

"C'mon, I know this is a difficult situation, but surely you can see the connection between *Hutterite* and *Hooderite*?!"

Ethan tried for a weak laugh, but only managed a mumble behind his duct-tape.

There was a pause, and he braced himself for another wallop. It didn't come, only a long exhale. "Well, moving on...*I*, for one, intend to enjoy the process. It's not all about the destination, you know."

Psycho-bitch waxing philosophical. Ethan didn't have that on this morning's bingo card.

The doors again closed, and he heard something large sliding across the roof-rack of the van. Given the grunting that accompanied the sound, it was heavy, awkward, or both. Surely, she wasn't loading a boat — or maybe she was. Making people disappear in deep lakes was an age-old practice. Then he heard more scraping as she had loaded another heavy item.

Ethan heard what were probably ropes or straps being tossed over the roof and tightened. A couple minutes later, he heard the driver's door slam, and the engine roared to life. At that, a heavy aluminum blind that stretched from floor to ceiling clinked sideways across the van. When it reached the end, there was the sound of pins sliding into place. The van lurched forward, and his captor's voice came over a speaker.

"Okay, we're on our way." The woman had rigged up an intercom to allow herself to speak to her victims. *Monsters be monstering*, Ethan thought to himself.

They bounced over a road for about fifteen minutes before the van stopped. Once again, he heard scraping on the roof; whatever was up there had been removed. The van inched forward for a couple minutes, then stopped again. The senior psycho loaded the heavy objects back on the roof.

This process repeated itself at least four times as they traveled down what had to be a very rough track. About ninety minutes later, the jostling of the van stopped, and the road became smoother. There were right and left turns, and one that almost seemed like a roundabout. There were no roundabouts in the woods, so he reckoned she was trying to confuse him.

Then they were on a smoother road, but one that didn't generate the flying rock noise common to gravel roads. It occurred to him it might be a dirt road with sealcoat applied. Perhaps twenty minutes later, they were on an even smoother road; by the sound and speed of travel, it was a paved highway.

They had motored along for about fifteen minutes when they slowed down fast enough to make the brakes shudder. A few minutes later he heard, albeit faintly, a voice say, "Ma'am, it's going to take about forty-five minutes to clear the road...rockslide."

Then he heard his jailer and would-be executioner's voice. "We're going to be here a while. And I'm already bored."

The security curtain clinked open, and she stepped through the gap and slid the curtain closed again. She pulled a Bowie knife out of a sheath strapped to her heavy brown work pants and looked at him, tossing the knife back and forth between her hands.

Ethan not only knew that she was skilled with a blade, but that she was, right then and there, debating whether to kill him.

With lightning speed, she thrust the knife at him. He didn't even have time to flinch. Now there was a hole in the duct tape, and he could feel blood in his mouth. Then she pulled the duct tape loose from around his mouth.

"I'm enabling two-way communication, but with the flick of a switch, you're muted, understand? Give me grief, and with a flick of my knife, you're *really* muted."

"Got it."

She went back up front and closed the curtain.

"Radio check?"

"One RCMP officer in attendance."

"I hear you five-by-five, Mr. Birchom." She had used aeronautical parlance; Ethan reasoned she had flown a lot, or maybe even knew how to fly a plane or helicopter.

"As the saying goes, 'You have me at a disadvantage.' I don't know your name."

"And you *won't* know. Next question and *do* make it interesting. I'm easily bored."

Ethan considered asking about Reggie, but maybe Reggie was on their trail right now. There were so many things he wanted to say, so many questions he desperately wanted to ask, but he started with the innocuous.

"You don't see too many of these old four-wheel-drive camper vans anymore."

There was a pregnant pause. "Fancy yourself a van aficionado and a serial-killer-hunter, do you?"

This told him more than he expected. "No. Just fancied having one someday," he lied. "Uncle of mine had one; always envied how he could travel down all the back roads around here."

"Oh, what was his name?"

"*Quid pro quo*. Your name for his."

"My, oh my; you're a tricky one, Mr. Birchom."

"By the way, sorry for your loss — the guy I shot between the eyes."

"Oh, don't be! Just a contractor, and it's good to weed out the dumb ones. His colleague also passed, prematurely."

157

So, she eliminated the loose ends!

"Why did you chop off the Kayak Kid's arm? Was he about to get away? Or was it just depravity?"

At that, she moved from her front seat, opened the curtain, stepped through, and closed it behind her. Then, she backhanded him viciously across the face.

The woman had a hand of iron! Ethan had been hammered by bigger people, and had been prepared for it, but he tasted her power.

She opened the curtain again and peered forward before turning back to him. "Depravity? What an awful thing to suggest! As for 'the about to get away' part, yes, possibly. Regardless, he didn't suffer — much — after that."

"Shame he suffered at all. From what I heard, the young man was practically an angel."

"'Angel,' as in the delusional modern Christian definition? Like a special mortal being just waiting to get their wings?"

"Well, something like that."

"How convenient it is that we forget the true nature of the mightiest of angels. Maybe you know that the Angels of Vengeance were the first angels created by God. Some suggest the archangel Gabriel was the angel of death that killed the firstborn of Egypt and may have killed the mighty Nephilim. Or perhaps by 'angel,' you mean like Azrael, who was or maybe *is* the quote-unquote 'Angel of Death?' Then there is, and I quote from *Two Kings*, 'the angel of the Lord went out and put to death 185,000 men in the Assyrian camp.' Do you mean Rudy was practically that good?"

Ethan adjusted his name for her from 'Monster' to 'Biblical Monster.'

"I think you know what I mean. Rudy was just a kid with loads of potential."

"And that's why I gave the soup-kitchen kiddo mercy."

Biblical Monster's logic, or morality, if that's what one could call it, was as diverse as it was disturbing. And her tone oozed of something else: anger.

"It sounds like you were mad at him."

"More disappointed than upset. Here I thought he might be special — not 'angelic' special, but mentor-worthy. I took him under my wing after preventing him from being numbskulled, and what did he do but betray me and try to run away!"

There was so much to parse in that statement; maybe she thought that she'd said too much, for her eyes became wild, and she turned away.

Ethan knew he had to swing for the fences. "What would Hal Stead have done?"

His words caught her like a slap. "You — you know Hal Stead?"

It was the first time he'd seen any hesitation in her countenance, any opening he might pry wider.

He repeated Hal Stead's words. *"These hands have punched, choked, strangled, shivved, slashed, skewered, gutted, shot, hatcheted, and hung! These are the hands of horror and the Ten Commandments."*

"Wow, you said them verbatim! You're not just a reasonably good-looking face. It's strange to hear those words spoken by the uninitiated, like a truth spoken in a language you've never heard, but somehow understand. You didn't just fall off the turnip truck, did you, eh, Birchom? That takes some serious research! I commend you, and all the better reason to kill you dead before you ever speak of it again and ruin things for all of humanity."

"How did Rudy ruin things for you?"

"You found his name! Clever man. Rudy was going to rat me out the first time I tried to kill you."

"I suppose I can understand, in some weird way, but why torture the poor guy?"

"Sometimes methods must be employed in order to advance the craft."

Advance the craft? By torturing someone?

"But you seem to enjoy hurting people."

"Oh, don't confuse the raw action with the knowledge that can be acquired from it. The prospect of what I may glean excites me."

"So, you enjoy what you do, on more than just a physical level?"

"I enjoy my work — my 'Calling,' rather — on a *spiritual* level. It's my passion. Physical or sexual satisfaction is incidental."

Ethan thought of the saying 'It takes a community to raise a child,' only in *her* case, maybe it was more like 'It takes a cult to raise a serial killer.'

"Did you want to kill me because I was getting too close, or something — or *someone* — else?"

"Maybe it's a two-fer."

Ethan let that sink in; his heart ached at what crossed his mind. *No, it couldn't be.* He changed the subject.

"Could one not achieve more by instructing rather than killing?"

"It's a fair question, and to a degree, that is what I wanted to do with Rudy. But he blew it."

"I'm sorry, but to me, you threw away all the things *he* might've done to make the world a better place."

"I don't completely reject that statement, but the greater truth is, Rudy wouldn't have even been *born* if not for us."

Us. Another admission that more people were involved. "This 'numbskulling' you spoke of...is that what happened to Debra McGown?"

"I guess I shouldn't be surprised you know of that too. Anyway, *Debra* happened to Debra. She realized that what we were doing was for the ultimate good. It was unfortunate to lose her —"

He heard a honk, likely the vehicle behind them.

Quickly, she sealed the tape over Ethan's mouth and covered his head again, but before she closed the curtain she said, "After you die, you will learn the truth. As Slayer's Hatchets, we are exalted!"

'Hatchets' he understood, but the 'Slayer' thing? *Is that their name for God or something?*

They drove for about ten minutes more, and once again reached a very bumpy road. On two occasions, she stopped. Once, Ethan thought he heard a gate creaking on its hinges, and another time a *screeching-scratching*, like an old-fashioned wooden-post and barbed-wire gate being drug across the ground.

After driving just a few more minutes, the van stopped again. She opened the curtain between the front and back of the van. "I must hand it to you: You got me so riled up that I neglected to adhere to the process. Anyway, better late than never."

At that, she pulled a flask out of a pocket behind her seat and poured something pungent into a cloth. Would this be the end? *Suffocation? Poisoning?* No, she would want to see him suffer. *Another experiment.*

As the cloth pinched over his nose, he smelled chloroform.

Chapter Twenty-Three: Bait

Raspberry? *Kind of.* Vanilla? *Somewhat.* Urine? *Well, maybe if someone peed on a raspberry vanilla crumble. Oh, gross!*

Ethan shook his head, but the smell became overpowering, and he jerked his head to the side, or at least tried to. He opened his eyes to see a sack pressed against his nose and, behind it, his dark keeper.

"It's castoreum; you know, what beavers secrete from the base of their tails. But I have my own special recipe. I combine it with urine, as beavers do to mark their territory, but I also add brown sugar, some whole-wheat flower, and a few other spices. Marten, wolverines, wolves, they can't resist the stuff. Trapping supplements my income."

He wondered what her primary source of income was. Surely stealing whatever hitchhikers and homeless people had on them wouldn't put gas in the tank of her van, buy food, and rent henchmen.

Realizing the tape had been removed from his mouth, he murmured, "What's your name?"

"Few know that castoreum is a perfume ingredient."

"*What is your name?*"

She grinned at him: not a smirk, but a big, toothy smile. The woman had perfect teeth.

Ethan couldn't help but wonder how, in her line of work, she hadn't been bashed upside the skull or kicked in the face, two things Ethan sorely wished he could do right now.

"It's..." This time she did smirk. "None of your business. You can call me the Angel of Death if you want."

"I suppose it sounds more respectful than *Psycho Bitch!*"

She reached back to punch him, then composed herself and just smiled. "Funny, he called me that too, before I hit him with a shovel. He probably would've spoken more respectfully after that, if his face wasn't caved in."

The monster suggestively tilted her head to Ethan's left.

Ethan couldn't turn his head, but he shifted his eyes.

It was Reggie.

Ethan turned his gaze back to the woman with a look that would surely kill. It didn't.

He looked back at Reggie, blinking tears from his eyes. Reggie's head was down, but Ethan saw blood dripping from his smashed, dislocated jaw. Already there was a pool of blood at Reggie's feet, reddening the pine needles and sandy ground. Like himself, Reggie's body, arms, legs, and feet were tied to a tree. On the right side of Reggie's forehead, an 'h' had been carved into his temple.

As Ethan looked at him, suddenly, Reggie's head jerked up and they made eye contact, though one of Reggie's eyes was swollen shut. Reggie started to cry.

"We'll get out of this, Reggie." *Ethan wished he totally believed that.*

The woman affected a mocking laugh, then added, in a serious tone, "Stranger things have indeed happened under the sun, but not when *I've* been in charge."

"Eat-n, Et-an..." Reggie mumbled.

Oh, God, the poor guy. "It's okay, Reggie. I'm very proud of you, you know."

Reggie sobbed.

"Oh, for heathen's sake! I'm tempted to end his experiment out of sheer disgust and pity." The monster spit in the dirt.

Then, Ethan heard a dog — no, it was a wolf howling.

"Alas, the creatures will come a-callin'. I always learn so much from observing nature and human interaction with the beasts."

The woman walked back to her van and swung it around, so the driver's side door was facing them. She drank some water, then poured herself a hot drink. "Ah, nothing like Earl Grey to see the day into night." She howled like a wolf, and it was close to the real thing, which followed a minute later.

Ethan shouted at her, "In this life, or the next, I will kill you for this!"

She only smiled and tilted her teacup at him.

"Eat-n...scare...scared." It must've been torture for Reggie to say, and it was torturous for Ethan to hear. The pain in his heart became that much more excruciating when he realized Reggie was here because of him.

"I'm so sorry I drug you into this, Reggie. But courage to the end, my friend. Courage, to the end."

Reggie nodded, and when four wolves showed up, just as the sky was darkening, Reggie did his best to say, and exhibit, *"Courage to the end."*

The first wolf tore into Reggie, and as predators often do, they attacked below the belt. It seemed to break something inside of Reggie, probably his heart.

Ethan felt his own heart breaking, too, and by how hard it was pounding, he wondered if it might just explode. He tried desperately to suppress panic and looked up to see the monster jotting down some notes. She lifted a satellite phone to her ear.

Meanwhile, a second wolf had arrived. Whether it was mate to the alpha male presently chowing down on Reggie or the next-hungriest member of the wolf pack, Ethan didn't know.

It didn't matter.

The wind picked up, and suddenly Biblical Monster's van was spinning away, dust flying. Ethan's wounds had stopped bleeding, but one wolf walked up to him, gave his bare leg a sniff, and licked at the bandage job.

It was just a matter of time.

The wind was now blowing mightily. Limbs were rattling, sometimes screeching as they rubbed together. A loud crack preceded a tree falling across the small grassy area, the top landing not thirty feet from where they were staked.

Ethan closed his eyes and, despite the snarling, howling, and chewing, brought his heart rate down slightly. He couldn't decide if he should open his eyes or not.

He felt razor-sharp teeth sink into his leg. Before long, the wolf would go for his crotch. Ethan opened his eyes and looked down at the wolf. It released its bite and looked at him, even tilting its head in the way Twix sometimes did.

Then there was an enormous *crack!* From the corner of his eye, Ethan saw the limb, big enough to be a tree, land on Reggie and spin, striking Ethan a glancing blow; the smaller branches scratched his face and arms.

The wolves backed off; they weren't in a rush. In fact, the one that had been dining on Reggie was hobbling. The huge limb was partially caught on the rope that was holding Ethan's chest to the tree. Then, there was a thunderous *boom* and another *crack*. A second giant limb fell upon the one resting on Reggie's chest, and both limbs crashed to the ground.

Lightning flashed, and a minute later, rain fell. Shortly thereafter, dime-sized hail pelted down. Ethan moved his head free of the duct tape and saw that the ropes around his chest were loosened and frayed. Smoke was in the air. Lightning had either hit his tree, or the one Reggie was pinned to.

The wolves had not returned.

Now able to rotate his head, Ethan began chewing on the rope over his chest. His mouth was bleeding; he could see the rope changing color, but he didn't care. He kept chewing. One arm was pretty much useless because of his shoulder injury. He tried everything he could, but he couldn't quite pull out his other arm.

Across the clearing, through the rain, he could see the wolves. They would be back.

Ethan gave it all he could, but he couldn't free his arm. The rain stopped, and the wolves returned. The wolf that had tasted his leg now went for his crotch. Instead, it got a mouthful of bloody rope, which it tugged at, probably thinking it was Ethan's intestines. As it tugged, Ethan wriggled his arm out.

After figuring out what it was wolfing down wasn't guts, the canine came at him again. It launched toward his privates, but Ethan thrust his fist into the canine's mouth. It hurt like hell, and the wolf pulled so hard on his arm he thought it would dislocate his shoulder. With renewed vigor, the wolf tugged.

The pain was too much to bear; had his shoulder or elbow dislocated? Thunder barked again, loudly — no, it was a shotgun!

Seconds later, there was another shotgun blast, followed by an engine roaring and a horn blaring. Had the monster returned to finish the job, or just to watch?

The cacophony caused the wolves to disperse, but they still had Reggie and were dragging him into the night.

Then Caroline was standing in front of him. *Caroline? Is this a dream?*

Caroline held his face in his hands and said, "You're going to make it, Ethan. You hear me? You're going to make it!" Her fingers traced the cut on his head, and just as he was blacking out, he heard her yell, "Freepool!"

He came to as she muscled him into the back seat of her Bronco. He looked up at her and said, "Thank you, Caroline. How did you find me?"

She closed the door, and he drifted off.

Chapter Twenty-Four: Freepool

"Reg…" Ethan coughed, and he felt a straw pressed between his lips. Instinctively, he drank, the cool water vivifying and maddening.

Spitting the straw out, he barked, "Reggie!"

A firm hand gripped his least-injured shoulder. He squinted and blinked a few times at the morning sun before making out that Bert was sitting in a chair by his bed.

"Bert. Where's Reggie?"

Bert only shook his head.

The memories came flooding back. Ethan knew Reggie was dead, and that he hadn't done enough to protect him. With a groan, he rose, twisted towards the bed's edge, then sank back into the pillows.

Bert rested a big paw on his shoulder and said, "Easy now."

Ethan nodded and then promptly lifted himself up.

"For a guy that's been kicked, carved, shot, torn into, and lost a fair amount of blood, you're feisty."

At that, Bert passed him a water bottle, and Ethan drained it. "Reggie?"

Bert shook his head.

"Tell me."

Not meeting his eye, Bert answered in a quivering voice, "Not much left of him. We're going to get the bastard who did this; don't you worry, boss."

Ethan pounded his fist on the bedside table and exclaimed, "This time, the bastard is a bitch!"

Bert frowned, then clued in. "A *woman* did this?"

Ethan nodded. "More like a monster, a biblical one. Better take some notes and record this while it's fresh in my head."

Over the next two hours, Ethan regurgitated everything he could remember, from being pushed off the road to when Caroline saved him.

"Obviously, Caroline would've briefed you about the crime scene and anything after I lost consciousness."

"Ah, about that. After Caroline brought you in, which we have CCTV footage of, she dropped off the map."

"Huh?"

"In her defense, she did — as the doctors and nurses have raved about — an expert job tending to your wounds. She even pulled the bullet out of your calf. It wasn't deep; might've been a ricochet."

"But — but she's vanished?"

"Well, nobody has seen her since she left you at the hospital entrance. She submitted her resignation, her phone is no longer active, and from what I heard, her place is empty."

What on Earth?

"Credit card trace? Highway video? Anything, Bert?"

"Crickets. At least that's all I got out of our US counterparts."

"Has a missing persons alert gone out?"

"No. She resigned, and there's no reason to believe she is, by definition, 'missing.' It's more like she's avoiding everyone."

"But she's a witness to a crime! She can't ignore that."

Bert shrugged. "I don't know what to tell you Ethan, other than I'm sorry this is happening."

"How did you learn about Reggie if she left?"

"She left a note with coordinates." Bert pulled a small plastic evidence bag out of his pocket and held it up so Ethan could read the message.

All it said was, 'Officer down,' and a latitude and longitude.

Caroline had lied to him about her dad and kept her past secret. Ethan was even beginning to wonder if she truly cared for him. But why would she have saved him if she didn't care?

He had to admit that the monster who'd killed Reggie and aimed to see *him* dead reminded him of Caroline. Factoring in that he had seen the monster talking on the phone with someone and that, shortly thereafter, Caroline miraculously appeared, well… It couldn't all just fall into the realm of coincidence; it was enough to paint the woman he was sleeping with as a fraud, if not worse. *Maybe she had saved him to save herself, or, even, another!*

Bert was looking at him with concern and reached out and clapped the top of Ethan's hand.

"I vaguely recall something Caroline said as she was quote-unquote, *'saving me.'*"

"What's that?"

"It was a word, or maybe a name." Ethan rubbed his temples in thought.

"Be patient, it'll come to you eventually."

A moment later, it did. "I heard Caroline say 'Freepool' when she found me, just before I lost consciousness. I figured it was in reference to the person who killed Reggie and left me to die."

Bert jotted the name down on his pad. "I'll look into it right away."

"I'm coming with you." Despite the heavy bandages on his arm and shoulder, and stabs of pain that coursed through much of his body, Ethan started wriggling himself off the bed. However, something was making it very difficult.

"What the —" He held up an old phone cord and the beer cans that hung off it jingle-jangled.

Ethan looked at Bert, confounded.

"Angela's idea, but those are my empties."

A moment later, Ethan's doctor walked in. "He was going to leave, wasn't he?"

Ethan looked back and forth at the two men.

"This is some sort of conspiracy!"

Bert rested his hand on Ethan's good shoulder. "We're just looking after you; we knew, once you woke up, you were going to try to march on out of here."

Ethan sank back in his bed, half-exasperated, yet impressed; these people really cared about him.

No sooner had the door closed behind the doctor than an armed guard appeared.

Ethan looked from the tall, stoic young cop to Bert for an explanation, then answered his own inquiry. "Two attempts on my life. Mandatory watch. And — let me guess — they've put me on a leave of absence."

Bert nodded.

"How long?"

"At least two weeks."

"Fuck."

Ethan looked at his doctor. "Help me out here."

The doctor tossed his clipboard like a frisbee, and Ethan grabbed it before it hit him in the head.

"Hey..."

His doctor walked over and pulled the clipboard roughly out of his hand, then spoke as he wrote. "Full awareness of situation and surroundings. No mental impairment from injuries. Motor skills, excellent. Attitude? Taciturn and impatient, so 'Normal.' Shoulder to be reevaluated four days from now. Calf wound, fine. No infection. Patient is hydrated. No further signs of shock. Patient, free to leave. Sign here."

Ethan scribbled his name on the line the doctor pointed to. "Thank you, Doc."

The doctor pulled up a chair and sat beside him. "You're aware the perpetrator cut an 'h' into your forehead?"

"Yes, but I suppose it will heal."

"Oh, it will, but unless you go in for plastic surgery, you'll be scarred for life."

"I already am, Doc, but since I've never been all that much to look at, I reckon this will add some character."

"It will, but I always thought you were good looking, Ethan, as far as crabby cops go."

"Thanks, Doc."

The old doctor reached into his bag and carefully put some salve on Ethan's 'h' while he continued talking.

"In 1971, back in the old country, my sister and I were playing 'Ambush' in a park. It's a hide-and-seek game where you tried to scare the bejesus out of one another. It was her turn to frighten me, only she never did.

"People said a Baba Yaga got her, but I believe an evil person, not an old-world witch, kidnapped her. Nobody ever found her. I know you to be a determined man, and you're on the right track to finding something, maybe *someones*, both good and bad; otherwise, they wouldn't keep trying to kill you.

"My sister is gone forever, but if you find one other missing young person, it will go a long way to healing this heart of mine. Now, undo his telephone cord. He's taking up a bed for somebody who really needs it."

With that, the doctor walked out, leaving both Ethan and Bert speechless. Until that moment, the doctor hadn't said over thirty words, and had certainly never spoken about himself.

Bert unhooked Ethan, tossed the beer cans into the recycling bin, and helped him out of bed.

"I will speak to your minder. They'll park in your driveway until after your next appointment with the doctor. After that, I'll have them reassigned or smuggle you into the office or get what you need from the office. We arranged for Kim to stay at Angela's for a few days, until things calm down and you have time to rest and recalibrate. I'll also call Rudy Ingersson's contacts in Winnipeg and let them know that Rudy is no longer with us, and we will do our utmost to catch his killer."

"Thank for all that, Bert. I'd be lost without you."

"You would do the same for me."

"That I would."

Slowly, they walked out of the hospital. Ethan felt like a horse had dragged him through a cactus patch. Everything hurt, especially his heart.

They didn't speak until they got to Ethan's house, and then it was just, "Talk to you tomorrow."

His watcher waved at Ethan from a squad car. Ethan waved back, then pulled the curtains, an act that caused him more discomfort than he would've thought possible.

He made a note to inquire about a nice urn for Rudy's ashes, as little as there was, and to see if Josh Font would be okay with having the urn couriered to him. Rudy Ingersson deserved something to honor his life.

Ethan then called Caroline's number. It was, as Bert said, no longer in service. He checked his email. Nothing from Caroline. Stepping outside again, he noticed his security detail's head down over their phone. There was nothing in his mailbox. *Caroline, what gives?*

Tomorrow, he would call her former office and see if they could provide him with something, anything about her. He didn't know whether to be angry or afraid. She had saved his life, but clearly there was something big she wasn't telling him, and maybe those who wanted to see him dead now also saw her as a threat.

He drew himself a warm bath and awkwardly eased his aching bones, scratched, chewed, carved, tree-gouged, and shot up body into the tub. "I'm too old for this shit."

In his three previous decades of work, he had sustained remarkably few injuries. There were bruises and minor cuts, a couple cracked ribs, a few dislocated and broken fingers, and a sprained ankle, but nothing that required an overnight stay in a hospital. His worse injuries, a dislocated knee, and a broken shoulder, had come from skiing and snowboarding — the latter of which he would never do again.

But in the past few months he'd been fish-hooked, shot several times, suffered a concussion, been hand-grenaded, speared by a tree limb, kidnapped, all but eaten by wolves, and kicked in the head and slapped around by a psycho.

Oh, and jilted by a lover. He had to admit, that emotional gut-punch and taser-to-the-heart was bothering him more than his physical injuries.

Still, as some had mentioned — and correctly so — he had *mostly* 'dodged the bullet.' *How far are you going to push your luck, old boy?* He immediately supplied himself with an answer: *As long as it takes to find out what happened to Chelsea, that's how long.* The thought of it coaxed him to lever himself out of the piping-hot bath and into cold, hard reality.

Buck naked, he walked back into the living room and peeked through the curtains. His security person was still there, a guy in his mid-twenties, his head back on the car's headrest, fast asleep.

Ethan texted Bert. *Might be worth touching base with my watcher before his snoring wakes up the neighbors.* Two minutes later, he saw the man's head jerk up, and he scrambled for his phone. He glanced at Ethan's front window before getting out of the car and walking up to the door and knocking.

"I'm fine in here." Ethan spoke loud enough that it would carry past the door.

"Good, sir. I will be watchful."

While the person monitoring him could grab some shuteye, Ethan was too wound up to go to bed, so he limped over to his laptop to see what he could learn about 'Freepool.' After an hour of chasing rabbits, he hadn't even come up with a carrot, let alone a clue. So, as he had done more than a few times, Ethan went to his favorite encyclopedia: Angela. He dialed her number directly.

"I wanted to thank you for letting Kim and co stay at your place for a few days."

"Oh, no problem. They're a joy to be around."

"Yes, they are special. Say hi to them for me."

"I will. Now, what did you want to ask me?"

"You know me so well. It falls under the 'penny for your thoughts' category."

"Okay. Well, since it's after work, it might cost you some toonies."

"Fair enough."

"What's the subject?"

"A name, I think."

"And it is?"

"Freepool."

"Hmm...Immediate response, 'no-charge billiards.'"

Ethan chuckled. "That's not even worth a buck, though it is quite *loonie*."

"For a better answer, I need at least two dollars up front."

"Coins in the mail."

"Good enough. Can you give me some context?"

Ethan didn't really want to tell her everything, so just said, "Might be associated with the person who killed Reggie."

"Okay. Well, when you say 'Freepool,' I'm reminded of a French word with a similar spelling and pronunciation."

"You know *French?* I thought just Spanish and Portuguese."

"And Italian. I'm also working on Cree."

"Wow, you're quite the poly...polymurf...poly..."

"It's 'polymorph,' and thank you. Anyway, in French, *fripouille*, spelled 'f-r-i-p-o-u-i-l-l-e' means 'rogue.'"

"Rogue." Ethan rubbed the stubble on his chin. "Caroline knew where I was, and therefore had to know something of the woman who captured," — he swallowed hard — "Reggie and me. 'Rogue' could explain what happened to Caroline or the nature of the perpetrator."

"Makes sense. How are you feeling, anyway?"

"Like *Scarface* meets *Grumpy Old Men* meets *Die Hard*."

"I always thought you looked a bit like Al Pacino."

"Is that a compliment?"

174

"Oh, definitely."

"Well, thanks for that, Angela, and the fresh French idea on Freepool. I'll check out that angle, and you, Ms. Polymorph, will soon be the owner of some shiny new toonies!"

"Oh, goodie! Catch up with you tomorrow, then?"

"Yep."

"Have a good night; don't push yourself too hard."

"I couldn't if I tried."

Ethan put down the phone and then realized how selfish he was being, so he called Angela back.

"Umm... awful of me to have not said this earlier, but I'm sorry for your loss, Angela."

There was a pause; it was likely Angela needed to regain her composure. "And to you too, Ethan. Reggie was such a good young man. Like so many, taken *way* before his time."

"He will be dearly missed."

"Definitely."

"Talk tomorrow?"

"Yes."

"Oh, and Angela, I don't say this near enough, but I love you."

"I love you too, Ethan. Goodnight."

After having a glass of cold water to un-choke his throat, Ethan returned to his computer. He needed to take a different approach. Instead of 'Freepool,' he used the French spelling of *fripouille* that Angela had texted him. Unsurprisingly, he didn't find much, probably because he didn't know over forty words in French and most of those came from cereal boxes.

However, it occurred to him that, while the word might be of French origin, the crime was in an English-speaking part of Canada. Maybe he should apply a similar two-pronged approach to his searches. His mind flashed back to Caroline saying the word 'Freepool' and it did almost seem like the word was stretched, like a hyphenated word. *Or maybe it's two words that have one meaning?*

He nodded his head in satisfaction, which made him wince a little and reach up to his scar. "Freepool, free-pool, free pool..." There was something in that. He felt it, both on the surface of his head and in the grey matter underneath.

Ethan accessed his RCMP name search application and put Pool, Poul, Pouille, and Poulin in as possible surnames and then made the first name search a broad one, with the only parameters being the name would start with either 'Fre' or 'Fri.' Hitting execute, he went and got himself a beer.

It took him that beer and another before he boiled the list down to one name from his geographic area: Frea Pool.

He keyed that name into an advanced record search, which produced one result, Frea Pool, officially separated from Aaron Gamel Dell in 2006 — one year after Chelsea went missing. Frea's last known address, also from 2006, was a Post Office box in Complix, a community that no longer existed. Ms. Pool's last job was at the EK Horse Ranch, which he had never heard of, but would investigate.

She didn't even have a Social Insurance Number, a red flag in itself. There were no pictures, yet she presumably had a driver's license, so she either possessed a stolen identity, had changed her name, or used a fake ID to manage her life. It was a start. Plus, he had a former place of work, an ex-husband, and the name of her hometown, even though it was now submerged under the waters of the Hugh Keenleyside Dam.

Ethan also needed Bert to delve deeper into Miller Renfrew and how he managed to hang himself in a cell under the watchful eyes of the Jasper Spring's Sheriff department.

Chapter Twenty-Five: Rogue

The following morning, the man assigned to Ethan was re-tasked; his replacement wasn't due in until later that afternoon. It meant that Ethan was under the keen eye of Bert, which meant he could go to the office, where Angela was waiting for him with coffee and carrot cake.

"No Missing Persons Report, nothing. It's like Frea Pool dropped off the map."

"Or went rogue, as the name suggests."

"Good point, Angela, but why?"

"It's like that reality TV show, *When Relationships Go Bad*."

"I haven't heard of it."

"I'm not surprised; it kind of has a cult following, especially with women who've been jilted by their exes."

Ethan raised an eyebrow. 'Jilted' resonated with him.

Angela smiled. "Yes, that's right, Ethan, I watch it. When you've been with someone for a long time and they pull the rug out from under you, it can affect your mental health. Mind you, the women in this show are preoccupied with cash and revenge, whereas I spend an inordinate amount of time quilting or riding horses."

Ethan sighed. "I'm still miffed at Jim; haven't spoken to him in years. Mind you, Angela, I didn't *not* try to connect to him; he just buggered off, changed his cell number, all the signs of a man who desperately wanted a fresh start, or was ashamed, or both."

"Sorry our failed relationship ruined your friendship."

"No, don't apologize, Angela. I misjudged his character."

"Thanks for that, Ethan."

"No worries. While I don't quilt, I respect old-fashioned values, like loyalty."

"Well, on the upside, we have our friendship."

"We sure do, Angela, and I'm fortunate to count you as one of my closest friends."

"The feeling's mutual, *buddy*, but hey, I have to run, going to comb my horses."

"Roger that. I will keep you posted."

"After a while, crocodile."

"Uh, see you later, alligator."

Ethan sat on his desk and thought about Jim and *When Relationships Go Bad*. He might have to watch that show. It was wild how people could just bolt, whether it was to Fiji or completely off the grid.

Speaking of 'off the grid,' Bert had used available LiDAR and satellite imagery to find remote cabins. All the ones he located were legit — at least, the owners and agencies responsible for them had said so. Because Natural Resources personnel were vigilant about documenting cabins in the wilderness, Ethan had little doubt that the shack he sought had not been visited.

The attempt on his life, subsequent abduction, and the crime that resulted in Reggie's death all pointed to an in-depth knowledge of the area, and a base to coordinate actions. The obvious answer was a cabin with a dirt road or four-wheel-drive access. That he wasn't dead — and surely the killer would know this by now — meant they would act swiftly to erase evidence.

Modern technology certainly meant law enforcement had more tools in their collective toolbox, but to find that cabin would probably mean boots on the ground; Ethan was in no condition to go tromping through the brush, even *if* he knew where to go. He pondered that over a coffee and a piece of carrot cake, which he was going to have to thank Angela for. She made the best carrot cake. *She did so much for him!*

It might've been the sugar rush, but he had a thought. What if a cabin was out there, but had been there so long that it was disguised by tree canopy? He recalled branches scraping the van as they had pulled away. It was time to roll back the clock.

After a phone call and a second piece of carrot cake, a young lady from Natural Resources dropped off an armful of topo maps rolled into tubes.

He was about to sit them all on his desk when he noticed an official-looking card sitting on his laptop.

Ethan put the maps to the side and opened the card. It was an invitation for Bert and himself to be pallbearers at Reggie's funeral. After a quick call to Bert, he dialed the number associated with the name at the bottom of the card. He told Reggie's sister that they would be honored to be there for Reggie.

Life is rough. Ethan allowed himself a few minutes to feel sorry for Reggie, his loved ones, and himself, then returned to his work.

As the hours ticked by, an ever-growing layer of maps covered the table in the lunchroom. He'd had so much coffee that he was sure that if he looked in the mirror, he would see that Juan Valdez guy from the old Colombian coffee commercials staring back at him. His eyes were so tired that he put on the pair of reading glasses that had been collecting dust in his desk drawer for at least two years.

Ethan looked up at the clock. *2:30 p.m.* He had about an hour until Bert would collect him and take him home before his next babysitter arrived.

Ethan stretched the second-to-last map across the table and pinned it down with coffee cups. One of them, *Jughead's Revenge*, was Reggie's. It choked him up, but he had work to do.

The map before him was from 1961. As was the rule, roads were lines, trails were dotted lines, and rural dwellings were denoted by small black squares. Ethan had looked over and cross-referenced so many maps with imagery on his laptop that he was seeing contour lines as roads and vice versa. It took him looking over what he just saw three times to affirm his eyes were not deceiving him.

It was an old road that, because it passed through heavy, old-growth forest, no longer showed up in satellite imagery. At its end was a black square: a cabin.

Ethan glanced at the clock. Bert would roll in any minute. He snapped a pic of the area and the map's name; tomorrow, before or after Reggie's funeral, they could discuss it in more detail.

Chapter Twenty-Six: R.I.P

Fortunately, you only need one good arm to be a pallbearer; however, given it was Reggie, Ethan would've used the one dangling from his tree-speared, shot-up shoulder if he had to. It was an honor to be there for the young man, but with each limping step, a corpuscle of anger rose from his heart and joined the sea of red rage that had been born after Chelsea's disappearance.

They lowered the casket into the ground, and Angela cried on his shoulder. Reggie's family had come from northern Alberta, and it seemed they had brought half the province with them. Reggie deserved every flower, tear, and ounce of respect. Ethan felt like crying, thought he should cry, but except for the red rage in his head, he felt frozen.

He would catch Freepool — Frea Pool, or whatever her name was — even if meant going through Caroline, for as sure as God made little green apples, Caroline was involved. He knew it was wrong, but Ethan really wanted to kill someone, especially Freepool.

He squeezed Angela's hand, and she said, "I know. We'll get that monster."

Or monsters, he thought to himself.

The attendees trickled away, and then the trickle turned into a torrent. No, people weren't flooding away out of disrespect or a desire to get on with their weekend, but for many, closure would happen over months, memories, drugs and alcohol, or a combination thereof. As Ethan had experienced, people wanted to run from grief, but the faster they moved away from it, the longer it lingered.

He knew it was going to take him a long time to get over Reggie. Irreverent and incorrigible, Reggie had always kept things light, and they would never replace his innocence and exuberance. Reggie had made them laugh at one another and what they did, which kept them sane.

Now Ethan was having crazy thoughts, wishes and desires that would typically fall under the purview of a homicidal maniac. He cut himself some slack.

Seeing a friend slaughtered will do that to you.

Ethan was among the last to leave the graveside, and when he did, he stopped to visit Chelsea.

"Hi Chelsea. I miss you, sweetie.

"Well, where to start? Obviously, I haven't been by in a few days, but I feel being kidnapped is a pretty good excuse.

"No? Well, check out my 'Show and Tell' for next class!" He brushed his hair aside, so the scar was clearly visible. "Nasty, huh? But it is what it is. Carpenters get black and blue thumbnails, Mail Carriers get chased by dogs, and some cops get letters carved into their craniums. Angela said I look like Al Pacino in Scarface. That was a brilliant film, and since Pacino's considered a good-looking dude, I took it as a compliment.

"Regarding Angela, well, she's been incredible, as have Bert and Kim. Every day I thank God or the 'Blinkie-blinkie-big-guy, or girl, in the sky' for being blessed with such amazing friends.

"Sadly, we lost Reggie... I lost Reggie."

Only then did some of the ice in his heart melt to produce bitter tears, tears that stung where they streamed over the place where Freepool had backhanded him or where the branches of the falling trees in the meadow had scraped away skin.

"Here I came to have a nice little chat with you, and I'm blubbering!"

Ethan sunk to his knees and, not thinking about where he was or who might be around, wailed, "It should've been me, not him; it should've been me!"

He stood up and looked around. Nobody had seen him, so he wiped the tears from his eyes, straightened his shirt, and knocked some grass and dirt off his knees.

"Whoa, your dad's a bit of a mess right now, kiddo.

"But I have some potentially good news. I'm ashamed to admit it, but I had the records pertaining to you going missing in a cold-case folder. With what I've learned lately, I replaced the tag with 'Active Investigation.'

"I hope you can forgive me for not having the faith and fortitude to stay with the search. Turns out, I'm not the best dad or RCMP officer.

"I will make it up to you and Reggie, I swear I will.

"Well, going to go home before I start sniffling again. I love you more than words can say, Chelsea. Bye for now."

#

The following morning, Ethan could still taste tears on his lips. He seemed to recall crying in the night but couldn't be sure.

An empty mickey of rum was lying on the floor. He remembered having a drink or two, but not five or six.

Stumbling to the bathroom, he almost jumped back when he saw his reflection in the full-length mirror.

There stood a man, fifty-five, decent build, hairy chest, bandaged head, shoulder, forearm, and leg. He also looked like he was a scratching post for a tomcat. He pushed up the thin, straight hair that fell over the right side of his forehead. The scar was plain as day. Ethan turned around just enough to see a host of scars on his back and asscheeks. He then realized all he had on were his boots.

"Well, aren't we just fetchin'!"

He drank about a gallon of water straight out of the bathroom tap and for a couple minutes thought he might puke it all up, but he held it together.

Then he looked at the clock. "Eight!"

He checked his phone. No messages. His mind went to Caroline, and he wondered how he would feel if he ever heard from her again.

Two cups of coffee that you could stand a spoon up in, and he was pulling together his faculties and his belt buckle. Still, Caroline was in his head.

He promptly dialed her former Sheriff's office.

"Haven't heard from her, and don't expect to."

"Why? Wasn't she well-liked?"

"She was, but when you skip out on your brothers and sisters like that, well, there ain't any going back."

"I can see that, but she saved my life."

"Hmm."

"You have other thoughts?"

"I do, but, well, you know the drill."

"Part of an ongoing investigation."

"Yes, sir."

"Was Debra's body, and her cat, returned to her family?"

"They were. Thank you for all you did in that regard. We really appreciate how hard you and your department worked on her case and all the other missing persons cases."

"It's my duty. I couldn't live with myself if I didn't do my best."

"You set a fine example for others in the field."

"Thanks."

"Should I learn anything I can reveal, you will be top of my list to call."

"Thank you. Oh, one other thing — can you send me something that might detail if missing persons went up in your neck of the woods over the past fifteen years?"

"Uh, we can, but it might take us a few business days to compile the data."

"Whenever you can find the time, that would be great."

"Will do."

Chapter Twenty-Seven: Charm

Remote as it was, it was easy to spot the cabin from the helicopter. The smoke that rose from its smoldering ashes also helped. They overflew the cabin for a closer look, but there wasn't much to see.

"Bert, you've been to burned-out cabins before with your forestry friends. When do you think it was lit up?"

"Small cabin, but lots of trees nestled against it. Limbs, falling trees, heavy root systems would've kept feeding the flames, so I'm going to say three days ago."

"So, the chances of finding any useable evidence, just about nil?"

"Yes, but odder things have happened."

They searched for a landing spot and discovered a circular area, but it was too small for their machine.

"What could land there?" Ethan asked the pilot.

"Could easily put a Robinson R22 or an Enstrom F28 in there."

"Are they both two-seaters?"

"The R22 can only seat two. The F28 can seat three. Of course, one could hover over it with what we have, a Bell 206, and cable down."

They inspected the area and landed a further 600 feet away.

From there, they hoofed it to the cabin. Only some of the heavy outer walls and a burned-out stove remained.

"Lots of small coals. The building burned hot and fast; at least initially. She probably used an accelerant."

"I agree. But I think she missed something, Bert."

"What's that?"

Ethan pointed at a small, partly-burned building tucked into some nearby trees.

"The outhouse?"

"Yes; if she didn't leave something on the toilet seat, there will be DNA in the crap."

"Uh, yeah. Well, since that was *your* idea, you should reap the rewards of collecting the evidence."

"I guess I'm going to have to. The woman may be batshit crazy, but I reckon she poops like the rest of us."

The door to the outhouse fell off its hinges when he opened it up. Carefully, he used data-collection swabs to capture whatever was on the surface of the toilet seat. Then, with a long stick, Ethan scraped some fecal matter out of the hole. All were bagged and tagged before he rejoined Bert at the cabin.

"Was it everything you dreamed it would be?"

"Oh, I tell ya, Bert, it was the shit."

Bert clapped him on the back. "Well, I'm not sure what else we're going to find. It's a bad day when the best you can do is some 'do-do.'"

"Right, but let's do a search. You poke through the ashes while I investigate the perimeter. A place that's been here this long must have some stories to tell."

As Ethan hobbled around, the lack of a tool shed, or some old farm equipment surprised him. At minimum, there should've been an axe, maybe a splitting mall, old saws, shovel, rakes, snow shovel — the various things required to live in the sticks. Then again, the cabin might've been a three-season dwelling. It was still puzzling.

After venturing out in ever-wider circles and finding nothing, Ethan gave up and returned to the cabin.

"Anything, Bert?"

"Other than some old horseshoes and axe heads, nothing."

"Wish we could've come up with more than dump DNA."

"I know. Are you finished?"

Ethan kicked at the ashes and looked hopefully at the charred remains of cabin and trees.

"I feel like this place has something more to tell us."

"Well, I've learned to trust your feelings and niggles."

"Thanks. Let's cast out further. Do you want to check the higher ground while I check out the area near the creek?"

"Sounds good."

Ethan recalled his captor pouring water from a pitcher into a basin. Perhaps no water was being piped in from a crock, or the creek itself? Crocks and water lines set into them, or creeks, would often get choked with silt, or freeze and crack. Ethan moved farther up the creek, and as various aches and pains caught up to him, sat down on a boulder, took a rest, and looked around.

Freepool had picked a nice place to chill and kill. Fresh air, clean water, ample game, and nobody lived within miles. A gentle wind moved through the pines and aspen and caressed moss-covered stones, stumps, and deadfalls. As streams do, watery whispers were spoken, only in a language Ethan could not fathom. Light filtered through tree limbs, resulting in everything being imbued with texture and depth. It was idyllic. And then his eyes almost fell out of his head.

There, on top of a lid of an old wooden crock, sat his horse figurine. Beside it, weighed down by a rock, was a Ziplock bag with a note inside.

Ethan photographed the scene before he even entertained touching anything.

Is it a trap? Might he grab one item and ignite plastique or dynamite below the lid? Ethan steeled himself, then grabbed a long stick and, from eight feet away, crouched low and used the stick to gingerly move the figurine. No *kaboom*. Then he moved the bag. Also, no detonation.

He was *mostly* satisfied, but still not totally sure, so he radioed Bert.

"I found something up the creek about five-hundred feet."

"I'll be right there."

Bert strode up five minutes later.

"Is that what I think it is?"

"Yes."

"Any tripwires?"

"Not that I can tell. Figured another set of eyes would help."

Together, they looked around, and couldn't see anything foreboding.

"But of course, who knows what might be under the lid?"

"That's true, Bert, but I feel comfortable retrieving the horse and envelope."

"Go for it."

"Swab for fingerprints after I grab them."

"Will do."

Ethan carefully picked up his horse and, before tucking it into a small baggie and returning it to his shirt pocket, let Bert swab it.

Holding the keepsake close was powerful; Ethan blinked away the emotion.

"Now the note. Ideally, we should process this at the station."

Bert looked at him. "Yes, I suppose we *should*."

They both grinned at one another before Ethan opened the bag and pulled out the note.

"Note, I am only touching the edges."

"Noted."

Ethan held up the note, reading it aloud for Bert's benefit. In impeccable cursive writing, it read, "'*A gift opens the way and ushers the giver into the presence of the great.*' I also like the idiomatic expression, based on an old proverb, '*The third time's the charm.*'"

"Biblical bitch, isn't she?"

Ethan nodded. "Monster biblical bitch. The main thing is I have my horse back, and we know she'll try for me at least one more time."

"Right."

"Fancy a look into the crock?"

"Yes, but carefully."

"For sure. I'll get a longer stick."

They scoured around until Bert reefed out a twelve-foot-long, rail-thin dead tamarack, broke off its dead branches, and passed it to Ethan.

"That'll do, thanks. Now, take cover."

Bert eased his large frame behind a boulder, while Ethan tucked himself behind a stump and extended the pole to the lid of the old well.

Ethan pushed hard, and the lid slid an inch or two. *One more time.* He used a tree behind him for leverage and pushed harder.

Boom! The blast was vast, and shards of concrete and shrapnel raked and littered the surroundings.

"You okay, Bert?"

"I'm good. You?"

"I'm fine. Ears though, damn."

"That was loud! More than a couple sticks of dynamite there."

"'*Third time's the charm.*' Kiss my pucker, Freepool."

"That woman is a real piece of work."

They looked around. Besides bits of concrete, small chunks of tools were scattered over the ground, or in trees. Some rake teeth were stuck in a pine tree three feet over Bert's head.

Ethan pulled out the tine of a pitchfork from the tree next to him. "I proclaim the mystery of the missing toolery solvèd." It was perhaps his best Inspector Clouseau impression, and it got Bert to chuckling.

"Well, Bert, I think we've done all we can here. Let's get back to the chopper."

They returned to the heli and, under Ethan's direction, slowly cruised the old road from the cabin.

They began to notice that every mile or two, a deep gouge appeared that would've stopped any vehicle, even a quad, in its tracks.

It jogged a memory, and Ethan related it to Bert and the pilot. "I remember her stopping several times, and hearing something sliding across the roof. Each time, she would do it twice. They must've been heavy; as strong as the monster was, she grunted when she moved them. Then, about five or ten minutes later, she would reload what she had taken down. I think what she was doing was taking down heavy planks and using them to drive over the crevices that she probably made herself."

"If I can land safely at one, do you want to investigate?"

"Yes, please."

A few minutes later, the pilot spied such an opportunity, and they landed in a small meadow near the road. The pilot kept the heli running while Ethan got out and had a gander.

Sure enough, on either side of the ditch that bisected the road, trenches in the road were dug out to accommodate planks of wood. Freepool would place the timber in the ruts and use them to drive the van over. Then she would retrieve them to use again at the next obstacle.

When they got back to the main dirt road, they found old brush stacked up to disguise the road, or at least dissuade others from going down it. Time permitting, they would return and look for clues.

Chapter Twenty-Eight: Anagram

Concerning one of their first conversations about there *not* being a disproportionate amount of unsolved missing persons cases in the northwestern 'Mountain States' of the USA, Caroline had lied. Not only that, but, by percentage, fewer cases were solved in Montana than in neighboring states.

While Caroline had garnered a reputation of getting her man, the data Ethan received showed that murders were both solved and processed at a surprising rate. She was almost *too* successful.

He found that one 'Asner Duke' had provided a written alibi for Miller Renfrew. It was now highly debatable that Miller killed the Flower Shop lady. Miller's hanging also took place when only two officers, one of which might've been Caroline, were at the station. Asner Duke, who was the prime suspect in Caroline's attempted murder, had died in an altercation with her and several other state troopers. It was also noteworthy that Bill de Vandenbrough was noted as a "person of interest" in the investigation. If Asner and Miller could've exonerated one another, then that would've made Bill a primary suspect. Unfortunately, Rachel Steward's murderer would probably never be brought to justice. *Perhaps I brought the justice to him?* This, Ethan would probably never know.

For too long he had pined for Caroline; he'd lost sleep over her and checked his phone dozens of times, hoping that she would reach out to him. Now Ethan didn't care — at least he kept telling himself that.

Back at home, with his doctor saying he could physically return to full-time duties, Ethan waved goodbye to his security detail and scampered inside. He had also convinced his superiors and the RCMP psychologist that he was mentally fit to return to work. Still, he had to get security cameras set up to ping-in every few hours to affirm his well-being.

Another hoop he had to jump through was to submit a rough work schedule and travel itinerary every morning, so they knew where he was going to be at pretty much any hour of the day. Then, every evening, a summary of his daily events along with an online mental-health assessment. It was onerous, but under the circumstances, proper.

It was 8:00 a.m., and he had three hours before he needed to be at the office. Ethan had something just as important to do as trying to find Freepool's whereabouts and whatever the story was on her ex-husband.

Ethan dug out his rock-polishing kit. No, he would not tumble any stones today. Instead, he was going to make use of an already pristine artifact he cherished. He pulled his horse ornament from his pocket and laid it on a cloth beside a beautiful 2.5" by 1.5" by 0.5" piece of jet-black obsidian. It had been a gift from Chelsea.

With great care, he glued the horse's hooves to the obsidian and pressed them firmly down. He sat looking at it; it was a thing of beauty. The wee inscription Chelsea had affixed to the edge of the obsidian read, '*Papa, you are my rock.*'

Ethan couldn't pry himself from the irony that Chelsae was the stone *he* would forever cling to.

With nearly two hours to kill, Ethan elected to poke into the Hal Stead case, this time focusing on Alridge Pennington. Having earlier subscribed to a site that had immigration and shipping manifests for the period of interest, he found a passenger list for the Belfast to Dublin route the day Myles Blackworth was found murdered. He traced his finger down the screen until he arrived at an 'A. Pennington.' Pennington was one of fifteen surnames that had their final destination marked as 'New York, USA' via a ship called the *Hibernia* later that year.

In short order, he found the passenger list for *Hibernia*. Of the fifteen surnames aboard the *Belfast*, only one was missing: Pennington. However, it wasn't *really* missing; the name had been crossed out, and in its place was the name 'Arundel.' *Arundel? Arun-del!*

He flipped back to the data he had for Frea Pool. Yes, there it was. She had been married to Aaron Dell. *Arundel, Aaron Dell*, the names were just *too* similar to be a coincidence. Of course, two hundred years had passed, and it wouldn't be *the same* Aaron Dell, but some families were dedicated to honoring their forefathers by the reapplication of first names. It had long been common for the firstborn to get their father's name and the tradition had persisted into modern times.

If Aldridge Pennington had changed his last name to Arundel, he would most likely have done so to evade the authorities and arrive in America with a clean slate. It might be a bit of a reach, but Ethan was confident that Pennington had, in fact, killed Blackworth, and that maybe, just maybe, he did so based on a connection to Hal Stead.

Ethan did a quick search into the Arundel name and found it to be of Norman origin. *Norman, hmm*...that was also the people Bert mentioned with the stylized 'h' used on the Leadshat grave, carved into his own forehead, and on the hat that old man Leadshat wore.

The hatchet thing was prominent. Hatchets were on Freepool's wall. She had mentioned something about 'Slayers' Hatchets' and, of course, hatchets linked Hal Stead to the Leadshats.

Ethan sat back in his chair and looked at what he had just typed into the notepad: 'Hal Stead > Leadshat.' Like Arundel to Aaron Dell, the Hal Stead and Leadshat names were eerily similar. *No, wait; more than just similar! They both contain eight letters — the exact same letters!*

Ethan glanced at his watch; Bert would arrive in 15 minutes. He guzzled down his tepid coffee and started checking passenger manifests for ships that departed from Dublin to New York in 1828 and 1829. He tried, without success, all the 1828 ships, and then, when he brought about the names aboard the *Othello* in 1829, the Leadshat name sprung off the page.

"Holy shit!"

As portents and possibilities pulsed in his mind, another vibration reached his brain. It was his phone ringing.

"Hello."

"I'm outside. Tried calling you several times. I even rang your doorbell; was worried you might be dead or something."

"Sorry, Bert. I'm alive."

"It's okay. You want to grab a coffee before we go to the office?"

"Ah, ya."

"You don't sound so sure."

"Oh, I could use a coffee, maybe an *Irish* coffee."

"Good news?"

"I suppose it depends how we define it. I'll tell you shortly."

Ethan walked outside, his mind buzzing and stomach roiling from by what he had just discovered. *How am I going to tell Bert?*

Fortunately, Bert started a conversation just after Ethan belted himself in. "Okay, hey, did you see that Tree-Beard Derek has applied to become an RCMP trainee?"

"Yes."

"Thoughts?"

"I already recommended we give him an opportunity. We'll get him on some ride-a-longs here soon."

"We *do* need to replace Reggie." Bert paused, seeming shocked with himself. "I mean, we'll *never* replace Reggie."

"No, we won't, but we have to keep on keeping on."

They rolled down the street, and almost to a one, each person they passed, whether walking, jogging, or driving, waved. Some extended the thumbs up. Then Ethan noticed something else, people's red and white T-shirts. Across the tees was written '*R.I.P. Reggie*' with a small blue RCMP logo.

Two older women, both wearing the tees, were standing at a crosswalk, so Bert stopped the car. Rather than cross the street, they walked to the car. One lady came to Bert's side of the car, the other to the passenger's side. Both seniors expressed their condolences for Reggie's loss, and appreciation for what the RCMP did for the community and the area at large. It was nice.

After pulling away, Ethan asked the obvious. "Angela arranged this?"

"Yes. Our shirts are at the station. All proceeds are going to BC's Children's Hospital in Vancouver."

As a roller coaster of emotions swept over him, Ethan spewed out what he had just researched.

Bert stopped the car. "So, Caroline's family and these Dells or Arundels are involved, not just this Freepool woman?"

"It seems so." Ethan shook his head. "And to think, I was sleeping with the enemy — an enemy that might even had something to do with Chelsea's disappearance. God, I think I'm going to be sick."

Ethan opened his door, ready to vomit, but just spit out some bile. After a few minutes, Bert asked if he was okay.

"Yes; let's roll."

Bert idled the car forward. "It's not your fault, Ethan. There's no way you could've known. And don't forget, Caroline *did* save you."

"I suppose, but I probably would've never needed saving except for that bunch. And Reggie would still be alive."

"As you often tell me, all we can do is move forward. What's your plan?"

"Well, while you're making rounds and taking care of business, I'll try to learn more about Freepool by diving into whatever I can dredge up on her husband."

They made it to Brickwallaby, and after Bert fed Twix and grabbed his Reggie shirt, he went on patrol. Ethan put on his Reggie shirt and sank into his office chair. Twix was looking forlorn and let out a mournful sigh as she slumped down on the rug beside his desk. Ethan couldn't help but feel bad. With all that had been going on, Twix had not received the attention she needed and deserved. And since Twix was used to having one of Reggie, Bert, or himself around, she was probably feeling lonely and neglected. Ethan couldn't discount that Twix also felt a sense of loss. *Dogs were smart, and maybe even smarter than we humans tend to give them credit for.* Ethan got out of his chair and sat down on the floor beside Twix, and she politely offered her belly. "I'm sorry we haven't been doing our regular walks and frisbee tosses, Twix. I promise I will make it up to you."

As Twix's tongue lolled out the side of her mouth, her gentle eyes said, 'Just keep scratching my belly and I'll weigh your apology.' Ethan obliged, and after a few minutes, got back up. Just as he was about to continue his investigation into Freepool, Ethan spotted a Reggie memorial shirt that had been set aside from the handful that hadn't yet been sold. It was an XXL that had been torn at the collar. He held it aloft, looked at Twix, and after some careful measuring and cutting, fitted it around Twix's frame. Man and dog shared a hug. After Ethan sat down, Twix got up and rested her head on his leg, which prompted Ethan to pat her on the head. Twix laid back down, only this time, closer to his feet. *It was all good.*

Ethan got back to work. As he expected, there were no results for EK Horse Ranch. Clearly, Freepool had been living under the radar for perhaps as long as she had been Frea Pool. The idea gave him pause; maybe she hadn't *always* been 'Frea Pool?' But trying to find out when Frea Pool 'became' was something he didn't have time for.

Now, on to Mr. Aaron Gamel Dell.

Fortunately, there were some official records for Aaron Gamel Dell. Up to 1990, he owned land in both Montana and BC. In 1990, ownership of those properties was transferred to a numbered company. *Tricky bastard!*

Next in the downloaded file folder was a marriage license. Dell was married to a 'Ruth Pender.' There was no mention of Frea Pool. He searched for Ruth Pender and found several records for her, even a picture. It had been taken at a Charity Auction and captured by the *Kootenay Quarterly*. The short, round-faced woman bore no resemblance to Freepool.

"This doesn't make any sense!"

Twix looked up momentarily, then went back to the bone Ethan had tossed down to her.

Perhaps the 'Officially Separated' document was, like the EK Horse Ranch, official bullshit. But why? *A joke? A smear? An error?* Might Dell have had two wives, one on either side of the border, and with the law only permitting one, Frea Pool got *axed*, so to speak?

Ethan needed to speak to Aaron Dell.

195

Chapter Twenty-Nine: No Farmer in the Dell

Forty miles southeast of Gadsby's Gulch, a right turn took Bert and Ethan south on another highway toward the US border. In the rearview mirror were mountains clad in blue-green coats of fir and spruce. Around them, pines, spaced out by nature's design, dotted the landscape, at least until the shorter thicker-limbed trees took over on the higher mountain slopes, which in turn gave way to the withering limestone and shale of Canada's 'Rotting Rockies' to the east. As they continued south, the valley widened, and native fescues and wheatgrass waved from the undulating terrain.

Twenty minutes later, they turned east on a paved secondary road which snaked its way toward the Rockies. It was mid-September, and before long, the stands of aspen would start changing from green to yellow. The morning air was crisp, the flies less, the sunlight less potent, and the elk rut was in full swing. By the time they came to a cattle-guard and a gate across the road, they had seen twenty cows and two bull elk. The gate was unlocked.

Ethan glanced at his navigation screen. They were still on Collar Road, but here the pavement gave way to dirt. A posted sign instructed, '*Close the gate after you,*' and another sign said, '*Smile for the camera.*' If there was a camera, it was well hidden. They closed the gate after they passed through.

It had been another warm, dry, late-summer day and a dust cloud rose behind them as Ethan drove further east. Then, curiously, the dusty dirt road morphed into a single-lane paved road named 'Hills Mountain Road,' according to the GPS.

"A one-lane paved road? Did we just get transported to a bitumen byway in England?"

"It does make for a *jolly good* outing," Bert replied.

Normally, rural roads that poked their way into forest and ranch land were dirt or gravel. Pavement cost money, and a fractured and potholed paved road was much worse to drive on and far harder on tires and shocks than a good gravel road. Someone, other than the Department of Highways, was spending a lot of cash on this road.

The navigation screen told him they had arrived at their destination, 10849 Hills Mountain Road — Aaron Dell's home address. However, Ethan could see neither driveway nor home, so they drove onward. A few hundred feet later, they left Hills Mountain Road and were now on an unmarked road, with the GPS lady kindly instructing them to 'Drive Safe.'

"Maybe you should drive, Bert. After all, I've recently been at the wheel for two write-offs," Ethan joked.

"I thought of that. Insurance company messaged me to say you were now only eligible to rent a wheelbarrow and couldn't be listed as the primary driver."

"Good one."

"Do you really want to switch?"

"No, that's okay, Bert. Anyway, let's see where this lovely lane takes us. But before we go any further, let's lock and load."

They loaded their revolvers, unlocked their rifles, and put on their bulletproof vests.

As they drove down the single-lane bitumen road, an odd feeling came over Ethan. It was like they were in another time and place or simply not supposed to be here — or at the very least, not welcome.

"This place feels spooky, Bert."

"I'm with you there, boss."

They crawled down the road which, to add to the strangeness, zig-zagged along for no apparent reason. Then, at another zigzag, they spotted a camera with a bullet hole in it.

"That's ominous."

Ethan nodded his agreement and added, "It is. I suggest you roll down your window, Bert, and be prepared to fire." Bert did as he was instructed.

A half-mile later, they reached a tree line that divided the forest from grassland and yet another gate, which was rather expected. What they *didn't* expect was that the gate was ripped off its hinges, and multiple black marks defaced the asphalt. Ethan unsnapped the holster that held his sidearm.

At this point, the road twisted to the left. A round, convex mirror was fastened to an aluminum pole, positioned to give anyone coming from the northeast a view of the section of road he and Bert had just traversed.

"From here on my friend, we keep our eyes open, and our knackers covered."

Bert smiled. "In homage to Reggie, your use of 'knackers' and friend in the same sentence tells me our bromance is blossoming."

Ethan looked at Bert, who had used a witticism that Reggie would've employed and enjoyed, and smiled, before swallowing hard. "Man, I miss him."

"Me too."

"He was the best pain in the ass I ever had. Between you and me and the fencepost, if we encounter Freepool or whomever is responsible for Chelsea's disappearance, Reggie's death, etcetera, I might experience an itchy trigger finger."

"You and me both, but legal-like right?"

"Is there any other way?"

Their ensuing fist bump said they were in full agreement.

They made a thirty-degree turn north, onto what had to be the driveway to Aaron Gamel Dell's home. The surroundings stood in sharp contrast to how Ethan felt: inside, stomach-turning, outside, idyllic. They spotted more elk and even a sow grizzly and her cubs. Deer stood at a lake's edge, and ducks ducked in and out of the blue water.

As they slowed for a cattle-guard, the *chop-chop-chop* of a helicopter sent the deer running and ducks diving.

"Can you see the helicopter, Bert?"

"No."

"Must've left low and fast."

Ethan switched on the lights, but not the siren. As they crept to the next sharp turn in the driveway, they came upon yet another smashed-down gate, and a hundred yards on, Dell's residence.

Boom! The truck shook from a large blast, and a moment later, a propane bottle flew over the top of the vehicle, demolishing the siren assembly.

Instinctively, Ethan cranked the truck sideways to one: block anyone from leaving, and two: provide cover in case of gunfire.

Meanwhile, the barn door pirouetted and then slowly fell flat. The burnt and broken man, miraculously alive, raised a fist in the air.

"We should —"

A cacophony of small blasts interrupted Bert, and their windshield fragmented.

"We're taking on fire!"

Ethan instinctively reached across and pushed Bert downward. The shots continued frenetically.

"It's ammo going off from the barn and or the house. Stay down, Bert!"

A minute later, the buildings seemed to have run out of ammunition. Ethan craned his head out the side window to see what was happening. The flames had diminished, and whatever animals that had been in or around the barn had fled.

"Okay, let's take a closer look."

Bert joined him as they walked over to the man — probably Aaron Dell — impaled on the burning barn door. Numerous bullets had hit the old man's head, the damage substantial enough that visual identification could be problematic. However, Ethan had no problem discerning the hatchet-shaped pin on the lapel of his black wool work jacket.

After dousing the flames with his fire extinguisher, Ethan used a stick to flick the hatchet lapel-pin off the charred and nearly disintegrated shirt, and, after it cooled, put it in an evidence bag.

By the time they heard the fire engine and emergency vehicles approaching, most everything had burned to the ground.

"Please fill them in, Bert. I'm going to cast about and see what we have."

As Bert moved their truck out of the way and prepared to address ERT personnel, Ethan walked toward the smoldering house. He could see the scorched remains of a woman, probably Aaron Dell's wife Ruth, draped over an old sewing machine.

The only other deceased were poultry and pigs.

As he was walking back to Bert, the horse and wagon emerged from the trees. The panicked and badly-burned horse raised up on its hind legs and then, after it brought its

The air was filled with smoke and the sound of crackling flames, but no weapons-fire.

"Let's exit on my side and stay low."

Bert followed Ethan out, and after a few minutes of hiding behind the truck and taking some quick peeks, Ethan resolved whatever had happened seemed to have passed.

"Let's move in — slowly. I'll drive the truck. You tuck in behind. Provide cover, as is necessary."

"Roger."

Ethan got back in the truck and inched it toward the residence.

There was another loud bang and a series of *peeshew-peeshews*, like firecrackers going off. Then there was an enormous *whoosh* that seemed to pull the air from Ethan's lungs.

Bert rejoined him in the truck and as they crouched low to avoid projectiles, Ethan phoned 9-1-1 to get Fire and Rescue on the scene. Ethan chanced a look over the dash.

A horse was trotting toward them, its saddle dangling, with a section of fence in tow via rope caught on the saddle horn. Behind it, a big red barn was ablaze. As one of the barn doors swung open, a man, pinned to the door with a pitchfork, looked up at them. Then an explosion from the barn blew the doors right off, sending burning wood and hay flying.

The horse that had been trotting toward them broke into a gallop, and the section of fence dragging behind it smashed against the front of the truck. Singed chicken feathers floated down, and two pigs, wild-eyed and panicked, fled the yard.

Another black horse, shrouded in flames and towing a small wagon — which was on fire — broke out of the remnants of the barn. The wagon's wheels went over the man pinned to the barn door, causing him to wail in pain. As the wagon continued on, a rope from it snagged onto the skeletal frame of the barn door and flipped it, and the man stuck upright.

The tension of the rope caused the horse to swing around, and it and wagon then careened the remaining wall of the house that hadn't collapsed. The singed rope finally snapped the beast and its burden disappeared behind a stand of trees that hemmed in the southeastern portion of the yard.

front feet back down, took off wildly to the north, into the tall, dry grass. While the horse was no longer burning, the wagon was still on fire, and a line of fire trailed behind it.

This is bad.

The Fire Captain echoed Ethan's thought. "We have to get out of here! With the wind coming from the north, we need to make a controlled burn and be in position to save the houses to the south!"

Ethan felt wind gathering from the north and, sure enough, the fire began moving quickly toward them.

Not that further encouragement was required, but the Fire Captain's loudspeaker boomed a "Move out! We need to save the farms to the south!"

There would be no further examination of the crime scene today.

Chapter Thirty: Neighbors

The heroic firemen saved the homes to the south and, with the aid of a water-bomber, prevented the blaze from becoming a true wildfire. Another bonus was that four horses, one a yearling, were saved. Animal rescue believed they could even nurse the burned horse back to health. Several pigs had already made their home in a wallowing hole at a neighboring ranch.

The next day, Ethan kicked a hole in the ashes covering the scorched earth in the yard. Unfortunately, there was little of the ranch's buildings that weren't thoroughly destroyed. The home, barn, machine shed, and tack shed had all been reduced to ashes.

The Fire Marshall had already investigated the scene and made her conclusion: arson. It was clear to Ethan that at least two people had been murdered, and the fire was meant to destroy all evidence.

There was no flight data for a rogue helicopter, but those machines made a lot of noise, and fire kicked up a lot of smoke. *Somebody had to have seen something!* So, while Bert was putting out public bulletins, Ethan would be speaking to a handful of locals.

His first stop was a trailer on a two-acre parcel north of the Dell property. A right-side-drive Toyota HiLux was parked out front, and an Airedale Terrier observed him from a doghouse. The dog looked friendly enough — that is, until Ethan got out of his truck. It growled, then it barked and *barked* loudly.

Ethan waited, while the dog continued barking. Finally, a curtain was pulled back from the porch window, and a few minutes later, a tall, shirtless blonde man with a surfer's physique stepped out.

"Be quiet, Bogan!"

Ethan got out of the truck and walked forward, and the dog went ballistic.

"Bogan, *enough!*" The man yelled sharply, and the dog disappeared into its doghouse.

Ethan walked up the steps and onto the deck that jutted out from the porch. There, he introduced himself.

"And I'm Sam Quallie." The man said in an Australian accent.

"Good to meet you, Sam."

Just then, the clouds that had been threatening rain unleashed a downpour. After about twenty seconds, a pretty young lady opened the front door.

"Have some decency, Sam. Let the officer come in."

Ethan followed Sam into the house. By that time, Ethan's shirt was wringing wet.

The woman handed them each a towel.

"Honestly, Sam." She shook her head at him and then Ethan heard another man shout, "Smoko!"

"Do come in, Officer, sir."

"The name's Ethan Birchom."

"Hi, Mr. Birchom. I'm Sam's sister, Kate."

Kate walked away, and a minute later she was back, pushing an old man in a wheelchair.

Sam stepped from the porch through the main entry into the kitchen, and Ethan followed.

Ethan thanked Kate for the towel and dried himself off enough that he wasn't dripping on their floor. Sam only tossed his towel over a chair that sat at the kitchen table.

As quickly as the rain came, it stopped; mountain showers could be like that.

"Smoko!"

"Yes, Dad, I'll get you out onto the deck right now."

"Officer, this is our dad, Tex."

The old man grunted a "G'day," and turned to his daughter. "Kate, if I don't have a ciggy soon, I'm going to crack the shits."

Ethan didn't like the sound of that.

Kate wheeled her father out the main door, down the short ramp into the porch, and out onto the deck, leaving the doors wide open.

Over her shoulder, Kate said, "We shouldn't even let him smoke, but if he's going to fume, then it'll be outside in the fresh air."

Sam, arms crossed, said, "What can we do for you?"

Ethan got to it. "Were any of you home yesterday to witness what happened at your neighbors, the Dells?"

"No, we were all in town yesterday. Pops had an appointment."

"Are they okay?" Kate asked from the porch.

"I'm sorry to say they are both deceased, and the ranch burned to the ground."

"Oh, no. How awful!"

"Did any of you meet the Dells, see any suspicious activity, or have reason to think they had enemies?"

"Nope, negative, and no."

Ethan reckoned Sam wouldn't tell him anything even if he knew it.

"How about you, Kate?"

She looked at her brother and back at Ethan.

"No, we didn't know them."

"And how long have you lived here?"

"Two years. Though Kate's not been here a lot, she's got a gig in the Pilbara that helps keep us in the razoos."

"As in...?"

Sam crossed his arms. "Money, Copper, money."

Clearly, Sam didn't like him, and the feeling was quickly becoming mutual. "Oh. Sorry, I'm not worldly, and miss out on things some would understand."

"Forgive our Sam. He can be a bit of a mongrel in the morning."

"No problem. So, none of you ever witnessed any suspicious activities at the Dell ranch?"

"I *will* say that little green dragonfly on steroids they got nearly got me to going off!"

Ethan looked at the old man, who Kate had now wheeled back into the porch, and hoped he would clarify the statement. Since the old man just stared at him, and neither Sam nor Kate said anything, Ethan had to ask.

"'Green dragonfly?'"

"Is he daft?"

"No, dad, he's a policeman. Here they call them the RCMP." Kate said the acronym slowly.

"Oh... I see. By 'little green dragonfly on steroids,' I mean," and then the old man spoke slowly, "He-li-cop-ter."

"You saw a helicopter transiting to and from the ranch. Is that correct?"

The old man looked at Ethan like he was nuts, took another draw on his now dead "smoko," and added, "Yes, a few times. It flew too low for my liking — or for common sense, as far as I'm concerned. Anyway, I need to take a piss."

Kate wheeled her father back in and down the hall, then stood with her back against the door while the old guy was presumably doing his business.

Ethan took a quick look around the house. The kitchen table was covered in pill bottles, and a cardboard box held more on the countertop. There was also a small scale and a box full of what appeared to be mushrooms, though a towel over it made it hard to say for sure. The old man probably took a lot of meds, but Ethan had a sneaking suspicion something else was going on. However, he had more important things to worry about.

He turned his head toward the living room and saw a telescope pointing in the general direction of the Dell ranch.

Ethan was growing impatient, so got creative.

"That last Ursid meteor shower was really something, wasn't it?"

Sam's gaze shifted between him and the telescope.

205

"Crikey, yes."

Ethan knew the Ursid meteor shower occurred in winter, not summer.

"Well, anyway, I appreciate your time, folks. If you should think of anything that might help us solve the murder of your neighbors, please call me. I would appreciate it."

Sam didn't say anything, but Kate replied, "We will. Have a good day, sir."

At that, Ethan stepped out the door. The dog didn't stop barking until he was well past the end of their driveway.

Up to now, every Aussie Ethan had met was likeable. These, he wasn't sure about. It could be they brought their father here to help facilitate making and selling illicit drugs, perhaps fentanyl. On the other hand, they could be innocent, and he'd just caught them at a bad time. The telescope, though, that was an outlier.

Ethan's next stop was the Nablers. These people he'd met; they were long time residents.

The elderly couple were cordial and invited him in. After the requisite pleasantries, Ethan did what he was here to do.

"Were you both home yesterday?"

"Yes, we were. Fortunately, the fire was moving away from us. Isn't that right, Norma?"

"Yes, and my dear, sweet Gerald had put some of our most precious keepsakes and an emergency kit in the truck just in case the wind changed direction."

"It pays to have a plan." Ethan added.

The Nablers smiled at him and at each other.

"How well did you know the Dells?"

"We've lived here for forty years and met them fewer than ten times. Not that they were rude, just private people — like us, I suppose, hey, honey?"

"Yes, dear, though it's always sad to see people, particularly good country folk, lose their lives."

The old man looked at a picture atop a box near the door. It was probably the box of keepsakes he had organized. The picture was of another elderly man.

"Cousin just passed away recently."

"I'm sorry for your loss."

Gerald nodded and Norma said, "And we're also sorry to hear you lost a fellow officer."

"Thank you."

Ethan noticed a pair of binoculars on the ledge that divided their living room from the kitchen, and the large bay window that afforded southern exposure.

"Did either of you see anything unusual earlier in the day, prior to yesterday's tragic events?"

Gerald followed Ethan's gaze. "No, but I confess I generally use the binoculars to look at the birds or deer in my yard. My eyesight isn't the greatest."

"We both have cataracts that need to be taken care of," Norma added.

"Did you ever hear about the Dells quarrelling with anyone, or having any enemies?"

"No, not at all. Won't you join us for tea and biscuits?"

Clearly, Ethan wouldn't learn much here. "I wish I could, Mrs. Nabler, but I have so much on my plate, plus I had coffee and a breakfast sandwich before I arrived."

"Next time, promise?"

"I promise, Norma."

Ethan had only had three more stops to make. He hoped he would come up with more than what he had learned thus far — which wasn't much.

Twenty minutes later, he pulled into a yard that was furnished with old lawnmowers and wrecked bicycles. A man of about fifty, who looked a cross between a sheepdog and Tommy Chong, was chopping wood.

When he saw Ethan, he dropped his axe and walked into his cabin.

With caution, Ethan approached the door.

"Hello, Sir."

No answer.

He stood to the side of the door and knocked hard. "Sir, this is the RCMP. I need to speak with you, sir."

The door opened a crack.

"What do you want?"

A sweaty, swassy smell, with not-so-subtle hints of 'pot-pourri' wafted out of the cabin.

Ethan stepped back and asked, "Were you at home yesterday?"

"I'm home every day."

"Did you know the Dells?"

"If you mean the people who got burned out, then no."

"Did you see anything suspicious before the fire occurred?"

"Listen, I only rent this joint. I don't pay attention to shit."

"So, nothing unusual, Mr...?"

"Mr. I mind my own business."

"Thank you for your ti—"

The man closed the door in Ethan's face.

There was nobody home at the next address; records showed it was owned by some people from California. Owners probably just used the place as a base for hunting and fishing trips; they'd probably never know that firefighters saved their home.

The last house on his list sat on a parcel on the western border of the Californians. A 1960s Fargo pickup sat in front of a well-maintained rancher. There was a stout barn, shed, and chicken pen. A black lab that was more interested in its bone than Ethan's presence looked out from its doghouse. A horse stood near a hitching post, and Ethan could smell bacon cooking.

"Come on in, Officer. Door's open."

It was true, the main door was swung wide, the screen door held open with a wedge.

Before he stepped in, Ethan said, "Sorry to disturb you. I'm Ethan Birchom of the RCMP, and I was hoping you could help me out by answering a few questions."

"Can do, but not before brunch. How many eggs do you want?"

"Oh, that's okay."

"Nonsense. Three fried free-range eggs it'll be. Don't bother taking off your boots. You wouldn't have got them dirty at Nablers'."

"How did —"

"Saw you when I was riding in from my back forty."

Ethan pulled up a chair, and a wiry man of about sixty-five sat a plate with bacon, beans, and three over-easy eggs in front of him.

"Mighty kind of you, Mr. Stuberman — it is Clark Stuberman, right?"

"Yep, same as it was when you nailed me for speeding ten years ago."

"Ah yes, I remember that night. Sorry about that."

"Don't apologize. Best thing that ever happened to me — well, second-best. I took an anger management course and bought a new horse. Actually, *that* was the best thing I ever did."

Stuberman set to his meal and didn't say a word until he'd devoured it all and drank a cup of coffee.

"Got enough, Mr. Birchom?"

"Definitely, I'm stuffed. That was delicious, thank you. Please don't tell the Nablers I ate here; I turned down Norma's offer of tea and biscuits."

Stuberman laughed. "Good thing you did. Half the time her biscuits are hard-tack. And tea, heck, might as well strain water through a work sock."

Ethan liked the guy. Even when he nabbed him for speeding, he hadn't been an asshole about it.

"Truck looks great. Still running well?"

"Yep, but I only drive it every couple of weeks to get mail and groceries. No more eighty in a fifty zone." He grinned.

"I heard about your wife, Rebecca. My sympathies, Clark."

"Thanks, but it's okay. It's been nearly two years, and she went quick. I also heard about your young officer, so my condolences."

"Appreciated."

Ethan took a drink of coffee and was about to ask Clark — Mr. Stuberman — what he came here to ask when the man spoke.

"One day I was out riding at the northeastern corner of my property. Turns out, Dell was riding at the southeastern portion of his. I accidentally flushed out a cougar, which, in turn, spooked Dell's horse. Dell got thrown down hard and dislocated his shoulder. He got up hobbling, so must've turned his ankle too."

"Ouch."

"Dell sees me, and just tips his hat, like saying 'Howdy.'"

"I ask him if he would like a hand and he says nothing. Instead, he walks up to a fencepost and rams himself into it, straightening out his shoulder."

"Damn."

"There's more. But first, a refill. You want more coffee, Ethan?"

"Yes, please. I love camp coffee."

Clark pulled an old pot off the cook-stove and topped up their mugs. "Dell, it was like I wasn't even there. He walks up to his horse and gives it a right hook to the head that knocked the horse senseless."

"Wow!"

"The guy pulls off the saddle just as the horse falls over, legs sticking up in the air. Then, he bent over and whispered something in its ear."

"Did you say anything?"

"No, no, I didn't. I was shocked. Like, what kind of psycho punches his horse *and* hits it hard enough to knock it unconscious?"

"Then what happened?"

"Dell threw the saddle over his shoulder and walked away."

"What about the horse?"

"Get this — I wait until Dell is out of sight and walk over to the horse. It was *dead*."

"Are you serious?"

"Yeah, I know. Incredible, right? I tell you, when he was whispering in the horse's ear, it felt like the temperature dropped five degrees."

"Did you ever go back there?"

"Two or three days later. The horse was gone. Dell may have retrieved it, or scavengers took care of it."

Ethan couldn't help but associate that sort of sinister act with something Freepool would do.

"Did you have any other interaction with either of them after that?"

"Nope, stayed as far away as I could."

"By chance, were you around yesterday when they were killed, and their place burned to the ground?"

"Yes. I heard a heli flying in, thought it was Natural Resources or maybe a tourist flight, so paid little attention to it. When I smelled smoke, I busied myself taking care of my animals and hooking up my pump to my pond. I could swamp this place if I needed to. After that, I drove down the road a bit. I saw the fire crews doing their thing, so let them do it."

"Smart move. Anything else you found unusual about the Dells?"

The man's eyebrows perked up. "Oh, yes, I do remember something else. I saw them walking together once. It was about ten years ago, just before Christmas. It was freezing, nine p.m. and pitch black. A downdraft was driving smoke down the chimney, so I had the windows and door open to help air out the house. A gust of wind snatched my wife's favorite hat from off its hook and blew it out the door. I was casting about trying to find her hat and ended up a quarter mile from the house.

"At that time, I enjoyed my scotch, and I had a bottle stuck in a stump near my northern fence-line. Knowing I would get reamed out for losing Rebecca's favorite hat, I elected to pull up a stump and have a few snorts. As I sat there, I heard footsteps crunching over the snow. They walked within thirty feet and didn't see me, or at least they seemed not to.

"They were talking some strange language, saying things in unison, like they were in a trance. Dell had a hatchet in one hand and a Christmas tree over his shoulder. Mrs. Dell had a rabbit's head in one hand and a hatchet in the other. The moonlight was reflecting off their axe blades and their muttering continued until I couldn't hear them anymore. It was creepy as hell."

"That's the *definition* of creepy. Do you know if they had any enemies?"

"No idea."

"Frequent visitors?"

"Can't say I paid any attention to anything they did. There were times I would go down the main road and see a truck and horse-trailer or a truck with hay coming and going."

"Well, they had a large spread, so I reckon that's normal."

"True. Oh, wait — there is one other weird thing I recall."

"What's that?"

"A meeting took place about fifteen years ago. Maybe it was a family reunion. They always, and I mean *always*, had a fire burning, like an Olympic flame sort of thing in their yard. Went on for years. I could see it flickering away at night. After that get-together, no more flames. It struck me as odd, like a passing of the torch."

"That's interesting. Anything else peculiar that comes to mind? Did they have any close friends that you were aware of?"

"Nothing comes to mind. They *did* have some of the most beautiful black horses I've ever seen."

"Do you know what happened to them?"

"No idea, but I doubt he punched them to death."

After that, they talked about the weather and how much things had changed in the past thirty or forty years. As much work as Ethan had to do, he didn't want to go. It was nice to talk with a man his own age.

"Well, Clark, thanks a lot for all your help—and the eats."

"My pleasure. Hey, you should stop by again for a coffee and a chinwag."

Ethan smiled. "I'll do that. Thanks again."

Chapter Thirty-One: Proposal

Two days later, deep in thought, road flares caught him by surprise. Ethan didn't even radio in as he pulled in behind a Subaru with its hood up. He walked to the front of the vehicle.

"Problem?"

The person adjusted their ball cap up and smiled apologetically.

"Caroline?"

She slammed the hood down, walked by him, grabbed the pylon, put out the flare, and put everything in the trunk.

"We need to talk, Ethan."

Ethan could hardly believe it. "What? How... you?"

"Follow me." Caroline jumped in her vehicle and pulled off on a dirt road just north of where she'd parked. She swung an arm out, beckoning Ethan to follow.

Robot-like, he followed her off the road. Ethan cobbled together enough sense to back in and park beside her on the log landing that fringed the side of the dirt road.

He got out, and immediately Caroline had him in her arms, plastering him with kisses.

"Jesus Christ, Caroline!" Ethan pushed her away, but again she was on him like an octopus to a giant shrimp.

This time, he couldn't resist kissing her back. Ethan felt simultaneously joyous and sick.

Finally, as she started to unbutton his pants, he gathered just enough courage to take three steps back.

"Caroline, wait!"

She came toward him, and he almost straight-armed her. "Caroline, *enough!*"

Caroline pulled off her ball cap and tossed it into her car. "I know, I know. I have so much to explain, but please know, I love you, Ethan."

The tears in her eyes looked genuine, and his desire for her was obvious.

"I lo—" Ethan stopped and adjusted his trousers and straightened his shirt. "Five minutes, Caroline Leadshat, or Halstead — whatever name you and your family are using these days — I will give you five minutes."

"So, you know—"

"Yes, I know. The only things I don't really know are if you and yours were involved in my daughter's disappearance or if I should charge you with manslaughter, murder, or an accessory to her death, Debra's, Rudy's, Reggie's, or all of the above."

"Unless you know it all, you have no idea."

"Well, illuminate me. You have another three minutes."

Caroline pulled off her jacket and then her blouse.

"Caroline. We are *not* having sex!"

"I know, and that's unfortunate, but that's not what I'm doing. Here, hold this."

Caroline passed him a small flashlight, which he grabbed. She held her jacket over her head, providing some shade for her shoulders.

"Shine that flashlight here, on my right shoulder."

Ethan did as he was told and he saw the image of a hatchet, only about one by two inches, on her shoulder.

"A hatchet! How did I not see that before?!"

"It's a UV tattoo. It's one of the few new things the family uses. You couldn't see it unless… well, you know."

"Unless I had a UV Light."

"And we didn't have enough time together to explore our full range of intimacy."

Ethan recalled Caroline talking about psychedelic lighting and as with *anything* she suggested while they were in bed, he kept an open — or was it lustful — mind?

215

Ethen exhaled sharply, then regathered himself.

"Those days are gone, Caroline. What can you tell me about your kinky 'h' that I already don't know?"

As her head tilted down, Caroline looked profoundly sad.

"It's our symbol, and it's bequeathed, born, and branded into us."

"I'm sorry, but if you're looking for sympathy, you've the wrong man."

"You've never been the wrong man, Ethan. In fact, you're the only man beside my ex husband who's ever seen it. Others might've but..."

"They're probably dead."

"Maybe."

"So, you're a murderer too?"

"Not exactly."

"Not *exactly*? Do you know how that sounds, Caroline? Do you know what that means? We're Peace Officers, you know, 'laws and justice,' definitely not 'murder and cover-up!'"

"I can assure you I have saved far more lives than I've taken. In fact, I've never killed anyone because I wanted to. It was always at the direction of others. I didn't have a choice."

"Of course, you had a choice, Caroline. You could've said 'no,' gone to the authorities."

"My twin brother said 'no.' They killed him. My daughter ran away, disappeared, or was *disappeared* by my ex. And my son just died in an accident. You're all I have, Ethan."

"If that's the case, then I will ensure you get a fair trial. Your family — cult — and its twisted ideology must end."

"Twisted, perhaps. Wrong? Maybe not. Strong chance this world's most exquisite people, people like you and Chelsea, wouldn't have been born if not for —"

Ehan threw his arms up in exasperation.

"*Don't!*" Ethan felt angry enough to kill. "Don't *ever* use my daughter's name!" His head grew hot. "Don't stain what *she was* with what *you are*."

Caroline's hands fell to her sides, and she took a deep breath. "Ethan, what I am is a woman who loves you. I saved you, remember?"

"You didn't save Reggie."

"I came as fast as I could. It's not like we knew exactly what... what the suspect was up to."

"'We?' 'Suspect?'" Ethan felt like his brain was going to explode. "It blows my mind how you can switch between lover and cop and truth, or half-truth, or maybe outright *fiction* at the same time. You know damn well it was Frea Pool! I heard you say her name, and I *will* get that psycho if it's the last thing I do."

His vulnerable situation finally worked its way into his analytical brain. *What am I doing here? On a side-road, out of view of the highway, with a member of a family of serial killers — people that want me dead!* Ethan glanced over his shoulder.

"Nobody knows we're here."

Caroline's statement did nothing to assuage Ethan's concern. He had to go, but he had to take her with him.

"You know who tried to kill me, and you know who killed Reggie. You know a lot of unsavory characters and their crimes. Whether here or in the States, you can probably get immunity for testifying."

"I can't."

"You say I'm all you have, but you can't take that step!"

"I do that and I'm dead, and *you're* dead. You've only glimpsed a fraction of the reality, the scope of the enterprise — thousands of years, a myriad of connections..."

"What do you propose?"

"We walk away, together, right now. I know a place where we can be safe."

"I — I have a life here, and my duty, and..." He trailed off.

"And Chelsea. I'm sorry, Ethan, but you have to let go. We can be happy together."

He didn't question her sincerity, only her logic and sanity. "I will never stop looking for Chelsea. *Never!*"

Caroline's tears spilled down her face; she looked so lost.

Don't you feel sorry for her Ethan, not for one second!

Suddenly, Caroline fell to one knee and pulled a box out of her pocket.

Light filtered through the conifers and sunlight glistened off both her shoulders and the item she held in her hand. "Ethan Birchom, you're the best man I've ever known. Will you please, please, do me the honor of being my husband?"

This was insane! He'd loved this woman — maybe still loved her — but it was impossible. All he could do was shake his head, lacking the courage or conviction to say 'no.'

She gathered herself up, her fragility shattered, her bloodline and strength renewed. "So be it. This is goodbye, Ethan." She turned to walk back to her car.

He heard himself say, "I can't let you go, Caroline."

Caroline stopped. Without turning, she said, "You would have to shoot me."

"It doesn't have to be like this."

"Unfortunately, *Officer Birchom*, it does."

Just as she opened her door, he rushed forward.

Caroline bent forward slightly, pivoted, and suddenly the sole of a hiking boot was in his face.

Instinctively, he rolled to the side and grabbed his Taser. Another kick sent it flying into the bush. He grabbed his gun and pointed it at her.

"You won't shoot me, Ethan."

"No, but I can shoot your tires."

He pointed at her front passenger side tire and let off a round. The tire seemed unaffected. He shot it again. Nothing. He looked at his gun and at her.

"You could empty the entire clip at those and get no result."

He emptied the clip. She was right. As he reached to his belt for another clip, she rushed forward and kicked him in the chest.

He tumbled backward and, as he straightened for the fight, her shoulder pounded into his gut, launching him backward. Ethan used everything he had to hold on to her, and they tumbled down the gentle grassy slope at the edge of the roadway. When they came to a stop, she was lying on top of him.

Their eyes locked.

"I'm sorry about kicking you in the head, Ethan. Your nose is swollen; it might be broken."

"Coupled with the 'h' carved into my forehead, my fledgling modeling career is surely over."

She laughed, and then he laughed, and for an instant that lasted minutes he wondered if he really *could* run away with her.

She kissed him then, a soft kiss that spoke to her sincerity and passion, and like innocence rediscovered, Ethan let it linger.

He also let her unbutton his shirt.

"We shouldn't —"

Caroline placed a finger over his lips, but it wasn't necessary; he was already mute.

Like a goddess astride a mechanical bull, she rode him hard. The entire time — about twenty minutes — their eyes stayed locked.

She slowly rolled off him and they lay side-by-side.

"You know, I can't, Caroline."

"I know, Ethan."

She started to rise, and he flinched as if about to get up.

Before he knew it, a knife was at his throat.

"Don't get up, Ethan."

"Okay."

Caroline got up and walked away. Ethan was still lying there when she drove off. He was still there as the sun, mockingly, winked behind the horizon.

Chapter Thirty-Two: The Blót

The ritual remained unchanged. The year was 2023 — or perhaps it was 1100?

Only the light from the fire that passed around the hanging strips of flesh and glittering axes, large and small, revealed their loose, woolen cloaks to be as dark as the burbling, fire-blackened cauldron. Of the nine, three were men, three women, and three were of indeterminate sex, their features hidden by the hooded woolen cloaks and wooden masks they wore.

They chanted. It wasn't so much a song, but a monotone, metered *thrumming*. It went on for more than an hour, and though there never seemed to be a harmonic change, the sound became nearly ear-splitting. Even the natural world stood still, beguiled, and bewildered by the stentorian tone.

Then, a deafening quiet descended over the gathering and, indeed, all within a forest mile. Each member of the masked trio led an animal toward the fire: a goat, a sheep, and a horse.

The axes, which hung from chains, had been sent into motion, spinning and shining, shining and spinning. The invocation started again, but as a whisper, a sound like tall blades of grass brushing against one another, or perhaps that of air parting before a wing.

The animals — collectively mesmerized by sound, scene, and that which was added to their feed — were calm and quiet. Only the fire crackled its hunger.

One of the shadowed figures dispatched the goat, though all three drank of its blood. Hung from its rear legs, the goat swiftly bled out into a large four-handled vessel that two of the hooded trio dipped lengths of braided hemp rope with frayed ends into.

One walked clockwise around the gathering, while the other moved counterclockwise. Each swung the ropes, splattering the group. What remained in the vessel was poured upon a huge black stone previously pulled to the fire by horses on a stone-boat.

Servants, stupefied in the same manner as the animals, came and removed the goat's carcass. Two took part in dispatching the sheep. Again, its lifeforce was imbibed and potency spread.

Generally, this sacrifice would be enough to ensure fine weather, ample fertility, a bountiful harvest, and provide a reaffirmation of the holy covenant. However, this year, more was required. There was a new leader and participants must be welded to him, their common ancestors, and the divine purpose bestowed upon them in the most ancient of days.

All present then took a part in yielding up their most honored beast. Steel met with firelight, flashing crimson. Cloaks were blackened with blood and the cauldron filled with meat. Hours passed, until all bellies bulged from the feast.

The Supreme Being was sated. Harvests would be bountiful, bloodlines would be bolstered and renewed, and wondrous souls — perhaps the best to ever occasion the Earth — would be born. No offering was without honor. No sacrifice was too great. Humanity was worth it.

This was the way it had been since time immemorial.

Chapter Thirty-Three: hQ

No one claimed the remains of the Dells, and an anonymous donor paid for their cremation.

Ethan heard the land was going into a farmland trust, which he understood to mean that its ecological value and heritage would be preserved. The 'ecological' he could understand, the 'heritage,' not so much.

They also found homes, temporary or otherwise, for all the animals.

Ethan had been confident they would receive some leads from the public bulletins, but two weeks on, they had nothing. While it surprised him that nobody noticed where the low-flying chopper was going, it *was* a sparsely populated area. Also, people had become accustomed to tourist flights, as well as flights related to utilities monitoring.

He wondered how easy it might be to disassemble a smaller Robinson or Enstrom helicopter. He jotted that down on his ever-growing list of things to investigate. Truthfully, Ethan wasn't overly concerned about finding out who killed the Dells for *their* sake as much as his own, and to further cases for Rudy Ingersson, Chelsea, and even Debra, though that young lady had somehow turned to the dark side.

Ethan gave everything he could to Interpol's Ms. Lexsmith. She said they would look further into Frea Pool, Aaron Dell, Caroline, and all the Leadshats, and get back to him as soon as possible.

While he fessed up to having an affair with Caroline, which was hugely embarrassing, he didn't divulge all the details of their last encounter. Yes, Ethan had called in her location, but not promptly. He'd also opted to say she had incapacitated him, which, no matter how hard he tried to justify it to himself, was a lie. To Ethan's recollection, it reflected the only time he'd ever falsified a report about what he did or observed during his time as a Peace Officer.

Ethan had to admit that what happened with Caroline — both at their last meeting and how he "handled" his official duties afterward — revealed a flaw in his character. He was going to have to live with that. It was like the 'h' on his forehead, only carved into his soul.

He shook his head, thinking about it, which hurt his nose. Fortunately, Caroline hadn't broken it. Hindsight, as they say, is 20:20; maybe if he had acted immediately and appropriately upon seeing her, she would be in custody.

It was conceivable, though, that her survival instinct would've trumped her feelings for him; if so, he would be dead right now. Even without all his injuries, Ethan doubted he could 'hang and bang' with Caroline. She had as many martial arts black belts as most people had waistbelts and was in incredible shape. No, she would've kicked his ass — or worse.

If there was anyone who could evade capture, it was Caroline. All her years in law enforcement would give her an edge, meaning she would always be a step ahead of her pursuers. Mind you, technology and the surveillance apparatus were highly evolved, so security cameras and associated facial recognition software might reveal her location.

Still, Caroline had spoke of 'a myriad of connections.' No doubt, she knew people who would help her. By now, she might be 'Mira Jukic' and living in Croatia. It was anybody's guess.

Would he look for her? If they couldn't find Frea Pool or her associates alive and convince them to tell their sick stories, then he might *have* to. The next time, he wouldn't let her say a word before stunning or otherwise incapacitating her.

Twix had been resting her head on Ethan's foot long enough that it had fallen asleep.

"Sorry, Twix, but I have to move."

Twix's "*Urmph*" said she didn't really approve but understood.

One cool thing that had happened recently was that Kim's relationship with Mitch had blossomed, and she and her kids had moved in with them. The children also adored Twix, so, when Twix wasn't on duty sniffing for explosives or narcotics, she stayed with them. It was better than her bouncing back and forth between Ethan's place and Bert's. Plus, Mitch's place not only had a big yard, but it backed up onto Crown Land, so they could take her out for walks. A dog needed room to run and smell the roses, or animal poop, whatever suited its fancy.

Ethan got up, refreshed Twix's water bowl, and gave her not one, but two doggy treats.

Twix looked at the two treats, and then at him, as if to say *Are you sure about this?* Then, smart dog she was, she picked up one treat and pushed it into his hand before garbling down the other one.

Ethan pretended to eat the treat, then secreted it away for another time. Previously, when he'd thought about his best friends, Twix didn't come to mind, and that was an oversight.

"I love and appreciate you, Twix." He scratched her behind the ears, and she licked his hand affectionately.

Bert came in. "You didn't give her two doggie treats, did you?"

"Who, me? I would never!"

"Ya right," Bert chuckled. "I asked because I gave her two earlier."

"Ah, well, it's okay to spoil her now and then."

The phone rang. It was Angela.

"You didn't get my message yet, did you?"

"Not yet. Sorry, I've been brain dead today and only answering the main line."

"It's kind of a big deal."

"Hang on. Checking out my cell right now." Ethan dug his mobile out of his jacket pocket.

The message said, *Stella from the stables thinks she knows who has Friesians, and they must have a lot of them.*

"I just read the message. Wow! How did she figure it out?"

"I'm here with Stella now; I'll let her explain it to you."

"Okay, please put her on. Thanks, Angela."

"Officer Birchom?"

"Yes, this is Ethan. Please go ahead, Stella. I have you on speakerphone."

"Alright. I'm friends with a doctor of equine medicine, a veterinarian, if you will. She, Paige, specializes in, well, horses, and is an expert in afflictions particular to various breeds. Friesians, as wonderful as they are, often suffer from chronic dermatitis.

225

Someone ordered a lot of triamcinolone spray, hydrocortisone, and a special medicated shampoo.

"The size of the order suggests the purchaser had an urgent need to service ten to fifteen animals. Paige wouldn't allow an order of this size to be placed unless she witnessed some of the horses. She saw them, and I have an address for you."

Ethan quickly grabbed a pen. "Okay, go ahead with the address."

"Box 12, Lonely Lane, Grassylands, BC."

He jotted it down. "Stella, I can't thank you, Angela, and Paige enough for this. It could be the break we need."

"Happy to help. Should I pass the phone back to Angela?"

"Yes, please."

Angela came back online. "I imagine you're going to act on this right away?"

"Absolutely! And before you ask: yes, we're going to bring in reinforcements, and act with an uber-abundance of caution."

"Okay, let me know the particulars, so I can be there."

"Well, I don't know —"

"I'm coming and that's the end of it."

The phone went dead.

"We're cooking with gas, aren't we, Ethan?"

"Major gas, major cooking, Bert."

"I will wrangle up some help."

"Great. I'm going to research this address and send it up the chain of command and to Interpol."

The men set to their tasks. Given that it was late afternoon and the remote location presented logistical challenges, they wouldn't be able to go until noon the following day.

There wasn't time for a tactical reconnaissance flight, so they chartered a Cessna 150 from the local airport, and Bert went up with a local pilot for a bird's-eye view from 3000 feet.

The aerial and satellite imagery showed there wasn't anything extraordinary about the ranch that corresponded to the address. Horse ranches usually had a good-sized home and the standard outbuildings — barn, stable, machine shed, some smaller sheds, corrals, chicken coup, an outhouse or two, etc. There was nothing unique about this ranch at the mountain's foot. It did, however, have an unusually large lawn. Most ranchers didn't have big lawns, but each to their own.

It didn't strike Ethan as a base for a serial-killer cult. *Then again, what would a base for a band of butchers look like?* Chances are they wouldn't be flying the Jolly Roger and have poison symbols painted on their buildings.

Angela's detachment in Elk Point could spare two people, plus Angela. Yes, she was licensed to carry a weapon, but Ethan planned to keep her well away from the action.

That night, Ethan could hardly sleep out of anticipation. Who and how many would be there? Surely Caroline wouldn't be there, would she? And Freepool? Caroline's father? And the 'Numbskulls'? Were they dangerous? The place could be another Waco, only with total whackos.

Ideally, he would have more intel, but waiting would only increase the chance of more innocent lives being lost. And, based on what Caroline had said, information trickling to the Hatchets, giving them time to prepare, destroy evidence, or even flee.

When his alarm went off, Ethan felt like he hadn't slept an hour.

Ethan had a cold shower and burned his tongue on his morning coffee. He then ate a banana so fast he wondered afterwards if he had peeled it first. Just as Ethan was about to pull out of the driveway, his phone beeped. There were multiple new messages.

The gist was that the powers-that-be did not see sufficient evidence to warrant tasking anyone from the CFSEU — the Combined Forces Special Enforcement Unit — and they could only mobilise Emergency Response Team members from Glyph's Gulch, Overlook, and Elk Point.

Their mandate was to visit and investigate, and, providing they gathered sufficient evidence, search or arrest warrants would follow. That he was being supplied any additional resources at all was 'prudent and cautionary.' To read behind the lines:

Nobody wanted to see another 'Reggie' incident. Ethan also wondered if his affair with Caroline might also have caused them to have less-than-100-percent faith in him.

Ethan wanted to reply with *Thanks for nothing* or *You must be fucking kidding me*, but reluctantly typed *Understood. Will advise.*

Once his anger passed, he grudgingly admitted that it made sense. Realistically, what did they really have but circumstantial evidence and 'horse sense'?

Arriving at Brickwallaby, Ethan discovered that apart from himself, only two ERT members, one each from Overlook and Elk Point, were present. Angela and one other officer were from Elk Point, and, of course, there was Bert. Six of them.

It was a skeleton crew.

Everyone introduced themselves to one another, though most had already made acquaintances. It turned out the ERT guys were named Fred and Barney.

Ethan's phone beeped again, this time with a message from Bert.

Barney and Fred? Reggie would've had a field day with that!

Ethan replied, *Flintstones, meet the Flintstones, We're the modern stone age underfunded RCMP.* He saw Bert turn away to hide his snicker.

They gathered inside and formalised plans. *May tomorrow end with arrests and answers.*

Chapter Thirty-Four: Sunk

Ethan gasped as the glacial meltwater swatted him and pushed him under. How did he find himself in the torrent again? Another vicious smack, and he felt his face go from icy-cold to itchy and warm. Was he succumbing to hypothermia? No, he must survive! He had to find her, and them.

"Chelsea!"

As her name burst from his lips and he sucked in a lungful of manure-invested air, Ethan realized he was not in the mountain stream.

"Chelsea. Your daughter, essence long departed, but for a worthy cause."

Another dousing of cold water accompanied the statement, and Ethan opened his eyes. Caroline's father stood looking down at him.

"You killed my little girl?"

"Not really."

"Huh? Who killed her? Where are her remains?"

"Torn asunder, hooves of thunder, driven to Earth, for better births."

Ethan recognized Freepool's voice.

"I'm going to kill you both. I swear to God I'm going to kill you, Freepool! And you too, Leadshit!"

"It's Lead*shat*, but you can call me Hal."

"Figures. Regardless, you're a fucking *dead* man!"

The senior Leadshat stepped aside. "Before or after we pull this lady limb from limb?"

To his horror, Angela hung in the air between two large black horses. Heavy ropes were tied from her ankles to the harness of one horse, while her outstretched arms, secured at the wrists, were connected to another massive and glistening black Friesian.

Ethan looked up at Hal. "No, please, please don't do this."

"Oh, I've no wish to; she's hardly kill-worthy."

"Then why?"

"The horses need work, and the stallion — well, he needs to learn who's boss."

Before Ethan could counter, the old man barked, "Taught!"

Each horse moved a few inches, in opposite directions, and Angela screamed, "Ethan! Help me!"

"Let her go!"

"Why should we?"

"She's innocent."

Freepool now stood beside Caroline's dad, cackling away. "Once divorced, two children, and out here trying to save the likes of you! She should be taking care of her kids or even the ones she's minding. No, she's far, *far* from innocent."

"I'll do anything — let me take her place."

Leadshat and Freepool stepped aside. Their discussion became animated as Ethan looked skyward in the hopes of divine intervention.

Everything had gone so wrong.

#

They had considered taking four vehicles, but given their experience at the Dells, it was reasonable to assume their hosts would have cameras alerting them to people driving up the six-mile long Lonely Lane, which appeared to be the only road access into the ranch. The first five-plus miles looked to be gravel; the last section was paved.

So, three personnel traveled in two Suburbans. Ethan, Barney, and Fred went by helicopter.

They planned for the heli to overfly the ranch at a discrete distance and, minutes later, meet the rest of the team where the gravel entry became paved.

They were counting on an element of surprise.

They counted wrong.

None of them had ever taken fire from an ARM — an anti-materiel rifle. Ethan recognized it for what it was, for he had fired one in his stint in the Canadian Armed Forces.

By the time they saw the person on the ground shooting at them, the tail boom was badly damaged.

"We're taking on fire!"

"Bring us down!" Ethan shouted.

"They've taken out a rear horizontal stabilizer; we're going down, anyway."

As the helicopter plunged downward toward where their vehicles were parked, Ethan could smell fuel.

"Call it in."

"I tried; I can't get through."

The ground was coming fast, and he could see Bert and Angela pointing up at them. About twenty feet off the ground, the cockpit window blew out. Ethan looked over at the pilot. The man lacked a hand on the control stick — in fact, his arm was entirely gone.

They crashed hard, less than two hundred feet from the vehicles. The heli's rotor blades dug into the dirt, disintegrating, and became projectiles. Ethan bent as low as he could and grabbed the door handle.

A sound like a radial arm saw encountering metal sliced through the smoke-filled air. Chunks of matter splattered Ethan as he struggled to get out the door. It wouldn't budge at first, but finally it let go, and he fell to the ground.

Ethan crawled along the ground as fast as he could, then heard a loud *Boom!* as the heli, with Fred and Barney trapped inside, went up in flames. Ethan was then dragged to safety by Bert and Angela's colleague, Jack, from Elk Point.

Together with Angela, they stood there in shock as they watched the helicopter burn uncontrollably.

Ethan looked down at himself. It felt like he was wearing a shirt made of raw hamburger. He ran his fingers through the gore, expecting to encounter a gaping wound, but he was okay — at least physically.

"Call this in, Bert."

Bert jumped into one vehicle, and then a couple minutes later went to the other one.

"I can't call out. I don't understand..."

Ethan tried his cell phone. No signal.

"Everybody, try your phones!"

Nobody could get through.

Ethan heard a whistling sound and then another *Boom!*

"Hit the ground!"

Angela, Bert, and Jack joined him, lying flat on the ground.

The *booms* continued for about two minutes. When they stopped, Ethan saw that the explosions had destroyed the road, along with any access to it from the forest or field.

The heavy rifle fire resumed, riddling the suburban parked closest to the ranch with holes.

"Get in the other truck, now! Stay low; let's go!"

They followed Ethan's lead and got into the truck.

Ethan didn't know what to do. The road behind them was impassable, but to go forward was suicide. He turned the truck off the road and pinned it through the grassy field. Maybe they would spot a trail out.

Five minutes later, they came to an uncrossable stream.

A helicopter appeared, with a man pointing a rifle at them.

"Get down!"

Bullets tore through the front of the truck and the windshield.

Ethan peeked over the dash to see people on horseback, at least six of them, riding up. He swung the vehicle through a barbed-wire fence and started snaking the truck through the trees, gunfire, and horses in hot pursuit.

He took a quick look around. "Is everybody alright?"

Incredibly, they were all okay.

They burst through some trees and into a meadow. Ethan tromped on the gas and then — *Wham!* — they had crashed into a concealed object. Beyond the steam rising from the hood, Ethan could see that horsemen had them surrounded.

Jack jumped out and started shooting. A few seconds later, he spun around from the force of several bullets and hit the ground.

Bert stepped out and held his rifle aloft. "Wait, we surrender!"

A man on a Friesian rode up to Bert. He barked, "Hoof!" The horse rose on two legs, and as it came back down, a giant hoof clattered into Bert's head.

"Stomp!"

The horse stomped twice.

"Oh my God! Oh my God!" Angela cried.

From every direction, rifle barrels pointed at them.

"Let's go. Get out of the vehicle!"

Ethan and Angela obeyed, then everything went dark.

Chapter Thirty-Five: Stretched

"We don't have time for this, Hal!"

Back in the equally horrible present, Hal furrowed his brow at Ethan before saying, matter-of-factly, "You're too conditioned, too boneheaded to see the truth or give up the case, so there's no point plowing that ground. We'll spare your friend, in our fashion, and you can take her place."

"What does 'in your fashion' mean? Will you still kill her?"

"No, but don't go thinking optimistically about her future."

"I have your word?"

"Yes; we will not kill her."

Ethan wouldn't quibble, not with Angela on the cusp of being stretched limb from limb. "Okay, let me take her place."

Freepool was almost drooling.

By command, the horses stepped closer to one another, and Angela sank to the ground.

"Zombie, untie her!"

The zombie person, who Ethan figured must be what Freepool referred to as a Numbskull, slinked over, untied Angela and hauled her away feet first, her head dragging in the dirt.

Then it was Hal dragging Ethan through the dirt and fastening him to the horses. In the distance, Ethan heard Angela yell, "I'm sorry, Ethan!"

Kicked, whipped, and smeared with enough manure that he could barely see, Ethan smirked.

"What on Earth are you smiling about, Copper?" It was Freepool standing over him.

"How you failed to kill me on three tries — three! *'Third time's the charm,'* you wrote! And now, *great slayer of children,* you leave it for horses to do your work. You're a pathetic loser!"

His face absorbed more blows, but it didn't matter; his truth was far harder to take, and Freepool yelled, "Taught!"

The horses didn't move.

Hal issued the same command, and Ethan felt himself lifted off the ground and stretched out.

"Any last words?"

Ethan had to know, had to hear it from the man himself. "Why? Why all of this?"

"For Humanity. For love. For the love of humanity. For these are the hands of horror and the Ten Commandments."

Ethan laughed at him. "Weak! Come up with some new fucking material!"

Hal smiled. "Any other requests?"

"Where is my little girl?"

Hal just shook his head. "Froth and Axel, *stretch*!"

As waves of pain swept through his body, Ethan thought of Chelsea. The pain of losing her and not knowing the truth far outweighed what he was now experiencing. He would see her soon, he knew it, and his parents, and Reggie, maybe also Bert. The realization calmed him, and Ethan spoke loudly, but clearly.

"The end does not justify the means."

He detected people hovering over him, so he said it again.

"The end does not justify the means. It never has, and it never will."

Again, he heard the word '*stretch*,' but instead of the pain becoming worse, it abated.

Was he dying, or dead? He heard himself cry out, "Chelsea! Chelsea! Where are you? I love you, Chelsea. Please forgive me. *Chelsea!*"

He felt his bum hit the ground and the pain ebb slowly from his joints.

What happened?

"Froth is doing what she's told, but Axel is backing up — Whip him! *Whip them both!*" Freepool screamed.

Again, Ethan was lifted off the ground. However, just as he was pulled horizontal, the tension eased, and he sagged down again.

"Axel, what is *wrong* with you?" Hal yelled.

"Taught! *Stretch!*"

The forward motion on one end was counteracted by back-peddling on the other.

Ethan tried to see what was happening, but all he could see was horse's asses. Clearly, though, one of the equines wasn't following orders.

"Unhook the horses. This is not the way."

"The way? The *way*? This has *always* been the way, Hal!"

"Oh, Frea? Coming from you, that's pretty rich. You've violated the code more times than I can count. It's easy to see where Caroline got her temper and irrational behavior from."

"Just because you knocked up your cousin's wife doesn't mean you get to disparage her and the product of your infidelity!"

"You stu— Now is not the time for this, *Rogue!*"

Ethan did not see the slap, but he heard it.

For a minute, there was silence.

"Enough, Frea. *Enough.* We'll finish this — one way or another. Zombie, cut him free."

Ethan slumped to the ground, and once again, he was dragged across the earth.

"Chelsea," was all he could utter, all he could ponder. Cold water splashed against his face, and Ethan regained enough of his vision to see he was being lashed to a corral post. Ethan knew Caroline wouldn't be saving him this time.

Freepool flipped a long hatchet in the air.

"Go ahead, Frea; let your hatchet guide you. I'm going to saddle the fastest Malwari for you, grab my mare, and make for our convoy."

"And then?"

"The wicked shall perish. The enemies of the LORD shall be like the beauty of the fields. They will vanish, vanish like smoke."

"You still remember my favorite scripture."

"That I do, Frea. Until next time, then."

"Until next time."

Ethan heard footsteps retreating, and he wanted to curse them into everlasting hellfire, but all he could do was blurt out, "Your daughter and I loved one another."

Hal stopped, turned his head slightly, and replied, "That mistake can no longer be lived with."

Meanwhile, Freepool had taken ten measured strides away from Ethan and turned to face him. Time, weighed down by impending death, crawled.

The Numbskull brought one of the horses to Hal, and he climbed atop the Friesian. Somewhere, the sound of horses at a gallop, the rumble of a tractor, scraping teeth of a backhoe, chains clinking.

And screaming.

The fine dust kicked up from all the activity in the corral hung suspended, then, ever so slowly, drifted down. It settled on Ethan's brow and caked his lips. All the while, the sun radiated indifference — except where it reflected off the hatchet's edge as it swung from Freepool's swaying arm.

Ethan's eyes met those of Hal Leadshat just before the man turned his horse to ride away. Ethan would've spat at him if he could've summoned the moisture.

When he looked back toward Freepool, a hatchet was tumbling through the air. They had taped his forehead to a post, but he turned his head just a fraction and the axe missed — mostly.

"*Just* missed."

Frea pulled the hatchet from the wooden rail. "The next one will be right between the eyes."

She picked up a bloody, wrinkled blob off the ground. "You won't be needing this." She tucked what must be part of his right ear in her shirt pocket.

"You might call it a memento. I call it a chunk of ear."

"I call it five — *five* — times you've failed. What's your proverb now, you psycho bitch? 'Sixth time's the charm?'"

Freepool laughed, but Ethan judged it as fake and as her fraudulent ideology. The monster licked her lips, smiling, and reached back as she fluidly moved into a crouch.

Ethan knew she wouldn't miss this time, but he wasn't looking away; he wouldn't give her the satisfaction.

Then, just as her weight shifted forward to propel the axe, a puzzled look came over her face. Like a plywood cutout, Freepool teetered and tottered. Their eyes met as she fell face forward into the dirt, his stub of ear squirting out of her pocket. An axe was imbedded in her back.

Behind her, the Numbskull that Leadshat had called 'Zombie' was in the follow-through position of an axe toss.

Ethan looked at the woman, but before he could say 'Thank you', she said, "Papa?"

Chapter Thirty-Six: Road Rage

"Wake up, Ethan, wake up!"

He felt himself being shaken. "Huh, ya?"

Ethan sensed ropes being pulled across and away from his torso, and even winced as some chest hair went with them.

"You fainted." It was Angela's voice.

Fainted! Ethan had heard of people fainting, but he thought it involved wearing Victorian clothes while witnessing a guillotine.

"Uh, *wuss* move," he muttered.

"Probably, the rope they had around your neck pinched your carotid artery."

"Oh."

Recollection — or was it imagination? — crept into his consciousness. Had the chaos and pain combined to produce a hallucination? No, a father would recognize his daughter, even after eighteen years.

"Chelsea?"

"Who? What?" Angela frowned.

Ethan started to rub his temples to clear his head but recoiled in pain. His right hand was bloody from touching where his right ear was or used to be, but the pain sharpened his mind.

"The Zombie. The Numbskull."

"The one who saved us and killed Freepool? She's in custody. They just put her in an ambulance. Not sure about her injuries. Bert's with her."

"Bert's alive?"

"The guy has a head of granite and a steel frame. Headache, and some broken ribs, but he'll be okay. Thank goodness the house had a landline we could use to call for help."

Thank the Heavens, Bert's okay!

"But, the woman — the girl — the Zombie…It's Chelsea." Ethan started to get up, but the strong hand of an EMT held him back.

"Please, sir, not so fast. We need to address your wounds and check you out."

"I'm getting up."

The EMT shrugged and Angela helped Ethan to his feet. Immediately, he stumbled toward the departing ambulance, only to find himself face-down in the dirt.

Again, Angela was there to help him, this time untying the rope around his ankle.

Getting up, he thanked her and added, "Angela, please listen to me. That Zombie…" he corrected himself, "That young lady…the one that saved us, is Chelsea — *my* Chelsea."

"Oh…kay."

"We need to follow that ambulance. I can't let her out of my sight, not again."

"I'll drive. Let Tim wrap your head and check you out. Apart from your missing ear, your face is pretty chewed up. Get in the backseat; I put your ear on ice."

Ethan didn't argue, and with Tim, the EMT, at his side, he bailed into the back seat of Angela's vehicle.

Angela pinned it, and ten minutes later, they were right behind the ambulance.

"Borrow your phone, Angela?"

Angela passed her phone back to him, and Ethan dialed Bert.

"Hello?"

"How is she?"

"Ethan?"

"Yes. That's *my girl* you have in there. How is she?"

There was a pause, and then "Chelsea?"

"Yes."

"Seriously? I'm afraid that axe lady took off more than your ear."

"Nope. It's Chelsea, Bert. Believe me. How is she?"

He heard Bert ask the EMT how the patient was.

"Says she's in stable condition."

"Good. Be ready for anything. I have a feeling we're not out of the woods yet. Anybody in front of you?"

"No."

"Okay. Unlikely they would return to what we left behind, so we'll swing in front of you."

"Understood."

"Who else do we have available?"

"Not sure."

"Call Derek, have him go down for support. Yes, I know he's a civilian, but under the circumstances…"

"Roger."

"Hold up, Ethan. Vehicles are blocking the road ahead."

"Describe."

"One looks like a jackknifed dual-axel truck with a horse trailer. The other is a big SUV, maybe a small pickup."

"Slow up and let us go ahead of you."

"Roger."

"Pulling out front."

"Copy that."

"Oh, and Bert. I am *so glad* that you're alright."

"You too, Ethan."

Ethan had Angela creep past the slowing ambulance, and just ahead, he spied a long snake lying across the road with spiky segments that caught the light.

"Stop! Nail belt! Stop!"

Angela hit the brakes, and they skidded to a stop just before the spiky obstacle would've flattened their tires.

"Good job, Angela!"

Ethan wanted nothing more than to check on Chelsea, but, as it so often did, practicality forced his hand. He had a duty to protect the public and those under his charge, so Ethan got out of the vehicle to check out the scene. He crouched beside Angela's SUV and heard the distinctive, yet distant *chop-chop-chop* of a helicopter. Turkey vultures and large, black corvids appeared overhead, and the sound of wounded animals bawling filled the air.

He yelled toward the two vehicles blocking the road, "This is the RCMP! Step away from the vehicles. If you're injured, we can help."

There was no response, only the plaintive wails of animals in agony.

Ethan observed the horse trailer behind the dually. It was up on one of its two wheels at a twenty-degree angle, wedged against a road sign.

Angela got out of the car.

He shook his head at her. "Wait, please, Angela. If things should go sideways, please make sure Chelsea gets to the hospital."

"Will do."

As Ethan crept forward, he heard an ambulance door slam shut. He looked over his shoulder to see Bert, head and chest taped up, slowly moving up beside him.

"You look a mess, Bert."

"Says the man that looks *and* smell like shit."

Ethan smiled at him. *Even that hurt!*

"Anything, Ethan?"

"No, but I'll try again." Once more, Ethan bellowed, "This is the RCMP. Step away from the vehicles If you're hurt, we can help!"

The only response was groans and *neighs*.

"We'll check out the dually first, Bert. You take driver's door; I'll be on your right."

"Roger."

They proceeded stealthily to the Dodge Ram. Nobody was inside.

"All clear, Ethan."

"All clear in the rig, Bert."

Ethan looked into the canopy of the vehicle and saw a heavy sniper rifle — or, perhaps, the same ARM that had brought down their helicopter.

His eyes moved past the blood-spattered hood; it was clear what had caused the accident and what was making the mournful sounds: Five elk lay on the road, and two were still kicking.

They holstered their weapons, and Bert moved past the front of the truck as Ethan stepped over the hitch that joined the horse trailer to the truck.

Between two dead elk, a man, covered in blood with only one usable arm, was giving CPR to an elk calf.

Ethan walked over; the man, blood spurting out of his various wounds, was counting chest compressions. Ethan rested a hand on his shoulder, but a withering, side-eyed glance caused Ethan to draw back. The man moved off to the side of the calf and was breathing into its mouth but couldn't move his damaged arm up so his hand could cover its nostrils. Ethan bent low and pressed his hand over the elk's nostrils. The wounded man gave the animal two breaths and then remounted it to press hard on its chest.

Visibly exhausted and losing blood fast, the man toppled over, and the young elk bounced up and ran away. Ethan knelt by the man, who looked to be in his thirties, and checked his pulse. It was weak.

The man slurred, "thirteen, fourteen, fifteen… sixteen…" and then died.

"Whoa." Bert's appraisal echoed Ethan's thoughts about the event.

Neither shock nor trauma can explain what we've just witnessed.

Then Chelsea was there. *His* Chelsea. There was no doubt about it, now. She got down on her haunches beside Ethan and stared down at the dead man. "They called him 'The Count.' I used to know his real name, before…"

Ethan looked at his daughter, his little girl swept away by years — and who knew what else? Her eyes were the same color but lacked their spark. And her face was tanned and strong, not like the rosy-cheeked girl he remembered. Still, she was his daughter.

"You remember me, Chelsea?" Ethan's voice quivered.

"A little. Enough."

Ethan threw his arms around her and after briefly pulling back, Chelsea put an arm around him.

Her hand caressed his head as it lay on her shoulder, his tears wetting her hemp blouse.

"We have to help Axel."

He reluctantly pried his head off her tear-soaked shoulder. "Axel?"

"The horse that saved you. Come." She stood and extended her hand, which he took — though it was Bert's arm around his waist that got him to his feet.

Chelsea pointed at the horse trailer.

Ethan took two deep breaths. He looked around; the crows were already picking away at the dead elk.

Bert, one arm now tucked around his own ribcage, stepped gingerly around a dead elk, and held up his torn RCMP jacket to stop an approaching vehicle. Ethan cast his view to the right to see Angela setting up cones and caution tape. A pang of guilt hit him.

I should be out front taking charge…

Chelsea's strong, calloused hand squeezed his own. "Come."

244

Her voice and touch vanquished his previous doubts. Where she would go, he would follow.

As they approached the horse trailer, he heard a blowing sound. Chelsea said, "It's okay, Axel," and was met by a soft whinny.

Arriving at the back of the trailer, Chelsea jerked at the door. It was locked.

"Keys; I will see if I can find the keys. They might be in the ignition."

Chelsea shrugged.

Ethan did a cursory search of the truck; no keys.

"I could check the dead — The Count."

Chelsea shook her head. "Not enough time. Can't you just use that?"

She motioned at the gun he didn't even realize he was holding.

"It'll scare the horse."

"Not this one." Chelsea whispered to the horse and then pointed at the lock. The meaning was clear.

Ethan moved Chelsea back, and after maneuvering to the side to eliminate the chance of a ricochet, he blasted off the lock.

Chelsea threw the doors open and then motioned for Ethan to stand back.

Slowly, but gracefully, a big black horse backed out from the trailer. The Friesian stallion was easily the most magnificent animal Ethan had ever seen.

Chelsea reached into the trailer and pulled out a carrot, which the horse ate gingerly from her hand. After that, the black beauty nuzzled Chelsea's neck.

"You can touch him if you want."

Whether Ethan sought a connection to Chelsea through the horse, or simply wished to interact with such a majestic creature, he wasn't sure, but Ethan placed his hand on the horse's neck.

Chelsea's hand glided over to his and his hand overlapped hers as they petted Axel in unison.

Immediately, his mind went back to the time Chelsea had saved a small foal, and Ethan realized that the colt that licked his face then was now looking him in the eye. Together, they had all saved one another; it was as undeniable as Ethan's love for his daughter. Ethan threw his arms around the horse's neck and hugged him.

A persistent voice dissipated the moment and the memory. It was Angela.

"Uh, sorry to interrupt, Ethan, but Stella is going to bring her truck and horse trailer. We'll look after him."

"Axel."

"Yes, Axel. We'll make sure Axel is well-cared for, Chelsea."

Chelsea looked at her. "I remember you, Angela...you're still pretty."

With that, Chelsea slipped down to her haunches. She stared off somewhere, or — judging by the look on her face — nowhere.

The EMT was there again. "She needs rest and her wounds treated, as do you, sir."

Only then did Ethan notice that Chelsea's shirt was torn and that she had a cut on her side. *How did I not see that before?* Instantly, Ethan felt overwhelming guilt... guilt for not protecting Chelsea, for allowing her to be stolen, for not doing enough to find out what happened to her.

Bert also strode up. "Angela and I will take care of this, Ethan. You two go. I've arranged for Derek to escort you to the hospital."

"Are you sure? Maybe you should ride in the ambulance too, Angela; you've been through a lot."

"I'm fine. Don't worry about me. And Bert's skull probably only hurt the horse's hoof."

The distant sound of rotor blades curtailed that discussion.

"Not again!"

They were coming back to finish the job.

Ethan turned to Bert. "Bert, I know you're hurt, but I might need your help getting something out of that truck."

"What?"

"An AMR."

"A what?"

"An anti-materiel rifle. It's what took down our heli."

"I'll help you — even if it kills me."

The gun only weighed about fifty pounds, so Ethan managed it himself, though Bert helped him set it up on the ground.

"How do we know it's them?"

"We don't, but if it is..."

As the heli got closer, bullets plastered the pavement. His peripheral vision caught Chelsea pulling Axle behind the horse trailer for safety.

"It's them alright!" Ethan, partly shielded by the truck, got down behind the AMR.

As the green Robinson came around, Ethan was sure he could see Hal Leadshat at the controls. A man in the passenger seat had a rifle pointed straight at Ethan.

A bullet took out a chunk of asphalt by his left knee. Ethan smiled and pulled the trigger.

Hellfire was unleashed. Ethan saw red splatter the interior of the helicopter's protective bubble, and the green dragonfly of death burst into flames. As it descended, Ethan tracked it with the gun and kept on firing. What was left of it disintegrated into the ground and Ethan kept on shooting. He fingered the trigger until the AMR's magazine was empty. *Is there another clip in the truck? I need more!*

Bert rested his hand on his shoulder. "I think you got them, Ethan."

Chelsea looked at him with wonder and then gave him a thumbs up.

Chapter Thirty-Seven: Rewind

The staff had stitched his forehead back together and sewed what they could of Ethan's ear back on, and father and daughter were released from the hospital at the same time. The old doctor bear-hugged Ethan like a long-lost son and, in his good ear, whispered "Thank you." As for Chelsea's injuries, they were superficial, save for the ones buried deep in her psyche. Some of the resident psychologist's point-form notes scrolled over in Ethan's mind:

- PTSD
- Low self-esteem
- Years of sensory deprivation may result in hallucinations.
- Vulnerable to authority figures
- Possible memory impairment
- No sexual trauma
- Cognitive functions relatively normal and trending to the positive

Focus on the good, Ethan. In time, Chelsea will be fine.

She also had a quarter of a lifetime to make up for... *How to make up for that?*

On the way home, they drove past the cemetery.

"I want to see my grave."

"Are you sure?"

"Yes."

They parked and walked over to Chelsea's headstone.

"That must've been hard."

"It was, but I came to visit you a lot."

Chelsea reached over and took his hand, then pointed at the grave. "I believe it. What's down there, if not me?"

"Just a small box of stuff you liked: keepsakes, toys, a few pictures. Your mom and I weren't sure what else to put in it; we were so messed up at the time..."

"That makes sense. When can we dig it up? I'd like my stuff, and to get rid of that headstone. It's so morbid."

"That it is. I will make the arrangements."

"Thanks, Papa."

He put his arm over her shoulder, which was now at least eighteen inches higher than it had been before, and she put her arm around his waist.

Standing with his daughter, looking at her headstone, might've been the strangest thing Ethan had ever experienced, and given all that occurred over the past few months, that was saying a lot.

"Papa, I don't want to come here again."

Driving home, Ethan barely touched the gas pedal. Chelsea was glued to the window, looking about, then back at him, then looking out again. Halfway home, her head sunk low. It was all too much. Ethan reached over and rubbed her back. She cried uncontrollably for the next two hours, and there was nothing he could do.

Later that evening, Chelsea caught up with her mom, though they only spoke for about twenty minutes. Chelsea was exhausted, and her mother was overcome with emotion. Alice was going to give Chelsea a couple of weeks to adapt before joining her. Totally drained, Chelsea went to bed shortly after the call ended.

After Chelsea fell asleep, Ethan called Alice. They agreed that Chelsea's well-being was a priority. The question *What happened to you and mom?* would come up, and they had to be on the same page about it. They didn't break up because of her, or her disappearance and presumed death.

In Chelsea's vulnerable state, they couldn't allow her to think their divorce was her fault. She didn't need that guilt weighing on her mind. The truth was, he and Alice hadn't been doing that well anyway, a function of his work and her longstanding desire to pursue an arts degree. Alice ended up getting her degree, was passionate about her sculpting, and had remarried eight years ago.

After they'd had Chelsea, Ethan had talked about having one more child, but Alice didn't want to entertain the prospect. Of course, Alice loved Chelsea, and didn't regret having her, but of the two, Ethan was the more parental. Ethan's stepsister lived in Yellowknife, and she and her husband had five kids.

Alice was the lone child of divorced parents. Yes, Chelsea's 'death' brought an official end to their marriage, but the writing had already been on the wall. At least, that was going to be their story, and they would stick to it.

With that challenging call concluded, Ethan waded into his emails and messages.

The amount to do and digest was overwhelming. Also, nearly crushing, was the fact that, for eighteen years, Chelsea had probably never been more than two hours away from him. He was going to have to live with that — but at least she was alive. *That*, Ethan could easily and happily live with.

He turned his black-and-blue eyes, set below a whip-scarred and h-carved forehead, back to the paperwork.

The gist of it was that the bodies from the Robinson that Ethan had shot to pieces couldn't be identified. Ethan wasn't positive if Hal had escaped him in life or in death. However, he was sure the man he'd seen piloting the Robinson was Hal Leadshat, and that was enough for him.

DNA analysis was being performed on the deceased, and the RCMP and Interpol were working on identifying all the participants and establishing a plan to bring down the larger organization, however and wherever it existed. In the sprawling complex beneath the lawn, searchers had found six Numbskulls in a recreation room, snacking on dried fruit and trail mix, watching — but not laughing at — Looney Tunes.

Authorities were working on identifying the individuals and reuniting them with their families. Ground-penetrating radar suggested there were over forty graves on the Dell property in the US. They also found a trunk in the barn with seven skulls in it — six humans and one horse.

The place had been vacant for at least a year. Interestingly, there was a humongous fire pit, and they dated some charcoal back to the early nineteenth century. How the Leadshat's discovered Ethan was coming had yet to be revealed.

Ethan hadn't been aware that the RCMP had deployed an ERT. They'd killed four people holed up in a cabin. Word was, those Leadshat holdouts had a Gatling gun that had malfunctioned, but they wouldn't be taken alive. The authorities captured some Numbskulls, but they'd had nothing to say.

A large cache of weapons and a sprawling concrete-reinforced housing and combat-training complex lay under the lawn. An artesian well fed both the house and the underground Doomsday dwelling. It was estimated that there were enough provisions to keep twenty people alive for several years.

Additionally, there was a large hydroponic operation that grew both foods and drugs. Authorities had yet to investigate all subsurface anomalies and were trying to crack into the handful of computers and hard drives that were left behind. Ultimately, the RCMP had only scratched the surface.

Funerals for the lost police officers were scheduled, and Ethan would attend them all. Near the end of what he browsed, though there was more there, he read that DNA analysis conclusively showed that Frea Pool was indeed Caroline's biological mother.

Ethan perused the photos of those unfortunates imprisoned and brainwashed by the Leadshats. One picture jumped out at him: The woman was about fifty years old, but she reminded him of someone.

He dove into his file folder of missing out-of-province teenagers and brought up two photos of Josie Daniels. Josie had gone missing somewhere between Vancouver and the Long Plains First Nation in Manitoba in 1993. *If that woman isn't Josie Daniels, I will eat the kayak in our evidence room!*

Ethan immediately sent his thoughts up the chain of command. Fingers crossed, he was right, and Josie's family could be located, and Josie rehabilitated.

Even as he sent that communique, more emails and report reminders were coming in. If the Leadshats hadn't killed him by gun, hatchet, or horse-stretch, bureaucracy was going to render him dead. For the first time, Ethan gave serious thoughts to quitting the force. He didn't know what he would do, but he'd figure something out.

To take his mind off things, he texted Bert, Angela, and Kim.

Bert was doing well — nursing sore ribs, but still using the treadmill and determined to enter some sort of cross-fit competition the following spring. The guy was an absolute machine!

Angela, sweet and supportive superstar that she was, had been busy finding permanent homes for the critters at the Leadshat estate, organizing fundraisers for those people lost in action, *and*, somehow, baking more carrot cakes. Angela was, as her name implied, an angel. It made Ethan think of Freepool and their philosophical discussion of Angels. *Take that, you Monster Biblical Bitch!*

Kim, who had already been in contact with Chelsea, was doing great. She and Mitch had big plans for his store, and they all sounded great, literally, and musically. Ethan was certain that interacting with Kim would help Chelsea's recovery immensely — and Kim would have her old best friend back. In fact, they were hanging out today at Drop the Needle. Music was known to work magic with the mind, so Ethan was optimistic today would be a good day for the girls.

The remainder of the day droned away with duties. When Ethan got home, he found Chelsea already fast asleep, and that helped him get a decent night's rest, for a change.

#

The following morning, Ethan made a full pot of coffee. It was quiet, unusually quiet. Kim was at Mitch's and Twix was with Bert. Ethan drank two mugs before Chelsea even got up. Then he thought, *Wait, maybe she hasn't had coffee before, or she might prefer tea?*

After glancing at the coffee pot and dwelling on how his parents loved coffee and his sister loved coffee, and *he* loved coffee, Ethan chuckled. No, Chelsea was a blood relative, she wouldn't be drinking tea!

Ethan hoped she still liked his pancakes.

When Chelsea came into the kitchen wearing pajamas decorated with SpongeBob SquarePants' characters, though, all she wanted was water. There was so much he needed to learn about and adjust to with his daughter!

They sat there like, well, *Numbskulls,* for a few minutes; then thankfully, mercifully, she spoke.

"You know that feeling or state when you're not quite dreaming, yet not quite awake?"

Ethan nodded. "Yes."

"Well, it was like that, except that you couldn't will yourself one way or another. Somehow — with drugs or spells — they kept us in that limbo land."

An examination of toxicology reports done on her, The Count, and individuals rescued at the Leadshat ranch told Ethan that naturally-occurring psychedelics played a key role in turning people into 'Numbskulls.'

"Sounds like a twisted form of suspended animation."

As they had learned from a wad of material found in The Count's stomach, a melange of potentially mind-altering substances — including select herbs, cacti, mushrooms, and honey — were largely, if not entirely, responsible for the state Chelsea and other Numbskulls found themselves in. There were also traces of venom, possibly from scorpions or wasps, and even bufotoxin from a toad — and *lots* of protein.

It seemed that Numbskulls ate well, and except for some minor cuts and bruises and memory loss, Chelsea was in excellent physical health.

Chelsea was staring out the window like she did on the ride home from the hospital and on yesterday's trip to the record store. Her psychologist, Evaline, said it was going to take Chelsea a while to fully come back to the land of the living — to be present in the moment. Thankfully, Chelsea adored the lady and enjoyed the therapy.

"You've always had such a resilient spirit, Chelsea. That you survived that nightmare just shows how strong you are."

"Actually, it didn't *seem* like a nightmare. It was like being stuck in a dream, or a dream within a dream. I didn't really have a sense of time passing. There was day and there was night. There was work and there were the animals. Evaline believes my interactions with the animals, especially Axel, were key in keeping my sense of self and not going bonkers."

"Makes sense. As for Axel, I'll always be thankful for him."

"I think he feels the same way about us. We built a connection when he was just a colt. Imagine what he's seen... and yet, when ordered to hurt you, he wouldn't. We were also *his* chance to escape."

"I never thought of it that way. Maybe all the drugs they gave you allowed you to see some things us mere mortals can't. I've read that altered states of consciousness can be beneficial."

"Well, maybe I could start up a 'Numbskull School for Dumbies' and get you a course for, like, half price?" She poked him playfully in the ribs.

Her mood shifted abruptly. "Besides, I don't even have a high school diploma or any skills that anybody would want."

She sank into her chair and sobbed, then cozied up next to him. Ethan kissed her on the head, like he had when she was eleven. Eleven or twenty-nine, she was still his little girl.

"Can we go see Axel now? He must be lonely and confused. Who knows, maybe they even drugged *him*, and he's going through withdrawals?"

Ethan hadn't thought of that either, and his empathy and investigative interests were simultaneously activated. *I'm definitely going to have Angela ask the veterinarian about that!*

"We can't today, sweetie. Angela texted me and said Stella's Stables is closed today. Plus, there is limited space there."

Chelsea's bottom lip sagged, and she said, "That's cry-ogenic, man."

"*Cry-ogenic*? Like, sad?"

"Yes, Papa. You really need to get out more and get with the times."

Chelsea's quip produced a smile on both their faces.

"You ain't wrong. Let me guess, you heard that word at Drop the Needle?"

"Yeppers, but I think it sounds cool. Anyway, I wish we could do something for Axel. Like Twix, Axel's practically a member of the family, right?"

Ethan nodded. "You're one hundred percent right about that. Anyway, I do have an idea. I met this nice man named Mr. Stuberman. He has a lot of land and a nice barn. It's an hour away, but it's a pleasant drive. He might be able to help us, as in Axel, you, and me, out."

"That sounds great! You the man with the plan, Papa!"

She got up and gave him a hug and then sat on his lap, almost knocking over his coffee cup.

"Oops!"

"No harm, no foul."

She brushed his hair back and said, "I really love you, Papa."

"I love you too."

Chelsea got up and poured herself a cup of coffee.

"Umm… what do I do with this? Sugar and cream?"

"If you want. You could try it black."

She took a couple sips. "OMG, this is great! I don't think it needs anything!"

"Well, you are sweet enough as you are, so I guess that explains why you don't need sugar."

"Aww, thanks! I'm not cry-ogenic anymore."

"Good. Oh, I forgot to mention that Mr. Stuberman has a horse."

"So, Axel would have a friend! Yippee! But it's too bad they took all the other Friesians away."

"Oh, about that. It appears the arrangements for one mare and one colt fell through. If I can swing it, we'll keep them at Stuberman's."

"For serious?"

"Yeah, but I won't know for a few days. I'm trying to get a sponsor involved. It costs a lot to keep and maintain horses."

"You can do it! I believe in you!"

Chelsea got up and, like she had when she was a kid, spun around in a circle with her arms outstretched.

For the average twenty-nine-year-old, it might be strange; for a young lady that had been in suspended animation for two decades, it was delightful. In time, Chelsea would become more mature, but as she had missed so much, it was going to take a while.

Ethan was going to be there for her as much as humanly possible. Thankfully, they had Angela and Kim. They would be invaluable resources to an eleven-year-old going on eighteen, and approaching thirty.

Suddenly self-conscious, Chelsea shrunk her head down a little into her neck. "I guess that might've been a bit weird."

"Heck, no; watch this!"

Ethan got up and did a series of pirouettes, flailing his arms and doing awkward kicks. He did enough turns that when he stopped, he stumbled around, dizzy, for several seconds, until he had to sit down on the kitchen floor.

Chelsea started to laugh and minutes later they were both on the floor and laughing hysterically. When they finally stopped laughing, Ethan's gut hurt. Yet, he felt awesome.

They lay there and smiled at one another.

"Where or where did you learn that?"

"It was post-Bolshoi, when I did solo ballet appearances."

Again, Chelsea chuckled.

"Ballet? That's so funny! I was thinking more like Riverdance, except instead of Michael Flatley, Elaine Benes from Seinfeld, and her little kicks."

Ethan started to giggle, and then surprise took over.

"You — you remember all that?"

Chelsea looked around, seemingly surprised. "Yah… strange, huh? It's like with every tear or laugh with you, I remember more."

They got to their knees and after sharing a hug, sat down and quietly, and happily finished their coffee.

If tears and laughter helped Chelsea remember things, she would remember a lot over the coming days, weeks, months, and years.

Chapter Thirty-Eight: Figurine

It felt like a lost cause trying to catch up with all the communications and reports. Ethan had been at it for three hours and was seemingly getting nowhere when Chelsea crept in, holding two to-go cups of coffee, and his set of truck keys.

She sat the cups on the edge of his desk and jingled the keys. "I also made bologna sandwiches."

"Hint taken." Ethan happily closed his laptop. *That shit can wait.*

"Let's drive out to where we might keep the horses."

"Are you sure? I mean, if you're too busy, we can go tomorrow."

"I'm sure."

They were halfway to Clark Stubermans when Ethan decided it was time to show his daughter the item he'd been clinging to all these years.

He dug into his coat pocket and placed his horse figurine on the dash.

Chelsea glommed onto it and looked at him for an explanation.

"I've held onto it for years. It was always in my pocket to remind me of you. Just recently, I put it on that piece of obsidian you bought me when you were ten."

He was expecting a major bonding moment, but Chelsea exclaimed, "I remember! This is how it happened."

"What?"

"Can you pull over?"

Ethan moved to the side of the road.

Chelsea stared at the figurine in her hands. "I was sitting in Pleasant Park and looked up to see a boy on a park bench. He was about five years older than me." Chelsea shrugged. "He was holding the same style horse ornament I had. You remember mine."

Ethan nodded.

"I was about to ask him about it and then, suddenly, he got up and walked away. It was strange, but I followed him. I felt I needed to know why he had the same horsey as me.

He rounded a corner, and for a moment, trees blocked my view of him. Then, I saw this woman grab him and put something over his mouth. The boy went limp. I screamed.

"The woman dropped the boy and ran after me. I tried hard to get away, I really did, but she was so fast and so strong…"

Tears were streaming down Chelsea's face, and she was shaking.

"I know you did your best, sweetie. It's okay, you're safe now."

"Holy cow!"

"What?"

"I just realized that the boy was The Count! His real name was Jeremy. I heard him say it."

"That's incredible! And knowing his first name will really help us find his family."

"I remember Jeremy lying there and thinking, 'Is he dead?' and then suddenly I was asleep."

"What do you remember after that?"

"I recall a van door opening and seeing Jeremy asleep. I don't know why he was still sleeping, when I was awake, but I sprang for the door made a run for it. Unfortunately, I only made it about fifteen feet before a rope was around me and they had me tied up. Then they — the woman I now know was Freepool, an older man, and a beautiful dark-haired young woman — all started arguing about our fate.

"The older man said something about 'the sacrifice' being 'tainted.' Freepool just wanted to kill us and be done with it, but the younger woman objected. As they argued, I got out of the rope and started wriggling under the van, hoping to make an escape. Freepool snatched me by the ankle.

"'I like her feisty nature,' the man said. Freepool agreed and said something about me being an excellent Numbskull.

"I remember looking at the younger woman and saying, 'Please, just let me go.' She only looked down and walked away. I remember seeing sadness in her eyes…I felt sorry for her — which, thinking about it now, sounds crazy. I don't remember much after that."

Ethan opened his console, pulled out an envelope, and took out a picture.

"Is this the younger woman you saw? Keep in mind, she's older now."

"Yes; that's her."

"That is Caroline Leadshat."

"The American sheriff...*the* Caroline that was your girlfriend?"

"Yes."

There was a pause; Ethan felt like throwing up, and the feeling was made worse by the thought she might ask —

"Did you love her?"

Ethan stared out the window, sickened by the truth of it all, but knowing he couldn't lie to his daughter. "I hate to admit it, but yes, I did. Not anymore. I'm so sorry, Chelsea. I should've seen her for what she was."

Chelsea looked at him and smiled, a genuine smile that eased his inner turmoil. "You couldn't have known, Dad. Maybe that's why I had some empathy for her back then, because somewhere inside her was goodness, a humanity she nourished in a secret place, a place she let *you* see. Plus, she was *hot!*"

Ethan couldn't help but laugh. "You better hook me up some of those psychedelics they had you on because," he voiced a *kaboom* and mimed his head exploding, "that was some serious wisdom and maturity there, girl!"

"Thanks. It's going to take me a while to even understand love."

That was probably true; *so much of her life had been stolen!* Thankfully, her innocence and sharp wit remained.

"As I'm sure you are already tired of hearing, 'baby steps.'"

"Yep, I'm baby-stepped out!" She laughed and passed the figurine and picture back to him.

"Anyway, shall we see what Mr. Stuberman can do for us?"

"Absolutely!"

#

As Ethan had hoped and expected, Clark was all for it.

"I couldn't be happier to help! I've got lots of room and plenty of land. All I ask is that you pay for their winter feed and take care of vet bills."

Ethan had already reached a deal with Paige, the veterinarian, and since he was going to install a security system, free of charge, at Stella's Stables, Stella was going to make sure he got bedding and hay for rock-bottom prices.

"That works for us — doesn't it, Chelsea?"

Chelsea's smile said it all: She was over the moon about it. "Mr. Stuberman, is it okay if I give you a hug?"

"For sure you can, young lady."

Chelsea gave him a big hug.

They talked for a while but had to pass on an afternoon snack. Ethan had too many things to do, and Chelsea wanted to see Axel and share the wonderful news.

He elected to take a slightly different route home, one that would take him by Aaron Dell's neighbors; the Quallie's and Nabler's.

As Ethan drove slowly by the driveway to the Quallie's, he noticed a 'for sale' sign with a 'sold' banner across it. It was surprising, but if they thought he'd been on to their possible fentanyl-opioid gig, they would've been motivated sellers. Maybe they just missed Australia, though; he'd heard of Aussies moving to Canada and then rushing home a short time later.

Five minutes later, they parked at the bottom of the lane that led to the Nablers. The mailbox was stuffed, so Ethan thought he'd better investigate.

They rolled up to the Nabler house. It was quiet. A drape had been pulled across their big bay window and a curtain rod over another window was askew, the curtain bunched up on and hanging in the center of the window.

"Wait here, Chelsea — this doesn't smell right. Keep the doors locked until I get back."

"Okay."

The screen door to the house was closed, but the main door behind it was open.

"Hello. Mr. and Mrs. Nabler. This is Ethan, Constable Ethan Birchom."

Through the door's window, he could see empty boxes in the living room. Angling to the side, he spotted broken glass on the kitchen floor. "Probable cause," he muttered to himself.

"Are you okay in there? This is the RCMP. I'm coming in!" Ethan waited a moment and then depressed the latch. It wasn't locked.

He walked into the kitchen; a basket of biscuits with a napkin mostly covering them and a teapot with one cup were in the middle of the table.

One more time, he called out, "Anybody home?"

Nothing.

There was a note on the table. *Oh, no, here it is: bad news…hopefully not a murder suicide.*

"Sorry we had to go, Mr. Birchom. You're a good man; blind to the truth, but a good man. You have our permission to keep Axel and any other horse you like on our property. That said, that Stuberman fellah might be okay with you using his land and barn. Regardless, we've got some fine grassland, and we paid the power and taxes to the end of 2029. You sure chopped down that chopper, Copper!"

Ethan sat down in a chair, dumbfounded. The nice, sweet old couple were complete frauds. Why, they might've even been involved in killing the Dells!

He resolved to get Bert to examine the place.

Ethan turned the note over. On the back it read, "Eat, drink, and be merry, for tomorrow we die. - Ecclesiastes 8:15 and Isaiah 22:13."

Ethan sealed the door with caution tape and messaged Bert.

He had been tricked, fooled, and bamboozled one too many times. It was mostly dumb luck he was still alive. Tomorrow, Ethan planned to submit his resignation letter. He'd receive a full pension — and have plenty of time for Chelsea.

Chapter Thirty-Nine: Room to Run

Axel and Susanna, one of Angela's three Morgans, were offloaded into a paddock at Clark Stuberman's. Axel took an immediate liking to Susanna. Angela had explained to Ethan that Moriesians, a cross between Friesians and Morgans, were a hot commodity; as she put it, Moriesians 'boast the intelligence and elegance of the Friesian with the utilitarian nature of the Morgan.'

As he and Angela watched Chelsea ride Axel through the high grass toward a distant hill — with Twix running along — Ethan felt the question coming on even as Angela posed it.

"Do you think they'll ever come after us? And by 'us,' I mean mostly you and Chelsea."

Ethan took the chunk of grass out of his mouth that he had been chewing on and replied. "No, I don't think they will. Nothing to gain from it but revenge, and as deranged as they and their ideology are, I don't see them being motivated by that. Plus, attention is the *last* thing they want. I wager they'll go to ground and, when they think the time is right, reconstitute."

"Plus, we're probably too old and *impure* to bother eliminating."

"Well, you're certainly not in either of *those* categories, Angela."

"Thanks, dear, ahem, I mean, Ethan."

She smiled affectionately as he threw his arm over her shoulder.

"Always, beautiful."

By this time, Axel, Twix, and Chelsea had reached the knoll that was Chelsea's goal for the day.

"Do you think Interpol, or some other agency will nab that lousy lot of Leadshats?"

Ethan grabbed another long stem of grass to nibble on.

"Well, we got some of them. Plus, Interpol now has a lot of info on them and their operation, so, I believe, in time, they will face justice."

"You may be right, but then again, look at Caroline; she and, presumably, some others, *were* police. It explains why they were always a step ahead of us. That implies a complex organization."

"Valid points, Angela, but I believe good will win out."

"It's refreshing to hear you talk like that."

"It's the optimistic, post-RCMP me. Oh, and though I've said it before, I just can't thank you enough for all you've done for me over the years, Angela. You preserved the best part of me for Chelsea."

"Well, since you and Chelsea saved my life, I think we're even."

"I would do anything for you, Angela. You know that."

They exchanged a look, and as Chelsea, Axel, and Twix started to make their way back to them, Angela's hand found his own.

Ethan smiled. Life was good.

His phone vibrated in his pocket. It was a message from Bert.

Thought you should know that they have reunited Josie Daniels with her family in Manitoba. Josie's 81-year-old mother sends her heartfelt gratitude. You did that, Ethan. You.

About the author

Edge O. Erin grew up in British Columbia and now resides on the island of Cape Breton in Nova Scotia, Canada. A passionate outdoorsman, the natural world is imprinted on his psyche. His surveying and remote sensing experience in disparate parts of the globe has informed his opinion on land use, the human condition, and the importance of biodiversity and environmental stewardship. Edge has authored five novels, Way of the Hatchet, Terraform Charlie, Odin's Tillit, Time Sneak: Emergence, and Legacy of Seconds. He is at work on his next novel, Parn.

Made in the USA
Columbia, SC
25 January 2024